DANCE IN THE DUST

Denise Robins
(Harriet Gray)

DANCE IN
THE DUST

G.K.HALL &CO.
Boston, Massachusetts
1986

Published in Large Print by arrangement
with Hodder & Stoughton Limited.

G. K. Hall Large Print Book Series.

Set in 16pt Plantin.

Library of Congress Cataloging in Publication Data

Robins, Denise, 1897–
    Dance in the dust.

    1. Large type books.   I. Title.
[PR6035.O554D36   1986]   823'.912   85–16342
ISBN 0–8161–3978–4

For my Husband

DANCE IN THE DUST

'Life, who art love, and love, who art low
    laughter . . .
What though thy beauty may one day be
    hid
In a green grave? Yet, unslain thereafter,
Life will lilt onward, dancing through the
    dust.'

From: *Maria Montes*
By LLEWELYN SLINGSBY BETHELL

PART ONE

CHAPTER ONE

On the morning of June 3rd, Esmond
Walhurst, fifth Earl of Mornbury, opened
his eyes at the unaccustomed hour of seven
o'clock, and resented the awakening so
deeply that he let out a muffled roar, his
face half buried in the large filled pillow.

'Wilkins! Where the devil are you?'

Thomas Wilkins, his valet, came running
into the dark vast bedchamber. Thick
brocade curtains were still drawn across the
windows. Contrary to all Mr. Wilkins's
beliefs and wishes, these windows were
wide open. His young lordship was partial
to the night air, which had been thought by
his illustrious father and grandfather to
hold poisons that could easily bubble in the
lungs and chest and set up a hacking and
often fatal cough.

Wilkins had orders to leave the windows
all open. He shuddered as he did so. It was
a habit which, the valet had recently
reflected, no doubt milord would change
when he was married. (Which, in fact, was

1

to be this very morning.) And mighty pleased was the old and devoted Wilkins, who considered that his lordship had stayed far too long a bachelor. He was now twenty-five and most of his friends and contemporaries had already steered the boat of reckless youth into the safe still waters of the matrimonial harbour. Whereas young Lord Esmond, until he met the Lady Dorothea of Shaftley three months ago, had been confirmed in his bachelor habits. He was in London during the greater part of the year, sporting with friends of whom Wilkins was sure his late lordship would have disapproved. Too much drinking and card playing. Too many late nights. They could play havoc with a young man. Mornbury returned frequently to this beautiful spacious house—built fifty years ago and recently modernized in the present elegant tradition of architecture—looking pale and weary. Lines of dissipation were already beginning to mar the perfection of a face that had been called the handsomest in England. It was lucky, in the opinion of his old valet and confidential servant, that my lord was as strong as an ox and had, therefore, a constitution to stand up to all the debauchery.

He was a godson of Anne the Queen, who was a good pious woman and did not like her courtiers to indulge themselves freely. She had sent a mild reproof to Esmond after one scandalous party which he had held in his residence in St. James's.

Queen Anne was an invalid. Dropsy and gout threatened her and she held Court as rarely as her royal predecessor, King William. But when she was not cloistered at Hampton Court or in Bath with her bosom friend and confidante, lady of the bedchamber Sarah Churchill, she was lending an ear to the counsel of her ministers and flattening any attempts by her subjects to give way to irreligious or licentious living. It was known that Esmond's father had been one of Her Majesty's favourites, which was why she had consented to sponsor Esmond. She was, usually, tolerant of his peccadilloes. But it had been by command of his royal godparent that Esmond had reluctantly turned his thoughts to marriage. Anne considered that he had spent enough time in the card-rooms and coffee house and among loose-living women. He had been ordered to get himself a wife. Loth though he was to obey his Queen, it had been lucky for Esmond that at that precise time the Lady Dorothea Bridges, only daughter of the Earl of Shaftley, came into his life.

This was to be the end of his bachelor days. To-night, mused Wilkins, a dainty and fastidious lady would lie in meek and modest slumber at her lord and master's side.

Wilkins prayed that Lady Dorothea would have the same good influence over his lordship that the late Countess of Mornbury used to have.

Esmond had loved his mother, and for long after she died, had been inconsolable. There were several portraits of her here. One hung over the carved stone mantelpiece in Esmond's bedchamber. It showed Catherine Mornbury in a low-cut velvet dress with a deep lace collar, sitting with Esmond, himself, curled at her feet. He was then at the age of ten. Mother and son both had the same bright colouring, the polished chestnut hair in long silky ringlets, the proud nose, the curled upper lip and fine, somewhat aquiline nose. It was said that Esmond bore little resemblance to his short and stockily-built father who had not been long in following his young wife to the grave, a victim of the dropsy. After this Esmond had been cared for by his aunt and uncle, Sir Arthur and Lady Rokeley.

Mornbury Hall had ceased to be a happy home once the Rokeleys were installed, for Esmond, when adolescent, found that his tastes and beliefs, both political and religious, clashed with those of his aunt and uncle.

Four years ago when Esmond came of age, he courteously but firmly suggested that his guardians should return to their own home in Lincolnshire. He then flung himself into the joys of freedom.

There were times when old Wilkins, who knew and loved his young master so well, blamed the Rokeleys for the young Earl's subsequent behaviour. They had been too harsh. Once the leash had been snapped the young man had broken out. But the whole household at Mornbury delighted in the knowledge that there was to be a mistress here soon, worthy to succeed the departed Countess. Angelic, but not uncomfortably so. When Dorothea last came here with her parents to visit her betrothed husband, the late Lady Mornbury's drawing-room had been opened up, and once again the strains of music had been heard in the Hall. The

Lady Dorothea played the spinet and the servants had heard her singing. It would be good to hear a feminine voice and feel the feminine touch once more at Mornbury.

Esmond rubbed his eyes and glowered at the old servant, who, in black, with white necktie and thin spindly legs, stood there beside the bed. Poor old Wilkins; he must be every year of seventy. Wilkins had long and faithfully served his family. In certain moods Esmond could be impatient and exacting, but he considered it ungentlemanly to behave badly to an inferior. But to his own social equals he could be quite ruthless. Few cared to offend or pick a quarrel easily with Esmond Mornbury. He was as fine a shot as any man in the country—and as dexterous with a sword.

'Your lordship requires his breakfast?' asked Wilkins in his somewhat high and quavering voice, while he continued to regard his master nervously out of eyes which were milky-blue; filmed by approaching cataracts.

'I shall ride, first,' said Esmond.

'Ride!' repeated Wilkins. 'Milord! On the morning of your marriage?'

'Yes, you old dolt; get ready my boots

6

and clothes. First bring me a tankard of ale. My throat is as dry as a dusting brush. Don't stand there gaping like a codfish!'

'Yes, milord. No, milord.'

Esmond leaped from the bed, peeled off his embroidered nightshirt and wrapped his naked body in a silk bedgown, yawning prodigiously as he did so, scratching his cropped head. He was a fine figure, thought the loyal old servant, standing six foot two on his bare feet, with a goodly width of shoulders and a slim line of flank. He had the shapeliest of legs. He had never known a day's illness nor been cupped by a physician. He bore only one small scar where his smooth boy's cheek had been laid open by a sword-point in a duel—the only mark to spoil his physical perfection. Handsome Horace, the old Earl his grandfather had been named, and Esmond resembled him.

All his friends from Oxford, or London, or from this district wherein he had lived all his life had gathered to wish him joy of his forthcoming marriage. Many of them were here still, sleeping under his roof and would attend the wedding to-day. His great friend, Archibald St. John, was here too. Archie, who had been at University with

Esmond and shared a few of his outrageous adventures. The Foreign Office was sending Archie at the end of the week to Edinburgh on Her Majesty's business. This year had seen the final union between England and Scotland and removed trading restrictions between the two countries. Archie would have work to do there for the Government. He was a charming, amusing fellow after Esmond's own heart, but more practical than the young Earl himself.

Archie approved of Dorothea, and Esmond gave thanks now that the ball to which he had been invited, and which celebrated the eighteenth birthday of Lord Shaftley's only daughter, Dorothea, had been the only one he had attended this year.

He had gone to that dance reluctantly knowing it was his royal godmother's wish. At last he was being forced to inspect the marriage market in English High Society; not dreaming that he would meet his fate within twenty-four hours of the letter which had reached him from the Queen. Then, suddenly he had danced with the Lady Dorothea—and was lost.

Hitherto he had known her as a child, of whom he had taken little notice when she came his way; which was rarely. He had

8

heard that she was now grown to young womanhood and of an excessively pleasant disposition and reputed to have looks as well as talents. But he had heard also that she was delicate. She had had fainting fits since she was in her teens. He could not bear delicate females with their swooning, and their attendants shrieking for burnt feathers and vinegar. The women whom so far Esmond Mornbury had chosen to take to his bed were strong handsome creatures who could respond to a man's passion and make him feel that he held flesh and blood in his arms.

Nevertheless, when he bent over Dorothea's little hand and led her on to the floor in the Quadrille he knew that the die was cast and that his fate was sealed. He had never seen anything more ravishing than Dorothea Bridges. When he had kissed· her hand and looked into her glorious eyes as he thanked her for the dance, his brain had reeled with the possibilities of taking to himself such an innocent and unblemished bride. Dorothea was one whom the Queen would approve— the Countess of Shaftley had, until recently, been a lady-in-waiting at St. James's.

That night Esmond knew that Dorothea was the one for whom he had been seeking.

He went home, madly in love for the first time in his life.

To-day, Esmond felt, Mornbury would be restored to the joy and promise of life that used to flood the place when his parents were alive. The splendid, exciting hour was fast approaching when he would carry his bride over the threshold.

This morning, while Esmond waited for the grooms to saddle Jess, he walked from the stables, strolled across a lawn that was like emerald satin silvered by dew and stood a moment looking at his home with pride, as he had done so many times in the past.

The early sun was slanting across the fine brick and stone house with the handsome side wings that had been added on to it. The open colonnades lent an unusual dignity. From the terrace wide steps led down to a square court in which stood a great basin. Out of this rose the statue of a man, astride a horse. Sculptured in grey stone, grown green with age, this was a remarkably magnificent figure of a rider with head flung back and arms outstretched as though exulting in the life and vigour of his mount. Gushing from the animal's mouth a sparkling spray of water fell into the basin with a musical sound. All his life Esmond had loved that fountain. As a small boy he had once escaped the notice of his nurses, fallen into the basin and nearly drowned, but he continued to love it.

Part of the old house was concealed by thick flowering creeper which Esmond had a mind to cut down, for he preferred the plain stonework. The library, with Esmond's own private suite of rooms above it, lay in the right wing. He enjoyed the magnificent sight of the beautiful wrought-iron work which had been spun like a web of black lace right across the pale stone walls. Wren had designed it. New, also, was the splendid door with fluted columns on either side, and graceful fanlight overhead. Nothing delighted Esmond more than these additions to his home, masterpieces of an acknowledged genius of modern architecture.

Turning his back to the house, he looked now at the beautiful double row of lime-trees and green clipped bays in large tubs. Pale rose-bricked walls flanked the formal flower gardens. To the right, a handsome park full of gentle, spotted deer. Beyond was the heavily wooded forest on the extreme borders of Surrey and Sussex.

The Mornbury Estate was rich and fertile. The meadows were full of cattle, providing meat and milk and cream for the owner. In the kitchen gardens the finest fruits and the sweetest herbs awaited the pleasure of a new mistress and housekeeper! Too long, thought Esmond, the simple delights of his ancestral home had lain unappreciated. It was, indeed, time that somebody stepped into his mother's shoes; and who better than his beloved Dorothea?

A sudden thrill gripped him at the thought of the sons that Dorothea would bear him, and who would inherit Mornbury after he was dead.

To the devil with last night's carousing, he thought, and hurried back to the stables where the men held the head of his fine spirited grey.

He mounted and barely touched Jess's satin neck with his crop. The familiar touch thrilled the mare with a joy to match his own. Her hoofs struck fire against the flagged stones of the stable yard. In a moment the rider was away, out of the gates and on the rough road. Esmond, bridegroom of the future, was at a gallop, speeding through the still-sleeping village of Godchester along the banks of the river; which was his favourite ridc.

CHAPTER TWO

The young Earl returned from that early morning ride with his ills sweated out of him, and in high spirits. As the grooms came running to meet him, he had a story ready to tell them of a fox he had seen slinking out of Rushhurst Spinney and how he had chased it for half a mile before it took cover again. But the story died on his lips, for he saw, following the grooms, the figures of several of his friends who were wedding guests at Mornbury. He did not expect them to be up so early. Among them was the tall, slight figure of his best friend—Archibald St. John. Esmond looked slightly puzzled as he dismounted. None of the men appeared to be dressed, but were in their various négligés. Archie, alone, seemed to have dressed more fully than the others, for he wore breeches and a powdering jacket. It looked as though he

13

had hastily put on peruke and powder before coming downstairs.

'What is this?' exclaimed Esmond gaily. 'A special deputation to greet me on my marriage morning?'

'My dear Esmond. My dear Esmond . . .' began St. John and stopped as though the words stuck in his throat.

Of a sudden, Mornbury sensed catastrophe.

'What has happened, Archie?' he asked in a low quick voice. 'Have you bad news for me?'

St. John bowed his head.

'Out with it. Enough of this hesitance.'

Esmond had noticed several of his servants gathered in the court-yard. They were whispering, one to the other. A premonition of the truth—an appalling truth—gripped Esmond by the throat.

'Oh, God,' he muttered, '*is it Dorothea?*'

St. John bowed his head. 'A youth has just ridden over from the Castle to say that she has been taken gravely ill, and that there can be no marriage ceremony to-day.'

To himself St. John might have added the words *or any other day* but dared not. He knew his friend too well; that mercurial and often violent disposition behind the façade

14

of sunny charm. Esmond would not be one to take bad news well.

'We grieve for you, Esmond,' spoke up one of the young men behind St. John. He spoke ill-advisedly, for Mornbury turned on him like a wounded lion.

'Grieve for me—pray why, Liftborough? Is my lady *dead* that you speak thus to me?'

No answer. Esmond had started to shake, and the sweat ran down his face, a waxen colour under the burn of the sun. Then without a word he turned, grabbed Jess's bridle out of the hands of an open-mouthed groom and swung himself into the saddle. He was away again out of the court-yard and through the gates.

The black rooks were circling and cawing noisily around the tall elms. Never had the countryside looked more glorious. Never had Esmond, fifth Earl of Mornbury, known a more deadly fear than that which rode with him during that five-mile gallop on Jess to Shaftley Castle.

'Dorothea!' he kept crying aloud that cherished name. '*Dorothea*, Heaven grant you are yet alive.'

But he knew when he reached the Castle that his frantic prayer remained unanswered and that she was dead. For as

15

he came to Shaftley a superstitious horror seized him. With bloodshot eyes he looked at the Castle. It stood on the top of the hill. Usually it was a fair sight; built in 1100 during the reign of King Stephen for one of the first barons of Shaftley, it could be seen for miles around. Esmond had often climbed to the battlements with his Dorothea and looked upon the fair Sussex Weald as far as Chanctonbury Ring on one side and the Guildford hills on the other. But this morning, when all else seemed golden and clear, Shaftley was partially obscured by a thick whitish mist which seemed to Esmond to curl maliciously around those dove-grey walls.

Only a few moments more, and Esmond was within the Castle. Two footmen opened the heavy doors to admit him. The Earl—a tall stooping grey-haired man clothed in dark grey, relieved only by the white Steinkirk at his neck, greeted him.

Esmond could see that the usually upright man, not yet fifty, had become quite old and quavered in his speech.

'How is she, Sir?' Esmond demanded hoarsely.

Lord Shaftley bowed his head.

'Dorothea will be bride only to Christ her

Lord, into whose merciful arms she has been gathered,' he said brokenly.

Esmond neither moved nor spoke. Dorothea's father added:

'Her lady mother lies in her bedchamber, too sick to move or speak with you. I, myself, shall conduct you to the chapel to our darling's bier, that you may take your last fond look at her.'

'What happened, Sir?'

'Dorothea rose at daybreak and called for her maid, and bade her send for us, for she had a foul pain in her heart. Before we could reach her, Esmond, that loving heart had failed.'

'Failed,' repeated Esmond, hoarsely.

'Yes,' said the Earl unashamedly sobbing now, 'you know that Dorothea has been subject to fainting fits which our physicians assured us were signals of a childish bloodlessness which would improve. But they were wrong. We have all been wrong. That beautiful and gentle flower should never have been allowed to take a step, or to strain her feeble heart with dancing or moving about with her more fortunate friends. She should never have been subject to the strain of a courtship and this forthcoming bridal. Yet last night she seemed so well, so gay. She spoke to us openly of her great happiness. She especially enjoyed the thought that she would not be residing far from her parents whom she respected and cared for so deeply. And you, my boy, whom she greatly loved—she talked like one intoxicated with pleasure in the thought that her life would to-day be linked with yours.'

'Stop,' said Esmond in a tone of anguish. *'Stop!'*

Shaftley wiped his eyes. Turning, he led the way through the high-roofed, galleried hall down a long corridor leading into the private chapel. As they advanced, Esmond groaned aloud:

'Have the doctors made sure that nothing could be done?'

'Nothing. Our physician applied every manner of restorative—in vain. I shall leave you with our darling in the chapel, to pay your respects. Later when you are better fitted to discuss the sorry details with me, arrangements must be made for her burying.'

At this word, Esmond Mornbury felt an almost maniacal grief and horror. *Her burying.* Dorothea, his love, the woman

18

whom he had chosen and should have called his wife—within the next few hours—to be buried. Terrible incredible thought! She, the light of foot who had so often danced with grace and agility. She, whose laughter had rung out, gladdening his heart, and whose mind had reached out to his, capturing his imagination; turning him from foolish rake into serious man, ready and willing to live soberly and in dignity, at her side!

Esmond, ice-cold, followed the Earl into the chapel. At first, after the glare of the sunlight outside, his eyes could take in nothing for the chapel was dark and gloomy save for the light of two waxen candles, four-foot tall, burning in heavy silver sconces at the head and foot of the corpse. At last Esmond's horrified gaze focused on that pitful figure. *The corpse of his Dorothea.* Pitiful, yet still ethereally beautiful and wonderful, she lay on a catafalque of fresh blossoms. The trestle was covered with a purple velvet cloth edged with silver lace.

He saw to his anguish that they had attired the dead girl in her wedding robes. It was as though she lay sleeping there in her finery—waiting for him to awaken her. Except for the waxen whiteness of her face which already bore the pinched look of death, it seemed to him that she still lived and breathed. The long lashes lay so sweetly on the delicate cheeks. The lips smiled—a secret wise little smile. They had set a chaplet of lilies on her brow, and her long white lace veil was folded about her like a nun's habit.

The rich cream satin of her high-waisted silver-girdled wedding dress fell in stiff sedate folds to the tiny upturned feet in their brocaded slippers. Between her clasped hands was a posy of dark red roses—the only note of colour in the rest of that awful whiteness. In anguish, Esmond stared at those roses, remembering how she used to love them. They had been her favourites. No doubt that was why her heartbroken parents had gathered them for her.

'I will leave you here, my boy,' whispered Dorothea's father.

Esmond nodded and gulped. He walked like a drunken man, swaying, nearer to the bier. He fell upon his knees beside it.

While he muttered prayers, he continued to gaze in anguish at the young girl's angelic face.

Suddenly he cried her name aloud:

'*Dorothea!*'

It seemed to him all wrong that she did not open her eyes to look at him with pity, to answer that wild cry and comfort him. Bitter resentment mingled with his grief. The first tears he had shed since he was a baby forced their difficult way out of his eyes and trickled down his cheeks. He tasted the salt of them and was half ashamed that he was being unmanly. All his heart's love was driven back into the very depths of his being. It was as though the sweetness and warmth of life for Esmond departed with her—never to be revived. There was nothing left to him but darkness and despair.

He bent and touched with his lips one of the delicate hands of that pitiful bride, lying there folded so tragically in her veil. The little hand was cold as ice. Shuddering, he drew back.

He whispered:

'All my life shall be buried with yours, my sweet love.'

Then he turned and walked quickly out of the chapel back into the Castle. He forced himself to speak again with the Earl whom this day he had hoped to gain as a father, but there was little to be said

21

between them. Everything had ended. The deeds of the lands that Shaftley was going to give his daughter as part of her dowry must now be torn up.

'My wife and I know how you loved our dear daughter and we suffer for and with you,' sighed the older man as he accompanied Esmond to the court-yard, where a man stood waiting with Jess.

'I thank you,' said Esmond. 'What I feel cannot be expressed in any words. I can only bid you adieu, Sir, until the unhappy day of the burial.'

As Esmond rode Jess downhill and into the village of Shaftley, he saw that the streets were lined with shopkeepers and their wives and children, huddled, whispering; some of the women weeping. As the tall handsome fair young man in his riding suit, with laced waistcoat, and cocked hat, went by, the men touched their foreheads. One or two girls, stirred by his manly beauty, stepped forward and called out:

'God save your poor lordship . . .'

Ere he reached the village church, he heard the death-bell tolling for Dorothea. That grim measured sound was almost more than he could bear.

He returned to Mornbury. He was conscious of the ominous silence that had fallen upon his stately home. The curtains were drawn across the many windows. Already, thought Esmond dully, death had winged its way from the Castle and settled here too, with all its Stygian gloom.

Drawing a hand across his eyes, he stumbled into the hall. He suddenly realized that for three hours now he had been riding hard and undergoing a considerable mental strain. He had not even breakfasted.

Old Wilkins came out to meet his master, rubbing his blue-veined hands together—peering at Esmond, with his sad old eyes.

'Oh, milord. May I offer my respectful condolences—' he began.

Esmond cut him short.

'Get out of my sight. Get out, I say,' came roughly from his cracked lips.

The old servant, who knew his young lordship and understood, fell back, shaking his bewigged head mournfully. He went to the servants' hall to tell them that my lord looked as though he, too, had been struck by the hand of death.

'Alas,' said Wilkins. He spoke in a voice intended only for the ear of Mrs. Fustian,

23

the housekeeper who had also served the late Countess. 'This fearful blow may, I fear, unhinge our young master and drive him from God's purpose. It will go ill with him.'

On the staircase, going up to his bedchamber, Esmond met his friend Archibald St. John, who was now fully attired for travelling. Esmond stopped, swaying as though drunk, and stared at his friend. St. John was horrified by the look of him.

'My dear fellow,' he said, putting a hand on Esmond's shoulder, 'you have suffered an extreme shock. Let me summon Wilkins to help you to bed and bring you a pot of coffee. Surely you need sustenance.'

Esmond pulled sharply away from those kindly fingers.

'I need nothing but to be alone. Out of my way, Archie.'

St. John, who could see that his friend was half deranged took no offence but persisted in his effort to persuade him to allow Wilkins to undress him and bring him food.

'You must bear this catastrophe like a man, Esmond,' he said gently. 'It is God's purpose.'

Esmond broke into a wild laugh.

'Is there a God with a purpose so monstrously cruel? If so then I forswear Him and my religion.'

'Nay, Esmond—' began St. John, shocked.

'I forswear Him and all that is good in life. What kind of a God is He who brings death to one so sweet, so fair, so tender as my Dorothea? I curse God. *I curse Him . . .*'

Archie licked his lips. From the bottom of his soul he pitied Esmond now. For a man to lose the woman he loved on their marriage morning must be hard to bear.

By midday, all the guests who should have stayed for Mornbury's wedding had left the sad, darkened house without even seeing their deranged host. They sent him polite messages of sympathy through St. John.

The last carriage rolled away. Archibald, with a deep sigh, mounted the stairs and knocked on the door of his friend's bedchamber.

'Will you not admit me, Esmond?'

A hoarse voice answered him:

'I bade you to go. I wish to be alone in my house.'

'My poor fellow,' said St. John patiently, 'everyone has gone save myself and I felt that you might need and appreciate my companionship—someone to lean on in this time of woe.'

'I want no one, I tell you. Go, for heaven's sake.'

St. John shrugged his shoulders. He descended the stairs again. He pulled the bell and summoned Wilkins.

'I fear this trouble has temporarily unhinged your noble master, Wilkins. He will not allow even me, whom he loves, to stay with him. I must respect his wishes. I will return to London. But if he finds he has need of me, I pray you send me word by post-chaise to my dwelling—Number 17 Charlotte Square. I shall not be going to Scotland until the end of the week.'

The old man bowed his head, a tear trickling down his nose.

'Alas, Sir,' he sighed.

'Alas, indeed. Farewell, Wilkins. Take good care of his lordship,' said Archie, and reluctantly took his leave.

He knew Esmond's nature too well to disregard that repeated request that he should leave Mornbury. Better perhaps to leave the poor fellow to recover alone, as he

26

desired. There was nothing really to be
done for him now.

CHAPTER THREE

For three days, the bells of Shaftley church
tolled their dirge for the soul of the Lady
Dorothea.

On the fourth day the pure, white beauty
of the deceased bride was nailed down in a
splendid coffin and laid to rest in the
Shaftley vault—among half a dozen little
sisters and brothers who had died in
infancy, before her.

The young Earl, who would never now
lead her to the altar, stood beside the coffin
for a moment ere it was taken out of his
sight. He laid upon the lid a long cross
fashioned of the red roses Dorothea had
loved. He was ashen-faced and so haggard,
the fact was remarked upon by the male
members of Dorothea's family. Themselves
overcome by grief, they huddled together
in their black garments, weeping, leaving
him for those few seconds alone to bid his
last farewell to the young girl he had loved
so passionately.

At length the Earl of Shaftley came forward and touched Esmond on the shoulders.

'Let us ride back to the Castle together, my poor boy. No useful purpose can be served by remaining here. It is all over.'

'I do not wish for company, Sir,' said Esmond.

For three days he had barely eaten save when Wilkins had risked being cuffed or sworn at and set a tray before him, and then the young Earl had merely picked at the food, lacing it with copious draughts of brandy.

Dorothea's father, however, insisted. The poor man was cut to the quick by the loss of his favourite child. His wife would never give him another. Like Queen Anne she had lost a large family, one after the other. Poor Dorothea's heart had evidently been weak from birth. It was a mercy, the Earl thought in his sadness, that she had reached eighteen summers, and stayed with them as long. He dreaded returning to the Castle. It was full of wailing females. The only other gentleman staying there was Sir Adam Congrayle, his brother-in-law by marriage whom he disliked, and he had little interest in his niece, Magda, who was also a guest. She had been the victim of some terrible accident in childhood and he never remembered seeing her without a veil over her face. Dorothea had pitied her young cousin—it was because of this at Dorothea's request that Magda had come to the Castle for the wedding, but Shaftley saw no reason to say anything of this.

Shaftley in his youth had been a gay lad—as gay, at least, as was possible in the reign of King William. Secretly he admired the brilliant young man who should have been his son-in-law despite the fact that some of his escapades had made him somewhat too notorious.

Esmond hesitated. He had no wish to go to the Castle. He wanted to be alone again with his grief, but the old man insisted and out of respect to his dead love's father, Esmond consented to ride up the long hill with him.

Shaftley got rid of the other mourning guests and at length sat by the window drinking brandy alone with Esmond, extolling the virtues of his dead daughter until Esmond felt that he would go insane. He had been near insanity ever since he had gazed upon Dorothea's corpse in the chapel that terrible morning. It already seemed a lifetime away.

'Thanks be to the Almighty that you are yet young and will find another fair maid who will take my darling's place and, perchance one day give you an heir,' old Shaftley said, too full of wine for discretion.

'It is an insult, Sir, to suggest that I shall replace Dorothea.'

'Come, come, my boy, 'tis only human nature. The first sharp pangs of sorrow grow blunt with time.'

'I shall never forget *her.*'

'Never forget, perhaps, but it is not meet for man to live alone and you, yourself, once told me that your Royal godmother decreed that you should take a wife to Mornbury.'

Esmond gripped the hilt of the sword that he was wearing until the knuckles gleamed ivory white.

'I prefer not to admit such a thing is possible.'

'Well, well,' sighed the older man, 'time will tell.'

Esmond began to walk up and down the room. The brandy he had been consuming for days and which he had just finished here burned through his veins. He felt as though he moved in a miasma; the world spun round him. As for the Queen, a letter had indeed reached Esmond from Bath, written in person by Her Majesty this very day, commiserating with him, but hinting that marriage for him must be only a thing postponed. As if one could replace an adored woman, Esmond thought; as one would go forth to buy another mare, should Jess drop dead in her stables. Maybe it was because he had led so mad, so egotistical an existence in the past, he had taken this first great love of his life too deeply to heart. It sickened him even to contemplate another woman as wife.

'I must go home,' he muttered, drawing a hand across his clammy forehead, and tugged at his neckband. The sun was struggling through the mists. The air was humid and he felt hot and dizzy. Peacocks, strutting on the lawn in front of the Castle, kept uttering their weird strident cries. Like the cries of a lost soul, thought Esmond. *His* soul was lost. God had turned His face away.

As in a dream, he heard the older man mumbling about politics; about the perpetual feud between Whigs and Tories; about the growth of literary and intellectual life in London which he missed at times down here in the country. He had been talking, he said, to the priest who had read the burial service for poor Dorothea, listening to him prattle about the Bounty which Queen Anne had just given her clergymen. Then the Earl began on the subject of the thousands of French silken manufacturers who were now permitted to practise in England. From this subject he ambled back to religion.

'Our own priest here favours the high Anglican service. He certainly does not care for the Calvinist Whigs. By the way, thinking of Whigs, did you see General Corsham at the burial?'

'No,' said Esmond dully.

Shaftley went into a fresh boring dissertation about General Corsham and his lady wife. They had recently occupied Swanley Manor, a small estate between here and Mornbury. They favoured the refugees from France, and had French relatives, to be sure. The General's niece was living at Swanley now—Mademoiselle Chantal LeClaire, who had met poor Dorothea at a party and sometimes ridden with her. That was when poor little Dorothea was well enough to mount her horse. A pretty girl, Mlle Chantal, added the Earl, looking it was said for an English husband.

On and on he droned, until Esmond felt that his brain would burst. Then suddenly the library door was pushed open. A young girlish voice said:

'Uncle Charles, pray pardon the interruption, but my aunt has sent me to ask that you would kindly go to her.'

The Earl staggered on to his feet.

'Tell her that I am coming, Magda, I am coming. . . .'

Esmond stood stock still. He, too, had sprung to his feet as he heard the girl's voice. It was so extraordinarily like Dorothea's. So much so that it had sent a superstitious thrill through his very being. He had not seen the speaker, but *could it be Dorothea's voice?* Was it her ghost? Or was he in truth, delirious, after too much wine and too little eating?

Shaftley staggered towards the door, hiccuping.

'Who in God's name spoke to you just now?' asked Esmond.

'Magda, my niece—poor Dorothea's cousin; daughter of my wife's sister, Jane Congrayle. Magda came here with her mother and stepfather from the Cotswolds for the wedding. Alas they will return home to-morrow in sadness and disappointment.'

Esmond, left alone, remained standing in the centre of the room, his hands still on the hilt of his sword, his eyes half-closed.

That voice. Magda! He had never heard of Cousin Magda; or if Dorothea had ever mentioned the name, it had not interested him sufficiently to make a mark on his memory.

Then the door opened again. His distraught gaze fell upon a slight figure robed in black, face and hair concealed by a black gauze veil.

'My uncle has asked me to offer, in person, my condolences, Sir, and entertain you while he is with my aunt—' thus began the veiled girl.

But, as though out of his mind, Esmond let forth a cry and rushed past her, maddened by the sound of her voice. Almost he knocked her down, brushing her aside in the doorway. She tottered but recovered herself, both hands against her heaving bosom, her eyes staring through the veil after the tall running figure. How wild he had looked, how distracted. But how immensely, intriguingly handsome. She had never seen a more handsome man.

His rough departure brought her no offence. It was rumoured that poor Cousin Dorothea's affianced husband was crazy with grief.

Magda turned and stared through her veil out of the window, the tips of her fingers pressed against her lips. She thought:

How wonderful to be loved like that. To have meant so much to any man.

When her uncle returned, she told him that Mornbury had gone.

CHAPTER FOUR

The rain was falling more steadily as the shadows of that sad day lengthened. It was heavy enough to soak the lawns at Mornbury Hall and weigh down the heads of the outraged roses.

Esmond strode along the lime-walk, his black cloak flapping in the wind, his tricorne hat in one hand, his ebony cane in the other. His wig was sodden, his face deathly. He had got out of his phaeton two miles away and started to walk home alone across the fields. His fine boots were mud-splashed, and his black breeches stained. His brain was quite addled with the fumes of drink. Now and then he flung back his head, turned his wet ghastly face up to the frowning sky and laughed aloud. It was laughter that made a farm labourer, trudging home from the fields with his cow, stop and stare and, being a Catholic, cross himself.

That night Esmond remained locked in his bedchamber until finally he staggered to the door to admit Wilkins. He howled for brandy in a ferocious voice that left the old man no alternative but to go and fetch it, although he feared that in another hour Esmond would be insensible.

When the grey dawn broke the old servant sat patiently beside the curtained bed, vigilant and deeply apprehensive of the future.

For twenty-four hours his lordship remained in bed and drank solidly until illness put an end to it. Weakened, feverish, he spent a few more days forced to take the medicines prescribed by his physician whom Wilkins hastily summoned. On the third day Esmond was up and able to eat a square meal. He was himself again. But the Esmond whom

Wilkins dressed when he was risen looked a sick and sorry man, and the old servant could see that he had undergone a change. He neither smiled nor joked with Wilkins as he used to. It was as though he was completely frozen. Yet the devil was there underneath the calm and Wilkins sensed it. A strange violence, born of grief, was caged behind the façade. Grief had unstabilized him. Wilkins was full of dread when, at length, on a warm summer's morning he saw the coach turn out of the court-yard at Mornbury and drive his lordship to London. No gay farewell. Gone that dazzling smile, that dazzling charm which Esmond used at times to expend even on Wilkins, his humble valet. Always in the past before he left for London he would clap Wilkins over the shoulder and say some such thing as:

'Good-bye, you old devil. I am off to the capital to make merry. Keep an eye on things for me here till I return, and do not take Mrs. Fustian's virtue from her.'

That was an old joke between them, because it was known that the housekeeper, being a widow, had at one time tried to involve Wilkins in matrimony, which he had firmly resisted.

When the dust from the coach-wheels settled down in the drive, Wilkins went indoors, feeling more than his age. He shambled into the hall and stood looking up at one of the many paintings of the late Countess.

Oh, my lady, my lady, if you were but here to take care of my poor young master now! he thought.

In London, Esmond went straight to his residence in St. James's, not far from the Palace. He wanted to see Archie and sent a messenger to Charlotte Square, but to his disappointment heard that St. John had already left for Scotland.

Almost immediately Esmond went to White's Chocolate House, where the *beau monde* of London frequently gathered to talk and gamble.

Tobacco was becoming increasingly popular. The cardroom was thick with smoke when Esmond entered. Gabbling voices were hushed as one and all turned to look at the tall young man in his black clothes, a black ribbon tying back his grey peruke, and his face a white mask.

Many of the gentlemen knew him and greeted him kindly. One was mistaken enough to offer sympathy in his loss and immediately Esmond sprung on him.

'I thank you for your pity, Sir, but I do not require it,' he said haughtily.

The other shrugged and moved off.

Esmond, looking through narrowed eyes from one to the other, said:

'Who would care for a game of cards?'

Nobody spoke in return. Rumours had already sped through fashionable London that young Mornbury was to be avoided, being in a devilish humour since the shocking death of his affianced wife. Impatiently, Esmond repeated:

'Who is for a game?'

Then a tall, dark-eyed man, handsomely attired in a richly flowered suit and wearing the now popular wig with pigtail queue, advanced smiling.

'I will play you at Hazard, Mornbury.'

Esmond stared. He knew well who this was; Philip Senthill, baronet, was no friend of his, although they met frequently in the gaming or coffee houses. Senthill had a wife and son whom he stowed away at Rixham Manor in Suffolk, which was his family seat. But he had no great reputation as a family man and was more often to be seen in London playing cards or in the company of some fashionable beauty. He was a great ladies' man. It had been this aspect of his nature which had brought him into conflict with Esmond. They had a duel over a woman—some question of honour— eighteen months ago. Esmond had won, and Senthill, although he had received only a scratch, had been disarmed and unable to use his sword hand for six months; to which fact, a long scar across his right palm bore witness. Esmond did not like Philip Senthill, who had in turn never forgiven Esmond for being victor of that contest. But the affair had died down and on the surface the two gentlemen had resumed some kind of cool if not affable association.

Esmond, normally, would not have bothered to play with Senthill, but to-night he felt almost as though he was provoked into it by that half-sneering smile on Philip's lips as he issued the invitation.

Did the fellow think that he was afraid to play with him then?

Esmond said:

'Thanks, Senthill,' and led the way to a table.

The rest gathered round.

By midnight the crowd of onlookers had increased. The air was so thick the players had loosened coats and cravats and unbuttoned their waistcoats. The sweat was pouring down Esmond's cheeks. He was an unhealthy colour—not yet fully recovered from his recent debauch. Senthill continued to smile in that slightly malicious way that always roused Esmond's hot boy's blood. But it was Esmond who was winning. His pile of gold pieces was mounting. Senthill was unlucky. And at length the smile faded altogether from Philip's face and the dark eyes narrowed furiously.

At one o'clock in the morning Esmond flung a pack of cards onto the table and rose.

'Methinks you are cleaned out, Senthill,' he said quite pleasantly.

Both men had been drinking throughout the game. Esmond gave little sign of it, but Philip, who had a poor head for liquor, was less controlled now than the other man.

Through his teeth he said:

'Luck favours you, Mornbury.'

'I would not have said so,' said Esmond, straightening his waistcoat.

'With cards and with your sword-play at least,' said Senthill in a sneering voice. 'Perchance not with your women.'

A gasp went round the men who had

41

been watching the game. One of them whispered:

'A plague on Senthill. He will say the wrong thing at the wrong moment.'

'Do you allude to any woman in particular?' Esmond asked in a tone of ice.

Philip was on his feet now. His brocaded waistcoat was stained with wine, his wig askew. He looked unpleasant. And suddenly he hated Esmond more than ordinarily. The scar on his hand burned. So, there burned in him a desire to hurt this young Earl who always seemed to outwit him at everything.

'To no woman in particular; only to your marriage prospects, Mornbury. But maybe some unfortunate girl will be offered to you as a holocaust in order to satisfy Her Majesty; now that Shaftley's daughter has been lucky enough to escape you!'

Esmond looked at his old adversary as though stupefied. There was little more than outrageous lack of taste in Senthill's insolent remark, but to Esmond's inflamed imagination, not only he, but Dorothea herself had been mocked. He let out a roar, and turned the table over. It fell with a crash, wine and cards spilling.

'You have gone too far, Senthill. On

guard!' Esmond stammered the words in a passion of rage and indignation.

Senthill fumbled for his sword.

One of the older men touched Esmond's shoulder.

'Be advised, Mornbury, and wait until you are both less bemused with wine—' he began.

But Esmond brushed him aside, his eyes glaring blue fire at Senthill.

'You have seen fit to mention a name sacred to me and to taunt me with my recent loss. I will kill you for it, Senthill.'

The circle of men widened. The two men divested themselves of all but breeches and shirts and faced each other, swords in hand.

The duel was short and sharp. Esmond was by far the superior swordsman and this time it was not only a question of disarming his opponent. The point of his sword went through Philip's throat. With a gurgling cry, Senthill collapsed to the floor the red stain of blood mingling with the wine upon his shirt.

The gentlemen who had witnessed the event all started to speak at once.

'Great God, you have killed him, Mornbury.'

'There will be trouble over this.'

'Trouble with the Queen when this reaches Her Majesty's ear. Mornbury is a hot-headed young fool, though I admit that Senthill provoked him.'

Esmond stood staring down at the man he had killed. For some strange reason the sight of those fast-glazing eyes and the whiteness of the pinched face unnerved him. He seemed to identify it with the macabre memory of Dorothea locked away in her coffin, now rapidly decomposing. He was horrified by what he had just done. He had not intended to end Senthill's life. He sheathed his sword, picked up his coat and stumbled out of the Club. Nobody stopped him.

Esmond was sober now. The night wind blew upon his livid face but could not cool the agonizing fires of the misery that burned within him. He raised a clenched fist against his forehead.

'God, God, what have I done? This time I am finished with life. . . .'

Once home, he woke up one of his men, ordered a horse and without changing his clothes, cantered down the Mall towards the outskirts of London. Out on the rough country road he spurred his horse to a gallop. He rode like a maniac, bareheaded, demented by the violence of his own feelings. After covering a mile or two, his mount suddenly stumbled. Esmond was thrown. He remembered falling from the saddle, but no more. The horse cantered on, riderless, under the moon. Till dawn, Esmond lay unconscious, bleeding from a jagged cut on his head.

It was there that he was found by two Dominican monks, going to market from the small monastery of Clemford on the banks of the river—one of the few Roman Catholic religious houses which had remained in England since the Reformation, even though frowned upon by the present Queen.

The monks carried Esmond through their gates. For twenty-two hours he lay unconscious in one of the good friars' cells, patiently nursed by them.

He did not come out of that monastery for almost six months.

CHAPTER FIVE

When Esmond left the monks it was to make the journey home.

Outside the oak-studded doors of the monastery the Superior bade him farewell. He was a grave-faced man of fifty but he looked little older than the young Earl as they stood together in the bleak grey light of the December day. Esmond had aged this last six months. His face had lost its summer tan. Two whole locks of the once bright chestnut hair had turned white as the holy friar's. The jagged scar across his skull under the short hair was fortunately not to be seen. That injury, caused by sharp stones, had laid the flesh open on that summer's night when his horse threw him.

He was soberly attired in a surtout with a cape to it, and high upstanding collar concealing his chin. His expression was stern; he looked as he felt—a man who had gained a grip of himself and his passions.

'I thank you, Father, for the hospitality and kindliness shown to me within your sacred walls,' he said when he bade the Superior farewell.

The latter replied:

'Go with God, my son, and may our Lord Jesus Christ strengthen your purpose and redeem that spirit which is imprisoned only for a brief time within the hateful flesh.'

Esmond remembered those words as the

46

coach jolted over the rough turnpike road.

London was behind him. And he did not want to go back there—at present. He could not if he wished, he thought, as he pulled from his surtout some letters among which were two bearing the Royal seal. Missives from the Queen, herself.

They had reached him soon after his accident. The monks had not allowed him to use his eyes for some time for he had been subjected to violent headaches and a partial paralysis of the optic nerves from which, fortunately he had now recovered.

Later, when he was able to sit up and take stock of the world again, the monks had brought him the letters. Several from Archie, of course. But it had not become generally known that Esmond lay in that sequestered monastery.

His Royal godmother wrote on a note of grave displeasure. She deplored the fact that he had been embroiled in the ugly episode with Senthill. She had sorrowed for him, she said, when he lost the Lady Dorothea, but she was angered now by his weakness of character—a weakness that had resulted in the murder of one of her subjects.

She said that she understood that he had

been sorely provoked. Many gentleman present had borne witness to the fact, and alleged that Esmond had not at the time been responsible for his conduct. Duelling was not in any case unlawful, but Her Majesty disliked it and particularly the fact that her own godson, whose father had been such a fine man and whose mother had personally waited upon her, should permit such a besmirching of his good name.

There followed many more stern reproaches, all written in Anne's own handwriting; difficult to decipher for she suffered from the gout and could scarcely hold her quill in the cold weather. But Esmond had had plenty of time to peruse and digest the words penned by that august hand, and much of it made disagreeable reading. She did not favour papacy, Anne reminded him, and did not wish Esmond to remain with the Romanish monks once he was strong enough to depart.

Esmond had answered the first letter as soon as he was able to write, offering formal apologies to Her Majesty for the sorrow he had caused her and assuring her that there would be no repetition of it. Now that he was sober and in his right mind he had

taken a vow never again to take strong
drink as consolation in despair, and that he
would in future endeavour to lead, as Her
Majesty wished, a more godly life. He had
then begged her to understand that without
Dorothea his life had no purpose, and that
he had half a mind to abandon the world for
ever and enter the Brotherhood.

This had brought an immediate reply
from Bath, more stringent than the last,
forbidding him to do any such thing, on
pain of immediate exile. It was the Queen's
wish that Esmond should return to
Mornbury and perform his duties there as a
landed gentleman in the way his father had
done before him.

'Let it never be said that a godson of
Anne should show himself to the world as a
coward unable to face the bitterness of a
loved one's death,' she wrote.

She had then reminded him of her own
sorrows ... the loss of the many Royal
children who, one by one, had been born
only to die. Yet must she continue to accept
God's will, and rule her people and remain
a consolation to what family was left to her.

She would give him another month in
which to mourn his Dorothea, but in the
New Year he was to seek another bride. He

must take heed of this Royal decree or suffer the consequence.

Never before in his chequered career had young Mornbury received such a severe reprimand or such a sinister threat from the Queen who, in the past, had shown herself tolerant and affectionate towards him.

Esmond brooded over the two Royal letters as the coach rattled on its way to Godchester. A moroseness had seized him and a stirring of conscience, concerning Philip Senthill. He had already given orders to his legal advisers to make sure that Senthill's widow wanted for nothing.

Last night there had been a frost. The wheels of the coach skidded a little, and now and again one of the horses slipped and stumbled and had to be pulled up by the postillions with much shouting and hallooing.

Curious, thought Esmond, to realize that he had not seen his home for nearly six months. He wondered how he would find Wilkins from whom he had received one or two messages of condolence and anxious inquiry, sent in a round-about way through St. John. But while Esmond lay ill in his cell he had cared little about what went on at home or on his estates.

One of the young monks with whom he talked, had told him that there had been great agricultural triumph in England this autumn. All the big estates were booming, and the farmers growing fat and prosperous because there was no tax on corn in England as there was in Italy. Esmond as he went along tried to take an interest in the pastures, and roused himself to notice that many new beechwoods were being planted and that there was a new draining system of the more marshy lands in progress. He also let his gaze rest with faint interest on one of the latest houses which had just been built with the new big sash windows that he favoured. Yes—England was a fair and pleasant land even on a December morning, and suddenly Esmond felt a nostalgia for Mornbury.

A paper dropped from his lap over which the coachman had placed a plaid rug, and warming bottle to dispel the extreme cold. He picked up the letter which was addressed to him in a female hand. A neat, slanting hand, and one with which he had grown familiar during his convalescence. It was signed: '*Magda*'.

A dozen or more from Miss Congrayle had reached him in the monastery,

51

uninvited and unwanted—yet with the arrival of each one, Esmond had grown more interested about the sender.

He had never actually spoken with Magda but he remembered her on the morning of Dorothea's burial. The small slender female, with face hidden from him by a veil when she entered the library at Shaftley Castle, and told him that her uncle had sent her to talk to him. She had addressed him (he shuddered a little even now at the recollection of that voice; its unforgettable likeness to Dorothea's), but he had been too stunned to reply to her.

He was surprised by the fact that Magda wished to correspond with him. She did so, he presumed, out of womanly compassion, and the love she had borne her late cousin. That Magda was tender by nature was obvious, for she wrote in romantic vein, quoting poetry which, in fact, Esmond yawned over and skipped whenever he came to such passages. He supposed that her lady mother had suggested she should write. What reason Lady Congrayle could have in thus thrusting her daughter at Esmond—in a literary sense—he neither knew or cared. He cared for nothing and nobody at this time. But he could not help but be impressed by the manner of Magda's writing.

Her sentiments were expressed with a simple girlish charm and she sympathized with his ills. She also acquainted him with what news she imagined might interest a gentleman. He had been surprised by her intelligent survey of politics and world events—unusual in a female. She told him of the present state of the war in France; and discussed the latest victories of that great soldier, the Duke of Marlborough. She seemed, personally, enthralled by the defeat of the French fleet off Malaga, and the landing of the English at the newly gained Gibraltar. And she also wrote on the one subject which particularly intrigued Esmond. *Horses*.

The Congrayles' house was in the Cotswolds near Stroud. Magda sent Esmond quite a stirring account of the first day when she had ridden with her brothers to hunt the wild boar which abounded in the forests there.

'I am ever happy in the Saddle, and prefer it to all other recreation, for which I am chided by Sir Adam' [she wrote in one of her letters], 'I do work in the

Home but I so much more dearly like to follow the Hounds and to feel the wind whip against my face and the vigorous grace of a strong Beast carrying me across the rough open countryside. . . .'

Esmond read that paragraph several times, for when it first reached him, it brought the tang of fresh air and the excitement of the Chase almost into the monastery for him. He could sympathize with Magda's tastes. At the same time, he was not sure he did not prefer a young female to be truly feminine. He had never cared for hoydenish women. It would seem, he decided, that Magda possessed little of Dorothea's delicacy or gentleness in her disposition.

Yet the general tenor of the notes which came to him regularly from the young girl was quite touchingly solicitous.

'I who have suffered, do realize, Sir, that you too, have suffered greatly, and that your heart lies buried in the grave of my sweet cousin whom I venerated and admired above all others in my family . . .'

For that sympathy, Esmond felt well disposed towards Magda. But what she meant by that bit about her suffering he did not understand nor bother to analyse, save for a fleeting moment when he wondered how so young a gentlewoman could have already experienced a deal of sorrow.

He even began to wonder what Magda looked like and if it was possible that her face resembled in the slightest, that of his lost Love.

He wrote to Stroud only once—a meagre return for the generous supply of her sympathy. But at least he wrote. Briefly, curtly, to be sure, offering his thanks. No more.

Since the end of October he had heard no more from Magda, and presumed that the correspondence was at an end.

It was late afternoon when he reached Mornbury Hall. He noted the redness of the berries on the holly trees; portents of a hard winter. The trees in the lime-walk looked gaunt and sad. A bitter north wind had sprung up and there were black clouds banking up in the sky, heralding the first fall of snow.

Esmond suddenly realized the completeness of the desolation that had fallen upon him as he stepped out of the coach and looked up at his home. There were lights in the windows. Servants came running with lanthorns on poles to greet him. The sharp cold air stung his cheeks. He was home again. *But to what? To whom?*

He felt a sudden wish to converse with his old favourite servant, the devoted Wilkins. Where was the old man? Why hadn't he come out?

Unclasping his cloak, Esmond strode into the hall. It was warmed by a great fire in the open fire-place. The Earl nodded in response to the row of curtsying, bobbing servants who had lined up to greet their master. There was not one of them who was not glad to see him back.

It was Mrs. Fustian, her face flushed and pink under her mob cap, who first came forward and spoke:

'Welcome home, milord,' she wheezed and panted.

'I am glad to be here,' said Esmond.

'We trust your lordship has suffered no permanent ill effect from . . . from—'

'I am well, thanks,' broke in Esmond.

Then, looking around him, frowning at the many faces, he added:

'Where is Wilkins?'

A little murmur went down the row of servants. They glanced furtively at each other. Mrs. Fustian bit her lips, bobbed nervously once or twice and then spoke to her master:

'Milord, your lordship will be distressed, I know, but he was took very sick, a few days ago. It was something inside him, the physician said. It had been causing him great pain for a long while. *I* knew, but he would not have me tell your lordship. He had no flesh on his bones. Oh, milord, poor Mr. Wilkins! . . .'

She stopped, hiccuping into a handkerchief which she pulled from an ample pocket in her frilled apron.

Esmond shut his eyes and clenched his hands. Wilkins *dead*. That old faithful heart had ceased to beat. Yet another death . . . another loss . . . and this time it struck not as intimately as the death of Dorothea . . . but it struck, nevertheless, right at Esmond's heart. In his fashion he had loved the old servant. Now he had nobody who really cared about him or whom he cared for in the least, except Archie who was, of necessity, often away.

He turned from the stare of the servants and walked quickly up the stairs.

57

That night, Williams, a new young valet, helped his lordship to disrobe. Esmond accepted his attentions but did not speak or look at him. The boy went downstairs and complained to Mrs. Fustian.

'When I removed his wig, I saw that the hairs on his head are quite white. He looks old and is gloomy,' the boy grumbled.

'Nevertheless he is young and you are lucky to have such a fine master,' said Mrs. Fustian crossly. 'Mind your p's and q's and remember what I have told you as to the way Mr. Wilkins used to behave. His lordship has had a deal of trouble and wants no more.'

Williams, who had an effeminate streak, bridled and whimpered.

'My last master was more jolly. I wish he had not died. I am afraid of my Lord Mornbury. He did not seem to see me, but to look *through* me. It was strange.'

Upstairs, at his escritoire, Esmond sat, quill in hand, writing to Archie by the light of three candles that burned in a silver candelabra.

'Come down and stay with me as soon as your affairs permit, for this House is full of Tragic Memories and during my

58

Absence my faithful Wilkins has died and lies buried in the churchyard at Godchester. There is a New young Fool here who simpers around and will infuriate me. I shall not look on Wilkins' Like again, I fear. Come soon, Archie.'

He quickly sanded this letter, affixed his seal and then began to walk restlessly up and down his bedchamber. Six months ago he would have sent for a host of friends and filled the place with pretty women, with music, with card-playing. But that was the old Esmond; those days had gone. He stopped to pick up the last letter received from the Queen. His gaze fastened on that most conspicuous paragraph:

'I will give you only until the New Year in which to mourn the Lady Dorothea, after which I command you to seek another bride and make all preparations for your marriage.'

He crushed the letter in his hand and hid his eyes against his sleeve.

'How can I so soon? *How can I?*' he muttered the words aloud.

It was then that he remembered Magda

and the letters she had written to him. A new thought, as poignant as it was sudden, struck him while he stood there, listening to the wild sound of the wind blowing tempestuously around Mornbury. Up till now he had been haunted by the memories of Dorothea lying at Shaftley in the chill of her dark and silver vault; of his fair gracious mother, long since mouldering in her own grave. Of old Wilkins, but recently taken from this house to his last resting place. And full of apprehension about the long lonely days ahead. But now this new idea gripped his imagination, bringing with it the first glimmer of hope to lighten his darkness.

If Magda but looked like Dorothea. If she, too, was beautiful and virtuous ... *why should he not consider carrying out the wishes of his Queen?*

Suddenly with a flush on his cheeks which had not been there before, Esmond sat down and picked up his quill again. It was to Magda Congrayle's father that he wrote, and the words covered several pages. At the end, he said:

'If, sir, you are willing, I would like you to send me the latest miniature of

your daughter, and hand it to my servant
who will be bringing this missive to you.
'I bid you farewell.

'Mornbury.'

PART TWO

CHAPTER ONE

It had been snowing now for a week.

Before the upper windows of a bedchamber in an old stonebuilt manor-house, a young girl knelt with her face pressed, like a child's, against the cold panes. She was staring out at a scene of considerable melancholy. Wild barren marshland beyond the grounds of the house which lay under the Cotswold hills some five miles from the village of Fenbridge. Land little better than a swamp in the winter.

It was late afternoon. It had been a short day if it could be counted by hours, for it was already growing dark, now, at four o'clock; but to Magda it had been as usual—a long-drawn-out martyrdom. She was always glad when she could creep to bed and draw the curtains to exclude the bitter cold that seemed to come through the very pores of the walls, and down through a roof that leaked in several places.

Wildmarsh Manor had much of beauty—

even magnificence—although so neglected and falling into disrepair. It had been built in the Jacobean period for a favourite of Charles II.

Sir Adam, Magda's stepfather, was born beneath this roof and married, as a boy of twenty-one, Jane, the widowed sister of the Countess of Shaftley. He brought her back here with her baby daughter who afterwards became known by his surname, for convenience's sake. Thereafter, Lady Congrayle produced three sons. So far as Magda was concerned, the boys, younger than herself, of course, were as good as full brothers and she loved them. They were the only people in this house whom she did love or who seemed to care one bit whether she, personally, lived or died.

They were out with their father now shooting wild duck. Lady Congrayle was abed, ill, expecting another child.

Magda thought of her mother with little feeling save pity. Jane Congrayle was such a weak, silly creature. Try though she would, Magda could not summon up much respect for her. Lady Congrayle went in terror of her husband (*that* Magda could understand), of her own feeble health and the constant child-bearing (her labour always went hard with her), and she was quite sure she was going to die now with this new one. She was no longer young and she had had two miscarriages and two stillborn babies after the birth of the last living son, Oswald, who was eight to-day.

Magda would have been sorrier for her mother if the unfortunate woman had shown any courage or honesty of purpose in the face of woe. But Lady Congrayle seemed unable to stand up either to her bully of a husband or her rough ill-mannered boys who were encouraged by their father to plague her and laugh at her feeble efforts to control them.

And never, since Magda could remember, had she tried to protect *her*, the child of her first marriage, from Adam Congrayle's cruelty. It was a sadistic cruelty which he showed to all women and to his servants and animals alike. He tyrannized his own sons but they were allowed privileges which had never been shown to the girl they called 'sister'.

Yet it had not always been like this. Crouching here by her window staring at the ever-darkening scene of snow-white desolation before her, Magda revived her memories of the past. She liked to revive them in order to prove to herself that there were such things as colour and warmth and true nobility in this world. Such things as love and tenderness. For all such elements were lacking in Wildmarsh Manor where life, Magda reflected, was as melancholy and often more brutal than the savage winter wind that raged across the marshlands.

Her own father had died when she was an infant so she could not recall anything at all about him although she had seen a miniature of a bearded gentle face which had suggested that he was the exact opposite of her mother's second choice.

She knew the history of that second choice from her old nurse, Tammy, who still served here as her mother's personal attendant. Tammy was, herself, a harsh domineering old woman but with a fondness for strong ale and when under the influence of it and alone in the house with the children, her tongue would loosen and she would relax from ill-humour into a gossiping mood.

Magda, always a lonely child, had learned much from Tammy's gabbling. It would seem that her own father had been a Cavalry Officer killed in battle. At this time her mother's sister became Countess of Shaftley. Jane, widowed and with a babe in arms, had none of Elsa's beauty but a certain amount of money, and this attracted a proposal from young Adam Congrayle, the squire of Wildmarsh. At this psychological moment it happened that Adam Congrayle needed a spouse who would help to enrich his own coffers.

Congrayle was by nature a lazy man who had never been known to do anything that others would do for him. He was also a spendthrift and of a greedy, grasping disposition. As landlord of the manor he became the most feared and hated man in the district. His outlook was positively feudal. To his way of thinking his farmers were there only to work for him and he extracted money from them and from his farms when times were bad, even though the unfortunate tenants were reduced by his despotism to penury and starvation.

For miles around Fenbridge, near Stroud, the roads were bad—too soft for wagon traffic all through the winter, and there was much disease among the sheep and the cattle. Congrayle employed bailiffs to bully the farmers into increasing their dues but in the period after Adam's parents had died, and he was squire of Wildmarsh, most of the large hedgeless swampy fields around the village were still being cultivated by the most primitive methods—none too satisfactory. The peasants, who looked to Sir Adam for help and good counsel, found none. Gradually his resources dwindled, and it was then that he met the young widow—Magda's mother—charmed her into marriage and grabbed the money that went with her.

Magda could not begin to understand how her mother could ever have accepted a proposal from an unattractive man of such ill-nature. But Tammy declared that the young Adam had been quite good-looking, and used to have a way with women. No doubt the widowed Jane had been lonely at the time and anxious not to pass the rest of her life alone, and was deceived into believing that Adam would make her happy.

She must have lived to regret it, Magda often thought with a cynicism unfitting in a girl not yet seventeen. For from the moment that Adam took possession of his wife and her fortune, he began to treat her as one of his chattels and to dispose of her money in the way that he had done his own.

Magda did not know but guessed that he spent a great deal of his time at the cock-pits (he liked gambling of all kinds), or up in the London taverns, among women of ill-repute. While he was away there was a certain amount of peace at Wildmarsh but when he was present, it was nothing short of an inferno—particularly for the highly sensitive imaginative girl who had grown to dread the sound of her stepfather's voice and the cruel sneer in his eyes when he looked at her.

Just for a little while, when she was small, she had known kindness from him. For then she had been pretty, Tammy told her.

'Sweet-faced you were, with your dark hair and your eyes of hazel-gold. The master often took you on his knee and petted you and said that you were better favoured than your lady mother . . .'

Her wretched mother! Magda had heard her stepfather shouting at the woman, calling her 'a bag of bones' and declaring that she was 'as poor at breeding as she was at pleasing a man in bed'. He wanted more sons, he said, to work for him and keep him in his old age. Oh, he was vile and he said and did the most abominable things. And he let even his home go to rack and ruin for he spent not a penny in repairing Wildmarsh, neither did he give his wife sufficient money for the food and fuel that she and her family needed for their personal comfort.

There were grand meals and lavish entertainment at Wildmarsh only when Sir Adam wished to impress one of his monied friends or acquaintances. Then the family would all be dressed up and paraded and Sir Adam would ape the charming husband and father. Little would the guests dream that as soon as they had gone, the fires would be let out (even in the depths of winter) and Sir Adam's charm would disappear as though by magic—leaving only the tyrant, before whom his family and servants cowered in terror. Their diet was often a loaf of black peasant bread washed down by local ale. Sometimes there was no one left to serve the Congrayles except one or two of the older servants—and Tammy—because the young ones frequently ran away, sick of being overworked and underpaid.

As for being lifted on to her stepfather's knee and petted—that had become only a vague memory with Magda. For when she was thirteen a terrible accident had befallen her and changed her whole life.

She had been out riding with two of her young stepbrothers. They often got up early and rode during the summer across country. The best horses in the stables were those that Sir Adam rode himself, but he liked his sons to hunt with him, and his little stepdaughter had shown herself, from an early age, to be as spirited on a horse as the boys—if not more so. Uninterested though he was in Magda he had had to admit that she showed every sign of becoming a remarkable horsewoman. So all the children had ponies and a rough country lad to help with the grooming, paid for by Sir Adam with his usual reluctance.

Magda's one passion in life was riding. She adored the Chase. But on that particular day of catastrophe, her mount attempted to jump a ditch, fell short and threw Magda, pitching her into a pile of scrap iron—the remains of an old rusted up farm wagon which was lying in a heap in the field where she fell. She had nearly died. Her face had been cut to bits and there was not a portion of her body that did not receive bad bruises.

It was a year before she could walk

properly or bear to look again in her mirror. When she did look—young though she was—she was appalled. *She was permanently disfigured.* She was ugly now. She would never receive a proposal of marriage from any man. That meant she was doomed to spinsterhood and to remaining here, at Wildmarsh, for the rest of her life.

Never would Magda forget the anguish and horror with which that young girl in her early teens had regarded her changed countenance.

Up till then she had been called 'fair'. Even her stepfather in his good moods, praised the excellence of her slender graceful form, her good features and that especial strength and vitality which she had always exuded.

'Your daughter, Madam,' he used to say to his unhappy wife, 'is more likely to turn men's heads than you have ever done. She has no dowry, but it is possible that her face and her abundant health may attract a suitor.'

But after the accident all was changed. Magda had grown painfully thin, and nervous of strangers, and although the left side of her face was unmarred and still had a certain beauty of brow and high cheek bone and tender chin, the right side was marred by criss-cross scars—welts which had healed but badly. One corner of her mouth was pulled down, giving her a crooked unpleasing expression. Nothing was left now, she could see, but the golden hazel of her eyes, and the slimness of her waist and ankles. Even her hair had suffered. It had grown scantier since her accident and there was one snow-white lock running like a pale band across the smooth dark head. Some might have found it an attraction, but to Magda it was just another horror. Her stepfather had implanted it firmly on her mind that she looked old and repulsive. During her illness Tammy had nursed her. Her feeble complaining mother busy with a confinement brought her little comfort, but Sir Adam, as usual, was sadistically cruel. When he had first come to see her after the physicians had finished their poor work, he had put his hands on his hips, straddled his legs and shouted at her:

'God's teeth! Miserable child. Wretched girl! For me to be landed with such a freak. You will frighten men away rather than draw them. Now I will have to keep you all your life. You will be nothing but an expense to me and a nuisance. It is a pity that your fall did not end your miserable life.'

The thirteen-year-old girl had listened to his frightful speech in silence, one trembling hand against that side of her face which was then red and angry with the newly-healed scars. She could remember to this day how sick she had felt and how unbearably humiliated. But she was the exact opposite of her cowardly mother and had a spirit that could never be broken even though her body was flayed alive. She had given her stepfather a bitter look, then said between her teeth:

'Your wishes are mine, Sir. I, too, wish that I had died.'

She had turned and limped out of the room, one foot being still injured, although it had healed since then and she could walk now as well as ever. Sir Adam had shouted after her:

'I will not have you spoiled and pampered, like your brothers. I shall dismiss one of the servants and you shall work in her place to recompense me.'

And he had seen to it that this cruel decree was carried out. Magda, henceforth, received no favours as the young lady of Wildmarsh. Except for the one fine garment into which she was always bundled when her stepfather wished to make an impression on a caller, she was forced to wear her mother's cast-offs and to aid the country girls who were the servants of the house with the dusting, the sweeping, the bedmaking.

Lady Congrayle protested. But her whole life was a protest against the monstrous man whom she had taken for a husband, and utterly futile. If she was indignant that the daughter of her first marriage should be treated badly she had neither the heart nor the strength to say so and to fight on Magda's behalf. She, too, was disappointed that the girl had lost her looks and might never marry, and often, with her customary tears and moanings, made Magda aware of the fact.

From the time of that accident onwards, Magda came to believe that she was a good deal more repulsive then was really the case. She developed a horror of her own looks. She shrank from the gaze of the world. Her brothers teased her and called her 'Scarface' which name did nothing to increase her self-confidence. But they were not unkind like their father, and often took her part when he was being especially brutal, or brought her tit-bits from the table, for she was often left hungry. Sir Adam saw to it that she had fared little better than his servants.

The one thing that the accident had not destroyed was Magda's innate love of the horses, and of riding. She had little time now to indulge in the sport but with the aid of one of the boys and in her stepfather's absence, she would steal away from the house and ride again. Then and then only she would feel fine and happy and in her rightful place. Born to the saddle; with the wind blowing against her marred face, the old excitement of the hunt stirred the sluggish blood in her veins. Then in her imagination she became Diana the Huntress, and ceased to be the despised drudge of Wildmarsh.

Then there were the times when her mother and stepfather exchanged visits with the Shaftleys. Lord Shaftley, being one of the richest men in England, commanded Sir Adam's respect. With such a brother-in-law, he was obsequious and smoothly hypocritical. Before him he aped the affectionate husband and the tender father. Jane, his wife, was far too frightened of him to dare open her mouth and tell the truth to her sister, the Countess. And Magda was not the type to complain. So, when the families met, all seemed on the surface quite normal. Magda was attired as befitted a young lady of her station and at Shaftley Castle she glimpsed what seemed to her, life in another world. Life as led by Dorothea. Inevitably Magda worshipped her lovely cousin who was always so kind and friendly and who never once allowed Magda to feel unsightly or unwanted. Indeed, she tried to comfort her with the sweetest words; remarking on similarities between them, rather than making such disparaging comparisons as poured from the lips of Magda's stepfather at Wildmarsh.

'Except that you are darker, we have much in common,' Dorothea would often say, 'We are similar in build and height, and our voices are *exact*. We might be sisters, dear Cousin Magda.'

'Alas, I am very different from you, Cousin,' Magda would reply, sadly but without envy. She loved Dorothea too much to envy her. And when she heard that Dorothea had become betrothed to the young Earl of Mornbury, Magda wrote many warm congratulatory letters, full of happiness for her cousin. She received in turn, the most glowing epistles from Dorothea describing the handsome, fascinating Esmond and rhapsodizing on her joyful prospects.

To Magda it had come as a crushing blow when this beloved cousin died so tragically on her wedding morning. She had accompanied her parents to Shaftley and shed bitter tears in the chapel, looking her last upon that exquisite face. That so much beauty should have perished had seemed a terrible calamity to Magda.

'Why, why was it not I, who am plain and despised?' Magda had asked herself in bitter grief.

She had set eyes for only a few moments upon the bereaved Earl and her girlish heart had fluttered and throbbed at the sight of his handsome anguished face. Her heart had gone out to him in sympathy. Long after leaving Shaftley she had remembered that curious moment when she had been bidden by her uncle to speak to Esmond and he had rushed past her as though he had seen a ghost. It had not struck her at the time that it was because her voice and her form had recalled Dorothea to him, although she knew that he had not looked upon her face because of the veil she had been wearing. She had often covered her face with a veil since her accident; not so much because it was necessary as because she could not bear to see the pitying glances thrown at her by any stranger who chanced to look upon her disfigurement.

But after returning home, she had thought much about Esmond in her sad lonely fashion when she heard of his accident. Out of deep sympathy, and quite unbeknown to the rest of the family, she started to write to him. So those strangely lucid delightful epistles had reached and impressed Esmond Mornbury.

When his first and only letter, thanking Magda for hers, reached Wildmarsh, Sir Adam suddenly realized what his stepdaughter had been doing. The letter was given to him before ever she saw it. After reading the contents, he sent for Magda and asked her for an explanation. She answered sullenly; she had no excuses, she said. She had just felt the need to console her dead cousin's unhappy betrothed.

At that, Sir Adam had burst into raucous laughter.

'As if anything that you, a freak, could do, would console a gentlemen of quality,' he sneered.

And he tore Esmond's letter to pieces, thereby robbing her of the pleasure of reading it, herself. Somehow that new cruelty roused the hot temper that was latent in Magda.

'You fiend—that was *mine!*' she had screamed at him, scarlet-faced.

Whereupon he had slapped her and sent her reeling to the floor, telling her that nothing was hers.

'Perhaps you thought you would lure the Earl of Mornbury into taking you for a wife instead of Dorothea,' he had shouted, and burst into fresh sneering laughter.

The young girl had rushed up to her attic room and wept with shame and fury, knowing in her poor bruised heart that she had never imagined any such thing. But writing to Dorothea's bereaved, unhappy lover had in some way brought her solace.

Now it was over. She had been robbed of her pleasure just as she was robbed of everything beautiful or exciting in life.

She was allowed only a few moments to

wrestle with her tears, and then heard old Tammy calling her:

'Magda! Magda! Coom to my lady. She is needing you.'

Magda wiped her face, smoothed a coil of hair into place and covered it with the white mob cap, with hanging lappets, which she usually wore. The muslin was so thin through constant washing and ironing, it had become like paper which she feared would crumble. But there was no money for a new one. She wore an ugly brown dress and jacket of rough cheap material. The sleeves were short and showed girlish slender arms and hands of extraordinary beauty with long slim fingers. She was at least spared by her stepfather from the indignity of doing the roughest work and so had preserved the alabaster whiteness of those hands and the perfect oval of pink nails. But at this time of the year those charming hands were usually red with cold and often swollen from chilblains.

She walked into her mother's bedchamber wrinkling her nose a little with disgust at the heat and the foetid atmosphere. Lady Congrayle abhorred the cold and when she was ill and about to give birth she was permitted by her mean and tyrannical husband to light a wood fire. Magda knew that the wretched woman was now approaching her time. She lay in the big four-poster, looking sick and dejected, her sunken eyes like an owl's in her pinched face.

Usually when she sent for Magda or spoke to her it was to nag, or remind her fretfully that she had not done this or that. To-day she held out a more welcoming hand. Magda, unused to any show of affection, took it in sullen silence and felt how burning hot it was.

'Have you a fever, Madam?' she asked.

'I am going to die, Magda,' said Lady Congrayle in a sepulchral voice.

Magda softened.

'No, no, Madam, you will be all right, I am sure. If I can help you—'

Jane Congrayle broke in:

'I have wondered if perchance I will die before the child draws breath. My head aches fearfully but your father refuses to send for Dr. Crabtree. He says the expense when the birth takes place will be great enough.'

Magda gave a laugh far too hard and bitter for one scarcely seventeen years of age.

'He, who boasted that last week in London he lost a small fortune at his dicing.'

Lady Congrayle looked fearfully towards the door.

'Sssh! If he hears you say such a thing he will beat you.'

The girl fingered the laces on her bodice and laughed again.

'He can do many things to me, my lady mother, but he will not beat me. He knows that if he lays hands on my body, I will tear his face to ribbons with my nails.'

Lady Congrayle whimpered again and brushed the tears away which were running down her long nose.

She was such a stupid weak-willed woman that she had no mind of her own, and what she had, she was too frightened to use. She would like to have made life easier for Magda but found it impossible to do so. Sometimes she had considered writing the truth to her sister at Shaftley and begging for the Earl's protection. But every time she took up a quill to pen that letter she dropped it, half demented with terror. The long years with Adam Congrayle had taught her that he was not sane and that he found his pleasure in torturing them all.

'Magda, Magda,' she began, 'what is to become of *you* if I die—?'

Then she broke off. Her yellowish face assumed a look of deep distress. They both heard the heavy clank of boots on the stone passage outside. Lady Congrayle put a warning finger to her lips. Magda nodded and stood with her hands clasped a trifle nervously behind her back. Sir Adam entered the room.

He looked in a good mood. His full red mouth was smiling and his small slittish eyes gleamed. He was handsomely and warmly attired with a fur collar, as befitted a country squire. He carried one of the latest pipes in one hand and a document in the other. He enjoyed this new smoking.

He glanced slyly at his stepdaughter.

'I trust you have recovered from your tantrums, my dear.'

Magda pressed her lips together.

'Answer me, you imbecile!' thundered Sir Adam and his pleasant expression altered to one of such passion that the sick woman cowered under her coverlets.

'Oh, Adam, Adam,' she sobbed. 'Do not be cross with Magda. I feel so poorly. I know I am not going to live.'

'Rubbish!' he said.

Magda stepped forward.

'I am truly concerned about my mother, Sir.'

He looked her up and down.

'Shut your mouth!' Sir Adam shouted, 'Am I to be plagued morning, noon and night to spend money unnecessarily? A doctor indeed—before even the pains begin. What abominable extravagance!'

Magda, afraid though she was of the man, felt the sudden desire to help her wretched mother. She said:

'If your lady dies before the infant draws breath, it will be upon your conscience.'

Silence fell. Rarely had anyone addressed the master of Wildmarsh in such terms.

Magda's gaze flickered nervously around the room.

The appalling gloom of her stepfather's house always reduced her to this state in the winter when it was not so easy for her to get out of doors.

Then suddenly she heard a gurgling cry from the bed and saw her mother sit up and put two clenched fists against her stomach. She rushed towards the bed followed by her stepfather and Tammy, who uttered a cry as she saw her mistress's face.

'God have mercy—she's dying!' Tammy

screamed the words.

It appeared that even Sir Adam decided that he had gone too far this time, for he seized his wife's clammy wrist and snapped at Tammy:

'Send for Dr. Crabtree. Tell one of the grooms to saddle a horse and ride to the village.'

The physician arrived. Magda and Tammy worked to help the old gentleman at a task which he had performed often enough but this one turned out to be a good deal more difficult than the others.

It was a long labour. One of the worst Dr. Crabtree had ever attended.

To the young girl it was all horrible. Enough to destroy all sense of romance for if this was the end of loving, God help all women, she thought.

She left the bedchamber only to see that the three boys were sent to bed, feeding them first with bowls of milk and porridge. They knew little about what was happening to their mother and cared less.

Oswald, the youngest, and Thomas who was ten leaped gladly into the bed they shared, roaring with laughter because their nightgowns split as they jumped. Thomas tossed his garment to Magda, and bade her mend it. But the oldest boy. christened Adam after his father, followed Magda out of the room and questioned her about his mother.

'Will she give up the ghost do you think, Magda?'

She stared at him bleakly. She did not dislike the young Adam. He was like their mother's side of the family, fair and blue-eyed and he had a nice side to him and none of his father's cruelty. But he knew nothing of love or loving, she knew that, for he had not been allowed to learn about the gracious things of life. His father had brought his mistresses to this house and Magda was aware that the twelve year old boy had seen them with his father, so regarded such things without feeling. He had no tenderness for his mother. But suddenly the rare tears blinded Magda's eyes.

'You would not be sorry if she did. No one would be sorry except perhaps Tammy,' she said in a choked voice.

The boy stared at her and straddled his legs in a way that reminded her unpleasantly of his father.

'Poof,' he said, 'you cry-baby. What does one woman less in the world matter? Father says it does not.'

'Get to your bed,' said Magda and closed the door roughly in his face. She heard him laugh uproariously the other side and join in a scuffle with his brothers.

They were untamed little animals, she thought. They should have been at school years ago, only their father would not pay for their education. Reluctantly he had employed the services of a tutor who called at Wildmarsh every morning to teach the lads to read and write, and to study Latin and Greek. It was necessary even in Sir Adam's estimation that his sons should not grow up as illiterate as the peasants.

The tutor was as greatly afraid of Sir Adam as the rest. He came here only because he needed the money. And it was from him that Magda had learned much that she knew. Without being found out, she had managed to attend daily the lessons that the old tutor, Mr. Bacon, gave to the boys. Often, in her garret, by the light of a stolen candle, she would work at her writing and devour the books that she found in the library of the former baronet. And she felt a certain fierce pride when Mr. Bacon complimented her on her progress and told her that she was better at lessons than the boys who were lazy with their homework.

Adam Congrayle forced the girl to read to him aloud in the evenings when she was tired out and always by a poor light which strained her own sight.

At midnight, Jane Congrayle gave birth to her eighth child; a sickly girl who died a few hours afterwards.

Magda fully expected her mother to pass into the Beyond with the infant. It was a wonder to her, to Tammy and to all that Lady Congrayle survived. Weak in every other way, her wretched heart was strong and continued to beat even though the unfortunate lady longed to die. Once the doctor had gone and all danger was passed, Sir Adam ceased his pretence at being the anxious husband and father, and stamped around the cold dark house, candlestick in hand, raving at everybody who came his way.

He cared nothing that the infant had died.

Magda, half dead from exhaustion—for it was long past midnight—was sorely in need of rest. But she was not permitted to go to bed. Sir Adam was in the mood to tax her strength and patience. He waylaid her just as she was about to ascend the stairs and dragged her into the library.

'You cannot be tired, my dear—you have done nothing, nothing,' he said. 'And now that I have been kept awake so long by your mother's miserable efforts at giving birth, I am wide awake and would like to be amused.'

Magda regarded him stonily.

'What do you wish me to do?'

He flung her a sheet of printed paper.

'Perhaps you do not know, but there is a war with France, and I would like to hear the present state of affairs. This print is poor. Read to me, girl. Maybe while I listen to your ugly voice I will fall asleep,' and he yawned prodigiously and flung himself into a chair, thrusting out his legs.

She looked at him in disgust. His breath stank of wine. The reflection upon her voice did not disturb her. Dearest Dorothea, who was dead, had had the exact same intonation and it always seemed to Magda melodious; so how could it be that *her* voice was so unpleasing?

Oh, God, how difficult it was to see by candlelight when one was so bemused with weariness.

Magda's slender hands shook as she held up the page and began to read it.

Defoe's Review.

'*Purg'd from the Errors and Partiality of Newswriters and petty Statesmen, of all sides . . .*'

'Louder!' blared Sir Adam, 'you are mumbling, girl.'

Magda went on doggedly. As she came to the words: '*May contribute to setting the affairs in Europe in a Clearer Light . . .*' she paused. For her voice was overshadowed by the loud and healthy snores of her stepfather, who had, as he had predicted, fallen asleep.

She cast a look of loathing at his open mouth and disarranged cravat, dropping the *Review*, and climbed the stairs to her own room. She sluiced her face with the ice-cold water which she poured into a small basin and combed her hair, but in the middle of unbuttoning her dress, she dropped down upon the bed and slept, half-clothed, completely exhausted.

CHAPTER TWO

Magda was so tired that she overslept. It was her stepfather's familiar blaring voice that roused her. He bellowed up the staircase:

'Magda! Magda, where are you?'

She rose, buttoning her bodice with icy little hands and simultaneously she heard the grandfather clock in the hall strike the hour of eight. *Eight o'clock.* She was horrified to find how late it was.

She drew her curtains and was surprised to find that it was a fine day. Through the diamond frosted panes, she could glimpse snow-covered gardens sparkling in the pale light of the winter's sun. Hastily she braided her hair, put on her cap and ran downstairs. She should have been up two hours ago.

She fully expected to receive a lecture for being late when she saw her stepfather and was amazed to find him waiting for her at the foot of the staircase with a broad smile on his face. It was a smile which was good-humoured but at the same time sly and objectionable. She immediately wondered what fresh misery he was planning. But he opened his arms wide.

'My little angel! My sweet Magda! Come to your father's embrace, my lovely rose,' he greeted her.

She stared at him stupefied, blinking,

hardly yet awake.

As he folded her in a bear-like hug and kissed her on both cheeks, tickling her with his beard, she began to wonder if he was mad. But he set her apart from him and looked her up and down with that same beaming smile.

'My chicken, my dove, my brilliant little daughter!' he exclaimed.

She stared up at him, her mouth open. Through the open doorway she noticed a stranger in riding clothes standing by his horse, talking to her stepfather's groom. Sir Adam said gaily:

'Do not look so surprised my love. Did you wonder why I let you sleep? Yes, yes, you must have plenty of rest and bring the roses back to those cheeks and I have told Aggie to bring you eggs and a bowl of porridge, and send to the farm for a jug of cream. You need fattening, my dear. Men do not like skeletons, and I think with added weight you would have quite a delicious figure. I believe—'

But now Magda broke in, feeling hot and even terrified.

'What is this about, Sir? What does it all mean? You speak in a foreign language.'

Sir Adam gave a loud laugh and turning,

led the way into the morning room where Aggie, a scared-looking maid, was placing a jug of coffee and a newly baked loaf on the table.

'Eggs! Where are the eggs, you simpleton?' bellowed Sir Adam. 'Did I not order eggs to be boiled for your young mistress?'

Magda really began to feel that her stepfather had gone out of his mind. As a rule, if she was lucky, she got stale bread and a bowl of butter-milk. As for being called 'young mistress' she did not remember hearing that name since her disfigurement.

'Sit down, my dear, sit down,' boomed Sir Adam and drew a chair up to the table for her.

She looked at him with her grave eyes which held a hurt too deep for any ordinary man to fathom.

'Why, Sir, are you treating me like this this morning?'

Sir Adam seated himself opposite her. He went on smiling. He was fingering a letter which, Magda noted, bore an important looking crest.

Suddenly she said:

'Something untoward has happened. Is

my mother—'

'Your mother,' he interrupted impatiently, 'is quite herself this morning, and there is no need for anxiety. You shall see her later. Meanwhile let me say how much I admire your wits, my dear. Oh! you must be the wittiest and most intelligent maiden in this house of idiots—or indeed in the whole of the Cotswolds.'

She gulped.

'To what do I owe your compliments, Sir?'

'Do you not remember,' he said, 'that some little time ago you received a letter from a certain noble Gentleman thanking you for the letters which *you* sent to *him* while he lay in a Dominican Monastery?'

She nodded.

'I remember well. You mean my cousin Dorothea's betrothed husband?'

'The very same. Esmond, fifth Earl of Mornbury.'

Magda put her hand to her throat.

'What of him, Sir?'

Sir Adam unfolded the letter which was inscribed with a dark purple ink.

'There has come this epistle from Mornbury Hall, this time inscribed to me personally—and brought by one of his lordship's grooms who has had three days' hard riding through the snow to bring the letter here, on account of its extreme urgency.'

'But what,' asked Magda, staring, 'has it to do with me if he has written to *you*, Sir?'

'Ah, my dear, you underrate yourself, as usual,' said Congrayle in a voice which was meant to be pleasing, but sounded horrible to Magda. 'No one save my rose of the Cotswolds would have dreamed of writing those clever epistles to a young nobleman. And clever they were, I am sure. And I deem you wise and most excellent to have joined your brothers' studies and read your books and gathered the knowledge which has singled you out from other less literate young ladies. I can also take a modicum of the credit, insomuch as I have allowed you regularly to read the world's news to me, and so instructed your mind rather than allowing it to be wasted on less urgent matters.'

He stopped, coughing. Magda was utterly perplexed, but it struck her as being an irony that he should talk of 'wasting her mind'—he who had wasted the last four years of her youth by forcing her to perform only the most menial tasks in this

95

household.

She tried to be patient, eyeing the letter in his hand.

'Will you not tell me what Lord Mornbury has said that should concern me, Sir?'

'Later you, yourself, shall read all that he has written. Now, in a nutshell, I will inform you. Her Majesty the Queen has commanded that the young Earl, her godson, should take to himself a wife. He writes that he is still grieved by the loss of your cousin Dorothea, and can think of no woman in the world who could replace her to his sincere satisfaction. Nevertheless, marry he must, he states, and his choice has fallen upon—whom do you think, my dear?'

'I do not know,' said Magda faintly.

'My modest flower. It has fallen upon *you*. You whose letters he describes as having intrigued his fancy because they were so tender, so full of kind sentiments, so well expressed. You whose voice, he says, when he heard it at Shaftley, reminded him of another's—one forever lost to him. He has asked that I send him a miniature of yourself. If it pleases him, he wishes no further meeting. He will then, he

96

says, with the permission of your parents, consider you betrothed to him. The marriage will take place, as commanded by the Queen, in the first month of the approaching year of our Lord, 1708.'

Magda heard these words like one in a trance. Her heart had started to beat so fast that it seemed to get out of control and make her dizzy. Her breath came in little gasps. She muttered:

'Me. Me. He would wed with *me*.'

'Yes. Is it not astonishing?' asked Sir Adam gaily. 'And is it not delightful that I should have a stepdaughter who has taken the fancy of one of the wealthiest and noblest Gentlemen in this realm? He wants no dowry. He has stated so. He requires only a sweet and virtuous wife who will please him and give him an heir. You, I am sure, my little chicken, will do both.'

For an instant the girl sat dumbfounded. The shock of this announcement was so great that it took several minutes before the full impact of it smote her. Her thoughts fluttered like frightened birds round and round in her head. *A man had asked for her hand in marriage*. And such a man as Mornbury. She could see Esmond as she had seen him at Shaftley on the day of

Dorothea's burial. Tall, handsome, splendid, even though that day he had been a figure of grief.

And *he* had asked to marry *her*. She who had never expected a proposal from any man, even a yokel. She could not believe it. It was too devastating—too sudden a magic transforming her black tormented world.

Aggie, the maid, came in with the eggs and fresh butter and honey and placed them in front of her master and with a terrified glance from him to Magda, left the room again.

It was a long low room with heavy black beams. The plaster was discoloured. The green velvet curtains were now a faded yellow; the furniture, dark heavy oak. The walls were hung with paintings of former Congrayles—Sir Adam's ancestors—each one looking, Magda had always thought, more unpleasant than the others, although none so repulsive to her as the present baronet.

In the warmth of the sunshine, a great cake of snow thawed and fell from the roof with a crash on to the stone terrace outside. In the distance she could see young Oswald and Thomas pelting each other with snowballs. They were barefooted and would catch cold, she thought dully. But there was no one to control them.

'So you see, my dear,' she heard her stepfather's voice, 'that is why I am so pleased with my little Magda. There is going to be a marriage, and you are to become Countess of Mornbury. No doubt your husband will make us all handsome presents, and come to my aid when he knows that I am so short of funds. The fact that my Magda will occupy such an exalted position will also help to appease my creditors. Do you wonder that I am amiably disposed towards you this morning?'

Then suddenly the girl came alive. She sprang to her feet. Her uninjured cheek was as white as the snow outside. The other, blotched with scars, burned red, as always, when she was upset.

'Enough of this,' she cried. 'You know full well that I can never become Countess of Mornbury.'

Sir Adam, pouring himself out a mug of ale, glanced at her over his shoulder, brows upraised.

'Do I hear aright?'

'I can never become Countess of Mornbury,' repeated Magda in a violent tone. 'The Earl has never seen me. If he had done so you know full well he would not want me for his wife. Have you not told me a thousand times that I am ugly ... a maimed creature that no man would take to his bed? You must be insane to suppose that the noble gentlemen who once loved my cousin Dorothea would ever put me in her place. Why, he would run from me as from the devil—if he saw me.'

Sir Adam digested these words in silence, gulping down his ale, after which he smacked his lips noisily. He did not know whether to wipe his greasy mouth with the cuff of his coat, or with the linen napkin provided for the purpose. In either case it would mean that he must pay for the washing thereof. Soap was a necessary article but expensive. Then, without looking at his stepdaughter, he said:

'You are quite right, my love, in thinking the Earl would not choose you in place of your beautiful cousin if he saw you. *But he will not see you.*'

'How do you mean?'

'Wake up, wake up, my chicken! Use these wits that God gave you, and which you have so far put to such advantage. You are not a fool like your mother. This marriage can be arranged and very soon will

100

be solemnized without his lordship ever having set eyes upon that face that has . . . ahem . . . been a little spoiled, shall we say, in an unfortunate accident.'

'Spoiled!' echoed Magda, with a harsh ironic laught. '*Spoiled!*'

'Ah well, maybe in the past I have been a little harsh in the comments I have made about your appearance. But from one angle, you still appear quite charming and with a few well-made clothes and clever, concealing veils, and the application of some of those new salves and powders . . . as used by the ladies of quality in London . . . you might still pass as a beauty my dear. Yes, quite easily.'

Magda shook her head.

'It is not possible . . .'

'All things are possible and I intend that this shall be more . . . it shall become a fact. *You shall marry my Lord of Mornbury.*'

'I tell you I cannot!' said Magda, her voice cracking.

Sir Adam broke off a crust of bread and began to chew it reflectively.

'Let me see. This is the beginning of December. Christmas is at hand. It is in the New Year that my Lord wishes to tie the nuptial knot. Yes, yes, quite so. But first he must see your miniature and approve of it.'

'There is no miniature of me!' Magda cried. And her eyes were dark with passion and misery. 'And even if a painter could straightway imprint my likeness upon a piece of ivory, it would be hateful ... displeasing to any man. Look at these— look at them. Do I not see them every day of my life!' she exclaimed, striking a clenched fist against the grooves and welts on her right cheek, and touching her pulled mouth.

'Tush,' said Sir Adam. 'You are determined not to use your brains this morning, my love.'

Then from the big pocket of his coat he drew a case and handed it, smiling, to the girl.

'Pray glance at this.'

She opened the case dazedly. She saw against faded sapphire-blue velvet, a miniature set in a gold oval frame. It shewed the head and shoulders of a young girl. A vacuous but quite pretty face with languishing big eyes, pink cheeks, cupid's bow lips. There were lace ruffles at the neck. The hair was tied back like a peruke, with a black ribbon. Hair of an indiscriminate colour. Stupidly Magda stared, then recognized the face.

'*This is my mother.*'

'Yes, it is she, as she was at your age, my dear. It has been my turn to show my wits. I remembered this treasure which she gave to me when we were first betrothed. True it bears no resemblance now to the bag of bones that lies upstairs. But do you not see a faint resemblance to yourself?'

'No, Sir, I do not!'

'Come, come,' he chided her. 'Looking at the untouched side, it does resemble you. Your hair, of course, is darker, but that does not matter. Anyhow, this miniature is going to be sent to Mornbury by his messenger now—at once.'

Then Magda understood. She let out a hissing breath. Her scars burned yet more fiercely upon her face and brow.

'No, *no*, it would be monstrous! It would be cheating. That miniature is not of me.'

'I say that the miniature *is* of you,' Sir Adam roared in his old hectoring voice, and his eyes warned her. 'It is of you,' he repeated, 'and now I see it again, I find also a resemblance to your dead cousin. Yes, Dorothea might well have been a little like her Aunt Jane, when she was sixteen summers.'

103

And he thrust the miniature under Magda's gaze again, pointing to the chin, and the snow-white slender neck.

Oh, yes, there was a family resemblance there, Magda had to agree, strong enough to impress the unfortunate Esmond, perhaps. The large hazel eyes might have been Magda's except for their arch expression which could never be called hers. Perhaps poor mother had been coy in her youth, but she, Magda, never. She was of a more serious mind.

'It can never be,' at last Magda broke out, trembling from head to foot. 'It would be a gross injustice to my Lord Mornbury. He should be asked to look at *me* before he pledges himself.'

'Look at you? Fool. Then you would lose the greatest chance of your life. And I would never get rid of you.'

'So that is why you want to foist me on to Esmond Mornbury; because you hate me and wish me out of the way.'

'That is as it may be. But this chance has come and you shall take it.'

'Surely he will have heard from my aunt at Shaftley that my looks were ruined as a child.'

'Your mother had her relations' word

that they would never disclose the fact to anyone and you were veiled while at the Castle.'

'Then Esmond will come here and visit me and see for himself,' panted Magda.

'He will not. I have already bargained for that possibility. I have written to him and to Shaftley to say that your mother lies ill and that your brothers have the pox and that no one may enter this house.'

She stared at him incredulously.

'Oh, you are sly and wicked!'

He laughed. He seemed determined this morning not to resent her insults. It meant too much to him personally to bring this venture to a successful conclusion. Esmond should see the miniature, he said, and approve, but he would not come all the way to the Cotswolds, to a house where there was the pox. In the fullness of time, once the so-called danger had passed, he, Sir Adam, would suggest that rings should be exchanged and the betrothal agreed upon. Then—because Wildmarsh would still be a poor place to come to with its sick mistress and ailing boys—Magda should instead be taken by coach down to the South and to Godchester, and be married there to Mornbury.

Magda listened to this plan, her whole soul rebelling from it.

'There is no pox at Wildmarsh. It is all a pack of lies. Lies to drag Esmond into a marriage which he would shrink from if he knew the truth and could see me as I am.'

Sir Adam leered at her.

'He will see you only in your gorgeous bridal attire my dear. Your face will be veiled, and by the time he unveils it, it will be too late.'

'It would be a crime. And I should be returned to my home as Henry VIII returned Anne of Cleves, once he saw what she was truly like. He, too, was deceived by a Holbein miniature.'

'You read too much history,' said her stepfather in a freezing voice, 'but if I recall the incident, King Henry saw to it that Anne was adequately recompensed. If Esmond returns you to me, it will be with a generous portion which will help to recompense me for all the money I have spent on your upbringing.'

'You are vile beyond belief,' she breathed, knowing that was what she had always wished to say to him.

'Nevertheless you will do as I command. Eat your eggs and take plenty of cream with your porridge. It is as well that you put some flesh on your bones before you go to your bridal, then what you lack in face you may make up in form.' And Sir Adam laughed unpleasantly.

'I will never consent,' she began.

Then he came to her, seized one of her wrists and twisted it so that she winced with pain.

'Imbecile! You will do this or I will make your life a living hell.'

'Do you think that it is not one now?' she asked.

His small eyes blinked at her under their bushy brows. He was astonished by this show of spirit. Never before had she defied him quite so blatantly. Then he changed tactics. He became cunning—like a fox that noses his way through the undergrowth, fearing that the hounds are upon him. He began to whine.

'Do not think only of yourself, Magda. My little Cotswold beauty, think of your mother who needs the things I can ill-afford to give her. As for your brothers—they should go to Grammar School but I cannot pay the bills. The Earl of Mornbury has wealth enough to make your eyes open. Your aunt and uncle at Shaftley have always spoken well of him.'

He went on gabbling, pleading, pointing out that it was Magda's bounden duty to her family to make this marriage should the Earl approve of 'her' miniature. She was less easy to handle than her mother. He had to adopt a caressing voice which almost made Magda laugh—it was so horrible.

'You have an excellent bosom. Perchance Mornbury will not reject you. Think how happy you would be as the cherished wife of so handsome and fine a man. You will be received by our gracious Queen. Is not Esmond Mornbury her godson? Ah, my dovelet, you could not let such an opportunity slip by. It would be a crime.'

Magda's head shot up.

'And is it not a crime to send Esmond Mornbury the likeness of my mother and allow him to believe it is mine?'

'No crime, my duckling. Only a little subterfuge. Pray listen, my treasure, and decide. Come—the Earl's messenger awaits our answer.'

Her mind was a maze of conflicting thoughts. Oh, yes! she would like to feel that her fortunes had changed and that she was to go forth to Mornbury as Esmond's bride; to get away from this fiendish man, this unhappy house. Yes, and yes again! *But could she do it?* Could she bring herself so to deceive an honourable man, and the one whom Dorothea had loved?

Her stepfather rose.

'I shall send the miniature to the Earl in any case, and we shall see the result,' he said, smacking his lips loudly.

'No—' began Magda.

But Sir Adam had gone.

She heard the clop, clop of horses' hooves. She knew that Mornbury's man had ridden away with the miniature. The Earl was to be tricked.

Magda began to tremble. She picked up the long closely-written letter which her stepfather had dropped on the table. Her eye caught one paragraph:

'It was in my mind to remain unwed, having no Heart to replace the Image of her for whom my soul repines. But if marry I must, then it shall be to One whose Voice recalls those lost and happy Hours and in whose Veins there runs the same blood; whereby some Child of ours might come to resemble that Fairest of all Lilies who has been gathered to the Angels. With some Eagerness therefore,

Sir, do I wait your reply and an expression of Willingness from your daughter whose tender youth can be entrusted to my care. She shall receive the Respect and Homage due to her Youth and Station in life and my gratitude for her faithful and devoted letter-writing while I lay so low and ill.'

A formal proposal. Every word of it, written from a sense of duty alone—an act of obedience to the Queen—without love. At least she would know that Esmond did not love her—but only the memory of her cousin which he imagined that she might conjure up for him.

What hope, Magda asked herself bitterly, had she of ever bearing a child who even faintly resembled Dorothea? She dropped Esmond's letter, her heart thudding with slow painful beats.

Dear God, I cannot do this thing.

Before her stepfather returned, she ran up to her mother's bedchamber. Lady Congrayle was reclining on her pillows trying to swallow the food that the old nurse was giving her. She still looked sickly and piteous. It seemed that already she had heard about the Earl's unexpected and

110

astonishing proposal. Her sunken eyes rested with some eagerness on her daughter. Immediately she began to appeal to her to accept the offer.

'I know that Sir Adam has not done right in sending my miniature in place of your own likeness. But if the Earl approves, I do implore you to let the betrothal go through.'

'She'd be a ninny if she didn't,' put in Tammy with a cackling laugh. 'What chance has the daughter of this house of getting a fine husband without practising a bit o' deceit.'

Magda's cheeks burned.

'You are all very anxious for me to commit this sin.'

'Oh please, my dear child, think of it not as sin but as an act of mercy towards your miserable mother,' wheedled Lady Congrayle. 'Consider the purgatory of my existence. Dr. Crabtree said last night that if I am subjected to another confinement it will kill me. All that your stepfather really desires is the money that Mornbury will send if he tells him how depleted his income is and how needful we all are. Do not infuriate Sir Adam by refusing to make the endeavour. Even if the Earl sends you home again, it will be with gold in your purse. He is said to be a generous man.'

'And you would have me treat a generous man so badly?' flashed Magda.

Lady Congrayle started to cry.

'For my sake, I implore you, Magda. Strike a bargain with Sir Adam. Ask that he will leave me in peace and allow me to lead a more endurable life in return for the benefits that your marriage will bring him.'

Magda walked to one of the windows. She stared blindly down at the snow. Two blackbirds hopped across the crust on the white grass. It was a dazzling winter's day. She longed for the fresh air and sunshine, and hated the odour in here. Everything about Wildmarsh seemed an abomination this morning. Goaded and nagged by both mother and stepfather, the young girl began to feel mentally exhausted and weak. And deep in her heart she knew that she wanted to do as they begged. To have a fine home of her own instead of the humiliation and drudgery at Wildmarsh. Temptation indeed! Yet somehow, she had built up a romantic idea of Esmond Mornbury and hesitated to play so low a game with him. To her he was the Great Lover sorrowing for his lost love. She had never heard of that other Esmond; the profligate, the ruthless fighter, the arrogant sometimes cruel Esmond. For he had shown himself always at his best at Shaftley Castle.

Magda turned suddenly to her mother, pale and tense.

'Madam, think what my position will be if the Earl likes the miniature and is betrothed to me by proxy in the manner he states, then having seen my face, he marries me only because he will be forced as an honourable gentleman to do so. Think how I shall feel about that!'

Tammy ran to the bedside clicking her tongue, as she bent over Lady Congrayle.

'Tch! Tch! You will be responsible for the death of this poor lady,' she muttered. 'Should not a right and proper daughter think of the one that bore her in travail such as you witnessed last night?'

And as she applied vinegar to Lady Congrayle's forehead she rattled on complainingly, and further confused the young girl's reasoning. Magda could but shudder with horror of the memory of last night's agony. True, the wretched woman in the bed deserved some pity if not thanks for giving *her* life, considering what a misery it had become.

113

She tried to comfort the weeping invalid by assurances that she would ruminate upon these facts, and then rushed away—unable to bear the atmosphere a moment longer.

But she went straight downstairs to further torment—a nagging from Sir Adam; which continued for the rest of that bleak winter's day.

Magda would gladly have escaped, done her usual work, or played with the boys, or at least taken some air. But when the sun went in and night fell upon Wildmarsh with a black gloom that portended a further fall of snow, her torture was renewed.

Hour after hour, Sir Adam alternately raved, ranted and pleaded until Magda was so stupefied that she hardly knew what answers she was giving.

She was sick with worry and fatigue when at last she crawled to her attic room, allowed to seek her bed. Up there, she fell upon her knees and rested her head on her folded arm. She felt nauseated. Her stepfather had made her eat a quantity of rich food to-day to which her thin young blood was unaccustomed and her stomach rebelled.

Still more did her mind rebel against the

thing which they were trying to make her do.

Soon, she reflected desperately, Mornbury would see the miniature and, perhaps invite Sir Adam to arrange the betrothal.

Oh, she thought wildly, what could be the outcome? She knew full well the rigours of the winter months on these roads from the Cotswolds to Surrey. To-day it had been difficult enough for Esmond's man to get through on horseback. To-morrow it might be impossible. Snow was falling again softly, relentlessly, through the night with a sharp wind to rattle the casements. The temperature of Magda's attic was below zero. She was so cold that she could not get warm in bed and dozed fitfully, rubbing her cold little feet together.

Sir Adam had promised that to-morrow she could change over to one of the guest rooms that was never now used, and have a fire, and that Aggie should personally serve her. She should receive fine warm clothes as befitted her new station, and live like a lady, and write again to the Earl, telling him how sad she was to leave such a good home.

Magda was human enough to yearn for

the pleasant alteration in her life which Sir
Adam held out as a bribe. With a special
cunning he had even offered to buy her a
better horse and see that she had time and
opportunity to ride it whensoever she
wished. But none of this meant as much to
Magda as his solemn vow that if she
consented to her bridal he would
henceforth keep out of her mother's way
and allow Lady Congrayle to live in her
own rooms. He would see that she ended
her days in peace.

When Magda bade her mother good
night, the sickly creature seized one of
Magda's hands, covered it in tears and
kisses and babbled:

'Marry the Earl if he sends for you. Say
nought of your disfigurement. It is for my
sake more than your own. Do not have my
death on your soul. I swear I will take
poison if you leave me to live my life as it is
now.'

The young girl rushed out of the room in
horror, asking herself if it was indeed her
duty to practise this fearful deceit upon
Mornbury and so save her mother from
suicide.

CHAPTER THREE

It was over a fortnight before the answer from Esmond Mornbury reached Wildmarsh Manor. Two weeks of the most bitter weather Magda could remember in the drear Cotswolds. Blizzard after blizzard raged until the crusted snow was piled high against the walls of the damp old Manor, accompanied by wild gales and an intense cold which seemed to grip everybody by the throat.

The whole family and all their retainers crept around the house muffled in their coats or capes with hoods over their heads. Even the spirits of the boisterous little boys were quelled. They, too, hung around dismally, coughing, while their mother slowly—all too slowly—gained strength, sequestered in her bedroom, nursed by the faithful Tammy.

It was a fearful time for Magda; even though she was given better food than the others, and allowed more leniency than she had enjoyed since she was a small girl. But she felt that her stepfather was watching her—that he followed wherever she went in the house; a dark threatening shadow, a hunter stalking his victim.

She was subjected to both cajolery and threats; given no peace. All the while, Sir Adam's voice droned on.

'You are putting on a little weight. Yes, you are a little plumper, I do declare. It will add to your attractions as a female. You will not be altogether displeasing to his lordship, I warrant. Eat more. Drink more, my dove; thus shall we have a pretty bride to send to Mornbury.'

Or:

'Your poor mother has a yellow look to-day, and, I fear, is not so well. She needs a change of air. I warrant it would do her good if I sent her to drink the waters at Bath or Cheltenham or even to The Hague to stay with my Dutch cousins. But alas, I cannot afford the fare. But you, when you are Countess of Mornbury will be able to do so.'

Or:

'Young Adam is abominably educated and will never grow to be the man of culture we all desire, unless he can get to St. Paul's. I would send him if I could afford it, but I cannot. But you, my dear Magda, once you hold the exalted position

118

of Countess of Mornbury, will do much for him and his brothers.'

On and on, until Magda put both hands over her ears and stifled her screams of mad irritation.

Night after night, Lady Congrayle, fastening on to her husband's suggestion that she should travel to Holland, added her appeals. There was nothing she would like more, she told Magda, than to go to The Hague, even though the Dutch cousins were stodgy and dull. But there would be peace in their quiet house on the water, and *she would be out of reach of Sir Adam.*

'Marry Esmond if he sends for you. Go to him, I beg of you,' she kept imploring the girl.

Then suddenly, a new morning dawned fair over Wildmarsh. The whole household wakened to see sunshine. The icicles thawed, dripping from the eaves. In the night a strong wind had blown away the storm-clouds. With remarkable speed the sky had cleared. A white, bright world replaced that gloomy nightmare and before midday, the first traffic moved again along the dirty, slushy roads. Bells could be heard jingling on the farm wagons that rolled behind their great horses. The nostrils of the beasts steamed into the air. Forty-eight hours later, the post-chaise at last got through to Fenbridge bearing a letter for the squire.

Magda had been sitting by her mother's bed embroidering when her stepfather burst into the room. It was easy to see that he had received good news. His wolfish teeth showed in a smile. He rubbed his hands together as he greeted the two ladies.

'I trust I find my dearest Jane much improved ...' he bowed with unusual ceremony towards the bed. Lady Congrayle gave him a sour glance and, in return, muttered a reply. He looked now at Magda. At once her body broke into a sweat and she felt the scars on her face tingling. She could guess what was coming.

Sir Adam swept her an even more stately bow.

'Salutations to the future Countess, and congratulations, my dear.'

Her hand tightened over the tapestry. The needle pierced her thumb and made her jump. She sucked the scarlet pinpoint of blood that began to ooze from the tiny wound. She was as white now as her muslin cap. Her large tragic eyes smouldered at her stepfather.

'The Earl has replied?' she asked under her breath.

He drew a letter from his pocket.

'In the most admirable fashion, my dear. Take it, see for yourself.'

Magda could scarcely read the words written in that handwriting which had become so familiar. The missive was dated a week ago, sent from Mornbury Hall.

She was in such a state of confusion and nerves that she could not really take it all in. She only knew that Esmond had received that miniature—and that it pleased him.

'It hath a Winsomeness and an Innocence which does indeed remind me of my Dorothea and therefore Evokes my Tenderness. I therefore do formally Request, Sir Adam, the Hand of your Daughter Magda in marriage. She, being willing shall Receive the Consideration and Affection which a Wife may expect from her lawful Husband. Having a Mind to the fact that your household is afflicted, and the Lady Congrayle sick-a-bed, it will perhaps be foolish for me to Expose Myself to the Infection and expedient for Magda to be brought to

Mornbury Hall and the marriage solemnized in my own private chapel . . .'

There was one part of the letter which went on to say that as from the date on which the letter was written Esmond would consider himself betrothed husband of Magda, and her, his future wife. With this letter he sent a ring, bearing his family crest. This gold ring, Sir Adam held up for Magda to see, grinning, chuckling. That ring was in itself a binding oath, he said. Further to this, Esmond wished that Sir Adam would deliver his affianced wife to Mornbury on the first day of the New Year.

The letter was signed with a flourish and had been sealed.

The paper dropped from Magda's trembling fingers. She sprang to her feet and rushed to the long mirror that hung in her mother's room. She looked wildly at that side of her face which was scarred and distorted. She pulled off her neat cap and let her long dark hair tumble about her shoulders, staring at the white band across her brow.

'I cannot . . . I cannot!' she gasped. '*Look at me!* What resemblance do I bear to the miniature of my mother? What right have I to practise such villainous deception?'

'Come, my dear,' said Sir Adam in a dangerously quiet voice. 'No histrionics, I beg. We have argued enough this last few weeks. I want no futher defiance from you. You shall do this thing or I shall lock all of you in this room *and then set fire to Wildmarsh.*'

He ended these words with an evil chuckle which sent a thrill of horror through the ladies, and brought a shrill scream from the one in the bed.

'Mercy on us. He would do it, too. He is a madman. He would roast us all and tell everybody that it was an accident.'

The old nurse shuffled up to Magda.

'Do as Sir Adam says, child, for all our sakes.'

Shuddering, Magda turned from her own reflection and hid her face in her hands.

'When Esmond has seen me, he will send me back,' she moaned, 'I could not endure it.'

'When he sees you it will be too late,' snarled Sir Adam. 'He has given his word and sent his ring. And as a gentleman of honour he cannot altogether refuse you on the grounds that you are physically repulsive to him.'

Magda sank to the ground. No tears came but her whole body was shaking.

Physically repulsive! Those terrible words did not give her much encouragement. She was appalled by the thought of what she would have to go through. Yet in a dim way she felt that her stepfather was capable of carrying out his fiendish threat to set fire to this house and burn every female in it unless she made a sacrifice of herself. Her fingers groped for the letter again and her burning gaze devoured the final paragraph.

'With respectful and tender greetings to her whose Letters comforted me in my Sorrow and who will shortly walk at my Side.'

A great sob tore her throat.

Would it not be the most wonderful thing in the world to walk beside Esmond Mornbury? Her mind teemed with the memory of him; so pale, so handsome, so desirable on the burial day of her cousin. But to go to him as a cheat and a fraud, less like Dorothea than any woman in the world . . . that would be despicable!

She felt her stepfather's hand on her shoulder. She sprang up like a creature at bay. He was not smiling now. He was looking at her through his slits of eyes, a demoniac hatred and threat in that gaze.

'Well?' he growled, 'do you go with me to Mornbury?'

'For God's sake, Magda . . .' broke in Lady Congrayle hoarsely. 'Even after discovering the trick, Lord Mornbury may allow you to stay with him. Anyhow it will be a better life for you than you have ever known here. And you will save us all.'

A better life? Magda wondered. Ill-treated though she was in her one home, she could at least deem herself honourable now. But to go to Mornbury, be branded as a cheat and looked at in horror by Esmond, would be to steep herself in dishonour.

'Well?' repeated Sir Adam, in a voice that froze her very marrow.

She thought:

If he killed me, alone, I would not care, for I have no wish to live. But I cannot let him torture these others . . .

Suddenly her mind was made up.

'I will go to Mornbury,' she said, in a flat voice that held no expression at all.

Her stepfather sprang towards her and

tried to embrace her. Suddenly her spirit flared up. She kicked him on the shin with the point of her shoe.

'Fiend—keep away from me, or I will go nowhere, save to my tomb. I will kill *myself*.'

He laughed insanely, bowed, rubbed his hands together and called her by loving names. He would send to London, he said, immediately, for dressmakers and materials for her trousseau. She must sit down now and write a letter to Mornbury, acknowledging his proposal and giving him her personal consent. Henceforth she should live like a princess until they set forth on the wedding journey to Godchester, one week after Christmas Day.

He clapped his hands, ordered more logs to be put on the fire in his wife's bedchamber; and sent wood to the library wherein Magda could sit and read and sew in peace.

'This is a great day for us all,' ended Sir Adam smacking his lips. 'From now on our fortunes will change. We shall receive the bounty of our rich and noble daughter. May the Almighty smile upon her.'

After these unctuous words, he withdrew.

Then Magda fell on her knees beside her mother's bed and burst into terrible weeping.

CHAPTER FOUR

It was the evening of December 30th. In London, the weather was mild and there had been much fog, but this evening it had lifted and there was better visibility.

Esmond Mornbury and his friend, Archibald St. John, had just emerged from their sedan chairs and were standing outside the door of Esmond's elegant little house in St. James's. The link boys who had lighted them home had gone. The chairmen had received their pay by the light of the lanterns which were attached to the front railings of the house.

The two gentlemen, both richly attired under their heavy, caped coats, and wearing fashionable hats of military style, laced, and with cockades, were discussing their evening's entertainment.

St. John was back in the diplomatic circle in London just now and had been only too delighted when his friend who had lived so long in seclusion and mourning, had opened up his London house and consented to spend the night with him.

They had just attended the most modish entertainment of its kind, the Marionette Theatre which had been opened by a famous poet of the day.

As the lackey admitted them into the warmed and well-lighted house, Esmond unbuckled his cloak and threw it to the man who hastily lit the candles in a small charming room where supper was laid for the two gentlemen.

Esmond yawned.

'We have had quite good fun, Archie. It seems strange to me to be back in London again.'

St. John grinned at his friend.

'Once I thought you would never return to us, Esmond.'

'I never intended to,' said Esmond in a low voice.

'Let us not enter into any discussion of the sad past,' said St. John hastily.

He had found Esmond in tolerably good health, and better spirits, than he had seen him since Dorothea died. Esmond's exile from London had, of course, ended once the announcement of his betrothal to

Magda Congrayle was made public. Immediately the Queen received the news at Bath, she had expressed herself pleased. Esmond told Archie that the letter he had received from his Royal godmother had expressed her extreme contentment that he had agreed to take a wife and settle down. The Queen knew little of the Congrayles, she stated, save that Jane Congrayle was sister to Lady Shaftley for whom her Majesty had a warm regard, and that the young Magda was cousin to the beautiful lost Dorothea. Her Majesty was sympathetic with Esmond's wish to ally himself to one so closely related to his beloved.

Archie, himself, had no particular feelings one way or the other about Esmond's second choice of a future wife. The Congrayles had never entered his own life; although, when mentioning Sir Adam at one of the Clubs the other day, he had heard that gentleman spoken of somewhat slightingly. He had been described as a person of some ill-humour and meanness. But of Sir Adam's private life nobody knew anything other than that he came from the Cotswolds and was squire of Wildmarsh Manor and that his family lived modestly and in seclusion owing to the squire's lack of means.

None of this had seemed of prime importance to Archie but he talked freely to-night over supper about Magda Congrayle.

''Tis indeed exciting to know that you have found someone who can and will fill that sorrowful void in your life, Esmond,' he said, once the two friends were seated at the round well-lit table, beside a brisk fire.

Esmond stretched his long legs before him and looked reflectively at his plate.

'The strange thing is, Archie, that I have never yet seen Magda.'

'I was astounded when you first told me so.'

'It happens that I have been unable to pay a visit to the Cotswolds. It is a long distance and besides her two brothers lie ill after the pox.'

'Let us pray that she will not catch it.'

'Her father assures me that she has not been in contact with her brothers and is out of danger.'

'So you marry without looking upon your bride's face until the day of marriage.'

'I do,' said Esmond calmly, 'but I have this to enlighten me. . . .'

And he passed Archie the miniature which had been sent to him. Archie studied it by the candlelight. He thought the face sweet if a little expressionless, but he said:

'She is charming.'

'And do you not see,' said Esmond is a low voice, 'how the turn of the chin, the tilt of the nose, the largeness of the eyes can well be said to resemble those of Dorothea?'

'I do indeed,' said St. John sincerely.

'They are of course first cousins, so it is not strange. And although Magda, poor child, can never be to me what Dorothea was, it shall be a satisfaction to me to know that the same blood runs in her veins.'

Archie returned the miniature and started to eat his pheasant. He was thinking:

I do not envy Miss Congrayle. She will ever be second in Esmond's mind and heart to Dorothea; and constantly compared with her.

'Do you understand how I have been feeling, Archie?' went on Esmond. 'The Queen insisted and who better could I marry than this pretty cousin of Dorothea's?'

'Who, indeed?' murmured Archie.

'It is of little account to me how my spirit

will react towards her when we meet,' added Esmond. 'All I demand of Magda is that she should be a loving wife and give me sons to fill my empty house.'

'I am sure she will do so,' said Archie.

'She has led a very secluded life in the Cotswolds,' went on Esmond.

He seemed disposed to discuss Magda with his close friend. He had not seen Archie for so long. To-morrow they were journeying together to Mornbury. On the following day, the first of the New Year 1708, Sir Adam was expected to arrive at the Hall bringing with him the bride.

'Not knowing her it adds a queer zest and excitement to this enforced marriage,' went on Esmond. 'I remember only the moment when she flitted into the library at Shaftley and spoke to me with the sweet and musical voice of my lost darling. I tell you, Archie, the similarity of their voices was remarkable.'

St. John nodded. Esmond had a morbid streak, he knew.

He was quieter than St. John remembered him before his long illness and sojourn with the Dominican monks. After the meal, Esmond opened up his heart to his friend again as they sat by the fire.

'I rode over to Shaftley Castle once the abominable weather improved, meaning to speak with Lady Shaftley about her niece. Until then I had not been able to bring myself to go near the place. But I went there in vain. The bereaved parents have been residing in Rome with Italian friends ever since Dorothea died, seeking to forget their misfortune. Lady Shaftley wrote to me—this letter which I received this morning.'

He tossed this missive to Archie who scanned it.

It was written by a heart-broken mother—expressing some astonishment at Esmond's sudden decision to marry her niece. It would have offended both her and her husband's susceptibilities, she said, had they not realized that it was the Queen, herself, who had demanded that Esmond should terminate the period of mourning. As for his choice, Lady Shaftley was in one way pleased, she wrote, and could understand why he had decided to marry her little niece. She trusted that he would not regret it. Magda had led a tragic life, and the home from which she came was far away in wild countryside, and not a happy one.

'My sister Jane is of a highly nervous Disposition and always ill. Sir Adam, my brother-in-law, appears hard put to it to find money for his family and when Magda came to Shaftley with her parents six months ago, I noted that she seemed of a desperate Shyness. She admitted to being Happy only when she was out riding ... It's a wonder she sits her Horse so well after the accident, about which no doubt you know.'

Lady Shaftley ended the letter on a more joyful note, by wishing him and Magda good fortune and happiness from the bottom of her heart.

'I am glad,' Esmond, 'that I am not to be divorced from the friendship of the Shaftley family whom I greatly respect.'

St. John looked up from the letter.

'So you have a wife who is shy and reserved? Well, they are not bad traits in a female. But what of this "tragic life" and what accident?'

Esmond shrugged his shoulders.

'I do not know. But if Magda has had some tragic experience, it will make her appreciate my own predilection for sorrow.

134

She will respect my feelings. As for her riding, that pleases me. I prefer a woman who can grace the saddle and join me in the hunt.'

'Well I am sure I hope it all turns out for the best, Esmond,' said St. John warmly.

Esmond added:

'Those letters which Magda wrote to me when I was at the Monastery pleased me greatly. The last one I received from Wildmarsh Manor intrigued me still more. In it, she announces her intent to become my faithful and devoted spouse and states that I am already dear to her. I can ask for nothing more can I?'

St. John laughed and shook his head.

''Pon my soul, you are a supreme egotist, Esmond. What will *you* give to *her*?'

'All that money can buy,' said Esmond coolly. 'I have already visited my legal advisers with a view to settling a handsome portion on my wife, and I will gladly go to the assistance of her parents since they are so impoverished. I have more money than I know what to do with. It is emotionally that I am destitute. As this girl has obviously been brought up not to make demands— she will suit me. She will not ask for love I cannot give. It will be as the French call it, a marriage of convenience.'

Archie began to look solemn. It did not, in his estimation, hold out great promise of happiness. St. John had other ideas on matrimony and females. Even the beautiful Dorothea had seemed to him a trifle insipid. St. John's own fancy at the moment had fallen on an extremely spirited and handsome young lady in Edinburgh, the daughter of a Scottish nobleman. His dear Alison possessed a frank, warm nature, which roused nothing but admiration in the affable young diplomat. He intended to return to Edinburgh and pay court to her in the near future.

In the morning, the two young men left London in Mornbury's coach, and reached Godchester on New Year's Eve. The beautiful grounds of the Hall lay under a white pall of snow. No birds sang. It was Esmond's wish that his marriage should be quiet and private. Only the near relatives, and his greatest friends were attending.

Esmond was in a curious mood that cold and frosty night which was to be his last of freedom. He drank a little more than usual, though not overmuch. Once attired for the night he dismissed his valet (Williams had never been able to take the place of old

Wilkins) and seated himself on the edge of the bed. He sat gazing for a long while at the miniature of Magda sent to him by Sir Adam Congrayle.

How would she strike his senses when at last she stood before him? He pictured her as this miniature suggested she might look. Big eyes, pink cheeks, charming little chin, slender build. Enough to waken a man's desire. Innocent and *tragic*. So Lady Shaftley had described her. Tragic, perhaps, because she had been so much repressed and kept in seclusion at Wildmarsh. Poor child, he would try to be gentle with her. He would be glad now to settle down. Mornbury Hall needed a mistress. What better than to marry one who was related to Dorothea?

Then Esmond scowled with some perplexity at the pretty painted face in the oval frame. Somehow it portrayed a character totally out of keeping with the one suggested by Magda's letters. She was of course still a child, barely seventeen, yet she had written with a surprising maturity and wisdom, and shewn remarkable learning. The girl in the miniature was sweet but did not suggest great intelligence, or a female of spirit. Could *she* ride a half-broken horse? He had to confess himself mystified, but quite agreeably intrigued.

'I have indeed created a mystery for myself, but to-morrow should prove interesting,' he thought with a short laugh as he placed the miniature back in its case, climbed into the big bed and snuffed out the candles.

Meanwhile the last twenty-four hours before Magda left Wildmarsh Manor seemed but a continuation of the nightmare in which she had lived for so long. That she was being better treated did little to lighten the burden of her feelings. She had made up her mind to go through this farcical wedding which she knew would hurt only one person badly—herself—and she did not intend to retract the decision. In her queer way she had a fixed determination and could not easily be moved from it. Nevertheless she suffered because of the wrong she knew she would be doing Esmond Mornbury. She suffered physically, too, because her stepfather went to drastic lengths to try and alter her appearance.

All through that time which she had to wait before taking the journey to Mornbury (Sir Adam kept up the lie to Esmond about his home being infected with the pox, and no one being allowed to pay a visit there) Magda was treated like a stuffed marionette. Sir Adam jerked the strings, pulling her this way and that, making her dance to his tune.

Women came down from London. Experts in cosmetics, in hairdressing, in dressmaking. The Manor became a hive of activity. While the snows melted under the pale December sun, much stitching and experimenting went on. It seemed that even Lady Congrayle began to take an interest in her daughter's trousseau for she rose from her bed and gave a hand with the fine embroidery at which, at one time, she had been an artist. The wretched Magda looked on, unsmiling.

Every day now, somebody new came to look at her face and examine her scars. They applied fresh lotions, paint and powder. She hated the smell of it. When it was over she would stare at herself in the mirror and feel that she looked worse then she used to do. She thought that this mask that the so-called experts made of her face, was horrible; with a red gash for a mouth in a doll-like countenance that had two pink blobs on the cheeks for blushes, and lashes heavily blackened. They even dyed the white streak of her hair so that it was all dark now. They crimped and waved it and tried first this fashion and then that. It was raised and dressed high on pads. It was put down and ringleted. It was interlaced with ribbons or poms-poms. It was given a Dutch look. It was stuffed under a wig.

Each night Magda went to bed feeling that the hairs had been torn out of her stinging scalp; her face burned with continual patting and smearing; her body ached from tight lacing or padding. She was weighed down by petticoats. They hung velvet, brocades and silks on her, cut, stitched, fussed, chattered and criticized. Certainly her stepfather spent money, feeling that it was an investment, since to make Magda palatable to his lordship, he must try to increase her attractiveness.

The trousseau swelled. Boxes and coffers were packed. Occasionally allowed to rest, Magda sat on the side of her bed, watching the women fold her new dresses and undergarments. Her face was expressionless. She did not feel one single feminine reaction of pleasure in any of these things. Her stepfather complained that she might as well have been witnessing the sewing of her shroud. Now and again he forgot to smarm and slaver and beg her to give him a good character, and shouted at her.

'You Death's Head! You Nincompoop! Are you not grateful for all that I am spending on you? You are going to your wedding with finer garments than your mother came to me. Why do you look so sour?'

Then he would make the weary yawning maids unpack again in order to brandish in front of Magda's stony gaze some of the trousseau. An embroidered stomacher gay with satin bows; a piece of Mechlin lace; a pair of white Persian gloves; silk stockings decorated with gold clocks; flounced petticoats over dome-shaped hoops; rich mantuas of pink or blue damask; thick silk bedgowns which he mouthed over in his evil fashion, slyly eyeing his stepdaughter.

'Milord Esmond should be overcome with desire by such naughty frippery, and forget your twisted mouth, my dear . . .'

He made these and other remarks which offended Magda's modesty and sent hot waves of anger through her slender body. But she said nothing. Her spirit burned but she would not be drawn into open battle with Sir Adam again. She had made up her mind to that. Only once she turned and said between her teeth:

'Have done with this mockery, I pray you. You are selling me into marriage like a slave and I have accepted the bondage for the sake of my unfortunate mother. Let this be enough and hold your peace, or I will never reach Mornbury alive. I will join my cousin Dorothea in the tomb and lie forever at peace.'

This quietened Sir Adam for he was only too anxious to get the marriage contract signed and sealed and so be excused his debts in London. He humoured her and said no more.

Some nights before her wedding, the young girl lay alone in the big bedchamber which had recently been hers and began to think about Esmond. So full were her days and so quickly did she fall asleep at night, she rarely had time or energy to contemplate the thought of him as a future husband.

By the light of two candles and a leaping fire, she sat up and read one or two missives that she had recently received from *him*.

'I do most grievously deplore the Foul

Disease that has affected your poor brothers and so restrained me from paying a visit to my Intended Bride. May your brothers soon be restored to Full Health and I am most thankful that you yourself have escaped the Plague. Each night I look upon your miniature and am resolved to love and cherish Dorothea's sweet cousin whose youth and beauty will not Fail, I know full well, to excite my affections . . .'

Magda's lips worked. The tears she had not allowed her stepfather to see, filled her large tragic eyes and rolled down her cheeks.

'*Oh God!*' she whispered. '*What will he say when he sees me and discovers how grossly he has been misled?*'

The very eagerness in his letters heaped coals of fire upon her head.

Through her tears she read another letter.

It was to thank her for her last epistle to him. She had, at Sir Adam's bidding, sent many such to Mornbury. One she had been ashamed of. She had sent it, suddenly feeling the overwhelming need to express some truth . . . some sincerity . . .

something that came indeed from the bottom of her broken heart. *She had written in terms of love.*

'Night and day, beloved Sir, my thoughts turn to you and I pray that Almighty God will make me worthy to be called the wife of Esmond Mornbury and to replace that Angel whom you loved so well. Whate'er should hap, know that Magda Congrayle has no wish but to please you and since we have never met but for that Fleeting Second at Shaftley, I trust that you Believe implicitly that I mean as well by You as You do by Me. I shall hope not to disappoint You.'

As soon as she had sent those words, she had felt the bitterness of shame and remorse. Yet it was true that she had begun to build up an image of Esmond as a fine and honourable gentleman whom any girl would be proud to call Husband, and whom she could love passionately. She had begun to idealize him. She was pitifully anxious to please him. But when she looked at her ravished face, it made her sick with self-loathing.

She sobbed aloud as she read yet another of his letters.

'You write so sweetly to me, dearest Magda. I know that you must possess a gentle and amiable Disposition. You need not therefore, fear to Disappoint me. I felt much interest in your excellent Description of the Wild Boar Hunt in the Forest and deem that you must be a commendable Horsewoman whom I shall be proud soon to have riding at my side.'

This letter he signed:

'Till we are for ever united on January 1st.

'I am,

'Your devoted Esmond.'

Her devoted Esmond.
Magda laughed suddenly but it had a harsh and unhappy sound. He would see her, shrink from her and maybe send her back to Wildmarsh Manor.

Writhing and moaning, Magda hid her face in her pillow.

'I cannot go through with it,' she gasped.

Then she thought of this madman whom

her mother had married, locking all the women in a room and burning Wildmarsh Manor to the ground and calling it an accident.

She began to argue with herself. What did it matter if Esmond rejected her? She could not be much worse off. At least she need not return to Wildmarsh.

Then she began to build up a feverish dream of Esmond Mornbury as her lover—finding her acceptable.

Suddenly she took off her bedgown and with hot eyes, examined her body in the flickering candlelight. It was unblemished, with beautiful small breasts and delicately curved flanks. Did not Sir Adam say that a man's fancy could be seduced by a lovely female form? She had put on a little weight, it was true, and was all the better for it.

She would be heavily veiled for her bridal. Esmond might through the fumes of drink, imagine her less terrible than she feared. She began to think of *him* taking her to his bed. She imagined the sweet pangs of shared passion. She, who had been starved of all love all the years of her life, experienced a new anguished surge of longing for the unattainable. It set her weeping again. Pulling the bedclothes over her she alternately sobbed and prayed and finally exhausted, fell asleep.

Then came the morning of departure.

Magda felt terrible; her head ached and her eyes were swollen with weeping. She rang for Aggie. When the curtains were pulled back she saw that the day was sunless and felt a bitter cold in the room where the little maid hastily lighted a fire. Looking out of the window, Magda thought she had never seen Wildmarsh Manor look more desolate or grey. The duck pond was frozen. There was no sign of bird-life in the stricken trees. This morning she would be setting out on the long journey to the south.

God help me and give me strength, she thought.

Tammy came bustling in, snapping her orders at the younger servants. Then a young modish woman, more highly trained than the others, joined them. She was to help attire the future bride and travel with her. Magda did not like Annette. She was by profession a lady's maid and had French blood in her. She wore a smart grey dress and white mob cap with hanging lappets. She was fussy and talkative and had a high screeching laugh which got on Magda's

147

nerves. She wore false red curls. It was Magda's belief that Annette was one of her stepfather's mistresses but nothing like that seemed to matter now. Annette had been brought down here in order to supervise Magda's wardrobe.

What she thought of the bride's appearance, she never said, but Magda fancied that Annette's sharp black eyes held a look of derison and malevolence whenever they turned to the scars on the injured face.

When she was bathed, rubbed down by Annette and given coffee and a steak for her breakfast in front of the fire, the three little boys came into the room to see her. They were more subdued than usual. They regarded her with awe and curiosity. Young Adam, as usual, was spokesman. He scowled to hide what was a very real grief because his half-sister was about to leave home.

'Shall we never see you again, Magda?' he asked.

'I do not know, but I daresay I may visit you,' was her reply.

'We shall have nobody to read to us,' put in Thomas and snuffled and rubbed a running nose with the back of his hand.

Young Oswald, only a scared child of

eight, drew nearer to Magda, picked up a
fold of her velvet wrap and touched her
long black hair.

'Where is your white lock, Magda?' he
asked dolefully. 'Have you cut it off?'

'No, it has been dyed.'

'Are you going to die, too?' he asked
horrified.

Young Adam, gaining courage, shouted
like his father:

'Stupid little fool. She doesn't mean *die*
like that but change the colour.'

Oswald started to cry and then the three
boys set up a wrangle.

'I don't want Magda to go away,'
whispered Oswald.

'Stupid fool!' repeated young Adam.
'She is going to be a Countess and send us
more money.'

Thomas, who was greedy, cheered up.

'Will you send me money to buy a new
saddle for my pony?' he said.

'If it is possible,' nodded Magda, smiling
ironically at their inherited avariciousness.

And she leaned her aching head on one
slender hand and stared unsmiling at the
little boys. The noise they made wearied
her. Yet she felt something approaching
pity for them. She had always looked after

them. God knew what they would do without her, left to their imcompetent mother and the old scared tutor.

Then Lady Congrayle came into the room, walking on a stick as she did these days, and looking like a yellow scarecrow. She sent the boys out, seated herself by Magda and began to talk to her in her sad whining way.

Life would not be the same at Wildmarsh Manor without Magda. Alas, alack, what misery, to be losing such a good daughter.

Then Magda gave a harsh laugh and said:

'Losing such a good slave, you mean, Mother.'

'Do not be unkind. I have so much to bear,' moaned Lady Congrayle.

'I do not want to be unkind, Madam,' said Magda, 'but I find it difficult to weep at parting from anyone here. Equally difficult to shout for joy at what awaits me.'

'You do not know, it may all turn out better then you think, child.'

The Jane Congrayle held out her arms, sobbing.

'Kiss your mother. Leave her a kind word.'

Pity and disgust, both, tore at the girl's heart. Her mother as well as her stepfather had driven her to play this dastardly trick upon Esmond and she could not forgive either of them. But she was aware that the weak-willed Lady Congrayle had been punished enough already with a husband like Sir Adam. So she knelt at the woman's lap and permitted her to play with her hair and stroke her cheeks and ape the fond mother. And indeed, Lady Congrayle felt a real regard for her eldest child this morning.

'Think of us here with compassion, even if your own lot be hard,' she whimpered.

After that, the master of the house thumped on the door and warned Magda to be ready. The journey must be started in an hour's time.

Magda was thankful that there was no more time for sentiment. Now all was bustling activity with last minute packing of her boxes and her own attiring. Much against her will, her face was painted and powdered. She was put into fashionable travelling clothes; a dress of dark green velvet, entirely covered by a tent-like cloak lined with squirrel skins. Her curled hair was covered by a fur-lined hood.

No one could see how tired or pale she looked under the mask of thick paint. Her eyes were heavy, fathomless and looked straight ahead of her. Sir Adam, himself, wearing a fine new travelling suit, peruke, and cocked hat, went about, organizing, gesticulating, driving the servants frantic with orders which he continually gave, countermanded, then repeated.

Now, in the courtyard, Magda saw a fine leather-covered coach studded with nails, with four horses; excellent roans, whose manes and tails were tied up with blue and white ribbons. The postillions were attired in the blue and cream livery used by Mornbury's personal servants. With a slight sense of shock, Magda realized more fully what she was doing and where she was going. For Esmond had sent this equipage to conduct her to his estate.

Because of the length of the journey from the Cotswolds, and the poorness of the narrow roads, Esmond had suggested that the journey be done in three phases. His future bride and her escorts were to stay the first night in Newbury at the house of friends of the Earl's who would be glad to extend her their hospitality. On the following day they could rest again at Guildford—this time with a cousin of Esmond's who would be following in his own coach to attend his kinsman's marriage.

On New Year's Day it would be but a question of twenty miles for the horses and the bride would reach Godchester by mid-morning.

The last goodbyes were said to her mother and stepbrothers. The miserably paid ill-nourished servants stood out in the cold wind snivelling, wiping their noses on their sleeves. All were sorry to bid farewell to Magda. The young girl, alone, in this house, had shewn them kindnesses and understanding.

Magda found herself in the Earl's beautiful padded coach with Annette, the voluble French maid, at her side. Annette clasped on her lap a special basket in which food for the journey had been packed, including a bottle of home-brewed wine for Sir Adam. The Squire of Wildmarsh, opposite the two women, sat smiling his pleased cunning smile, stroking his chin with one hand while he pressed a knee lasciviously against Annette's once the coach began to rock and sway over the rough roads. Excellent though my Lord Mornbury's coach might be in comparison with any the Congrayles had hitherto travelled in, there was much motion and Magda began to feel nauseated and tired before the horses had covered twenty miles.

In different circumstances, she might have enjoyed such a break from routine; she had rarely been away from home in her life. The last time was to attend the Shaftley family after the death of Dorothea and much of that journey had been taken in a public post-chaise, crowded and foully odorous. But to-day she felt like a dead thing, drawing slow painful breaths as she rode towards her fate. She looked, her huge eyes unseeing, at the villages through which they passed; at the tumble-down cottages of the poor; the mansions of the rich; the farms; the broad sweep of agricultural land bounded by low stone walls, typical of Gloucestershire; the wild winter-clad hills.

She saw nothing, could think of nothing but Esmond. She was convulsed with apprehension, visualizing the reception she must face from him on her wedding-day.

CHAPTER FIVE

New Year's Day dawned fair.

Over the Surrey hills the sun shone merrily, turning the recent snows to glittering silver. Clouds billowed like sails in a cool north wind; white ships skimming a sky of wintry blue. The countryside had a gay look to it, and Mornbury Hall was glorious, every snow-powdered tree and clipped yew hedge bediamonded.

At midday, Esmond was standing looking out of the centre window of his library, one slender hand resting lightly on his hip, the other nervously touching the fine Mechlin lace at his throat. He was very obviously in a state of nerves, thought Archie St. John, who stood just behind him, watching like the future bridegroom for the coach that would bring Magda here.

Esmond had spent two hours in his robing-closet. He had emerged in a poor temper, irritated by the fussy gentlemen who attended him; his wig-maker, his barber, his valet. Now he was resplendent in coat of cream damasked satin, the button holes laced with gold, gold trimming on the deep cuffs. His cream silk waistcoat was exquisitely embroidered and had gilded buttons. He wore diamond knee and shoe buckles.

A bunch of blue and white ribbons—his colours—dangled from one shoulder. He had chosen a full-bottomed wig of delicate grey. His handsome face was particularly pale, and the deep brilliant eyes flickered restlessly from side to side. But he looked, thought St. John, magnificent. On the window seat beside him, lay his large cocked hat buttoned up with diamonds.

Now and again Esmond glanced at the hat and the soft doeskin gloves with gold-embroidered gauntlets, and laughed at St. John.

'A fine sight, eh, Archie? Esmond Mornbury dressed up for the slaughter.'

'Is marriage then so murderous a custom?'

'Freedom dies for me to-day, does it not?' asked Esmond jokingly.

'No—when the lovely Magda drifts like a swan into your arms, all else will be forgot,' said St. John.

'You wax romantic, my dear Archie,' Esmond laughed again.

Then he ceased to smile and gripped his

friend's arm.

'She is here,' he said under his breath, and caught his lower lip between his teeth.

Archie followed his friend's gaze. The coach, with Esmond's uniformed coachmen, swung around a bend in the drive. The horses pranced now at a pretty pace down the lime-walk. There was a rattle, a cracking of whips, the sounding of a bugle and all the inmates of Mornbury Hall rushed out to catch the first glimpse of his lordship's bride.

And now *I* shall see her for the first time. My gentle correspondent—my pretty child of the miniature, thought Esmond, conscious of a sudden excited jerking of his heart.

The coach came to a standstill. The postillions let down the steps. Sir Adam emerged first, and bowed low to Esmond who was out in the drive now. It was not only the cold wind that whipped the blood into the young Earl's cheeks, it was the sight of that slender girlish form following Sir Adam that ravished his sight. She came towards him, followed by her French maid attendant.

He went to meet her. He could not see her face. It was hidden from his for she

157

seemed to shrink back in her velvet hood. She also wore a veil and held it against her mouth and nose so that he glimpsed only two large magnificent eyes of golden-hue, shaded by long black lashes. Eyes not at all like those in the miniature, Esmond noted, pleased and surprised; for they were more beautiful; and far more expressive. He had little time to examine them further. He bent and touched her small gloved hand with his lips.

'Welcome to Mornbury Hall, Magda,' he said in a low voice.

There came her answer in that haunting voice which he had longed yet dreaded to hear.

'I thank you, Sir.'

Then Sir Adam took charge. He stepped between the young couple; called to Annette to attend to his 'daughter' as he called her, and after greeting Esmond, suggested that the bride be at once permitted to go to a room in which she might bathe the dust from her face and be robed in her bridal attire.

'Our sweet Magda ought not to be allowed to see you, my lord, until she stands beside you in the chapel—is it not so?' he said unctuously.

'Most assuredly,' said Esmond, and with another poignant look at the girl who was so soon to be his wife, gave orders for two of the maidservants to conduct Miss Congrayle and her female attendant, to a guest chamber. She was not to see her own suite of rooms until after the bridal. He had a great and, he hoped, a pleasant surprise for her. His mother's rooms had been redecorated and painted and the loveliest furniture and draperies in Mornbury had been used to adorn them.

Sir Adam was entertained to a glass of wine in the library with Archie and one or two gentlemen of the Mornbury family who had come for the wedding. Sir Adam was most affable and not too talkative, and behaved in an exemplary fashion. Esmond did not particularly take to his prospective father-in-law and paid scant attention to his conversation. He also felt thankful that Sir Adam and his family lived far away in Stroud and that he would not see too much of him.

Although Esmond had announced that he wished a quiet marriage, the village of Godchester turned out to wish the Lord of the Manor good luck; all sympathetic; all remembering the tragedy of last summer and all aware—for rumour spreads swiftly—that this wedding was at the Queen's request.

Archie left the room for a moment and when he returned it was to whisper in Esmond's ear.

'It is time that we took ourselves to the chapel. Word has been received that your bride will shortly be coming downstairs.'

Esmond stood up. His finely featured face was pale rather than flushed. His lips twitched a trifle nervously but his eyes were warm and eager. He picked up his jewelled hat and said in a clear ringing voice:

'Shall we depart to the chapel, my lords and ladies?'

There were, perhaps, a dozen female guests here from London who had stayed at Mornbury last night with their husbands. Not for a long time had so many gaily attired and beribboned ladies been seen flitting through the Hall. One or two families in the locality had also been invited and already received by Esmond.

General and Mrs. Corsham, his neighbours from Swanley Manor which was just over the Surrey border into Sussex, had brought the young French girl, Mlle LeClaire, who was living with them.

160

Just for an instant, when first introduced to the young refugee from France, Esmond had felt the old stir of appreciation when he looked upon a really pretty woman.

Chantal LeClaire, at eighteen summers, was exceedingly attractive; rose-petal face, laughing eyes almond-shaped, and chestnut brown hair. She wore rose and gold brocade trimmed with sable and a high *fontange* sat on her dark curly head, giving her a Spanish look.

When she curtseyed she had thrown him a provocative look under her wonderful lashes. He had murmured that he was pleased that she had escaped to England and that he hoped her war-torn country would soon be at rest. She had replied in her pretty broken English that she was *enchantée* to be at Swanley Manor, living so close to Mornbury Hall and hoped to see much of Esmond and his new wife. She had then apologized prettily for her English uncle's Whig tendencies knowing that my Lord Mornbury was in the Opposition. But Esmond, with a flicker of his old gallantry, had bowed and said:

'When a man looks upon such a beautiful woman, politics have little significance.'

Yes, Chantal LeClaire was charming and

161

he could remember how Dorothea's father had spoken of her and urged him to see more of the Corshams.

He followed Archie out of the reception room and walked through the passageway into the Chapel.

It was with mixed feelings that Esmond finally took his place at the altar rails. The Bishop of the Diocese had come specially to perform this ceremony, doing honour to the Queen's godson. He was attended by two of the local clergy. The little chapel was soon filled. The organ swelled softly.

Then she came . . .

Esmond standing straightly with one proud hand on the hilt of his dress-sword, watched Magda walk down the aisle on the arm of her stepfather.

His throat constricted as he saw that girlish figure—in height, in build, resembling Dorothea's—although through the veil he glimpsed that Magda's hair was dark. She was a brunette and in that way very different from the blonde Dorothea.

The soul of the man was torn for an instant between love and dislike; love for the girl that Magda *should* have been; dislike for the stranger that she was. Eagerly he scanned but could not see her features through the lace of her veil. When she held out a small gloved hand and he took it, he found it trembled violently. He pressed it and, bending his head, whispered:

'Do not be afraid. There is no need.'

She made an inaudible answer but the trembling did not stop.

Magda Congrayle as she stood there beside her tall elegant bridegroom facing the officiating priest, wished, as she had done for many days, that the ground would open and swallow her up. She was terrified even while her agonized spirit must inevitably feel a thrill of joy. A joy which she knew would within an hour or two be wrested from her. But here in this hour, she, Magda, the unloved and unwanted, was to be made *his*. Oh, how she could have loved this man, she thought; the handsome imperial-looking Esmond whom Dorothea, too, had loved so well. Oh, that this had been a day of rapture that under normal circumstances would have made Magda the happiest girl on earth. Oh, that a miracle could happen and that her ruined face could be suddenly transformed, and she should be given the beauty of the angel in that stained glass window above the little altar. The terrible thrill of this moment; of Esmond's presence, with his hand grasping hers. She wanted to die. She wanted to live.

She wore rich cream silk damask over a white satin quilted petticoat. Winged cuffs, a necklace of pleated ribbons, a stomacher of ribbon and silver lace; it was a beautiful bridal dress. Magda's hair had been curled. It fell in ringlets on either side of her face, and was dusted with grey powder, and interlaced with frilled ribbons under the lace of her short concealing veil.

Onlookers kneeling in the chapel would have said, from the view they got of the bride, that Mornbury was marrying a beauty. But in one of the back pews one woman alone, knelt with her several chins wobbling and her small eyes bolting with a horror that she would have liked to shout aloud but dared not. *For Martha Fustian knew the truth.* A few moments ago she had called in at the guest chamber to see if the French maid needed one of the other maids to assist her. Annette had rushed to the door to slam it on her, but in that split second Mrs. Fustian had seen Magda Congrayle's face. *She knew what his lordship was taking to wife.*

She had retired to her kitchen quarters

too amazed and scared to speak of what she had seen.

'Dear God,' she had muttered, 'his lordship cannot know. *He cannot know.*'

The marriage service began. The Bishop's sonorous voice rang through the chapel.

Magda, almost sinking, heard little save those words:

'*Esmond Walhurst Mornbury*, wilt thou take this woman . . .'

And Esmond's answer:

'*I will.*'

When it came to Magda's turn and she heard her own name spoken, *Magda Jane Congrayle*, she had yet another moment of blind panic. She felt so faint that the rich colours in the stained windows began to swim and move like a kaleidoscope.

Now, she thought, I must say *no*. I must rush from this chapel and from his side.

But if she did . . . what then? Torture for her mother and herself and for all at Wildmarsh Manor, at the hands of a madman.

This was her moment of weakness as well as of strength. So now she heard her own little voice answering: '*I will.*' And after that it was all too late. The ceremony must

165

go on. The fatal knot was tied. She was no longer Miss Congrayle but the Countess of Mornbury—*his* wife.

Once the service ended she realized that it was customary for the bridegroom to lift his bride's veil and embrace her before all eyes. To give him such a shock and endure her own torture in front of so many prying eyes—whispering ladies and gaping gentlemen—was more than she could bear. The unfortunate girl played the only card left to her. She swayed and as Esmond caught her, gasped:

'Carry me out of this, I pray you. I do beg your lordship's pardon, but I can no longer stand.'

He thought that the wedding had been too much for her after the long journey from Stroud. He respected her feminine weakness and found it touching. Poor child! He lifted her up, and inclining his head to the Bishop, turned and walked down the aisle with the white-robed figure in his arms.

'Lady Mornbury has swooned, and begs to be allowed to rest for an hour before the reception,' he said.

A little murmur rippled through the congregation. Sympathetic eyes followed

166

the couple. Mrs. Corsham, standing beside the General who was in full uniform, tossed her bewigged head and muttered:

'These young modern females, tck! tck! No stamina, no courage. Mornbury, I fear, chooses from rather poor stock. A pity if Lady Mornbury turns out to be as delicate as her poor dead cousin.'

The bride was being carried upstairs, her deathly face hidden against Mornbury's shoulder.

'I rather like this diversion,' he said to comfort her. 'It is a delight to carry my newly made wife to her room and watch her first pleasure. Are you a little less faint now, my love?'

'Yes, my lord,' came her strangled answer.

'Tush,' he said, 'you need not use that title. I am Esmond, your husband, or have you already forgotten that fact?' he added gaily.

She made no answer. She had not forgotten. Oh, God, she thought, could she ever forget such a thing? Why, why, could she not stay the march of time itself, so that this moment in his arms might last for ever.

Her small hands—one bearing his ring— were locked about his neck. She clung as though he alone could save her from drowning in the stormy waters that were about to break over her head.

But once the two lackeys had opened the double doors of Lady Mornbury's suite, and Esmond carried her over the threshold, Magda felt that her little hour of desperate happiness was over. The most terrible moment of her life had come.

Over Mornbury's shoulder, her scared haunted eyes noted the bedchamber which seemed to her uninitiated gaze to be of fabulous beauty.

The previous Lady Mornbury's old bedchamber had been entirely redecorated by Esmond's command. The walls were papered in a stripe of pale gold and ivory. A dove grey carpet covered the floor. The furniture was of that excellent walnut now being made in London and becoming popular in this country. It had a highly polished golden veneer such as had never been used before, and was of charming design.

Three tall windows overlooking the gardens and parkland were framed in heavy curtains of dove-grey brocaded satin which hung from twisted golden poles.

The great fourposter bed in which

Esmond had been born and in which his mother had died, was draped in rich claret-coloured satin which had a gold thread running through it. Everywhere were touches of luxury beyond anything that Magda had ever imagined. The frilled beribboned flounces on the dressing-table on which stood gold stoppered perfume bottles and a gold toilette set bearing the Mornbury crest. A handsome carved and gilded mirror; an exquisite little chaise-longue piled with red satin cushions. On all the tables, great bowls of white roses. Everywhere, wax candles gleamed softly in their gilt candelabra. In the handsome white marble fireplace a huge fire was burning. It spread a delicious warmth through the whole bedchamber.

Esmond would have laid Magda on the bed but she struggled to be set on her feet.

'One moment, sir ... Esmond ...' she stammered, 'allow my maid to bathe my temples ... it is just a little giddiness ... it was so hot in the chapel—'

She broke off, clenching and unclenching her ice-cold fingers. Her breath came in great gasps. All of which Esmond put down to a natural maidenly modesty, but he was no longer going to be done out of looking upon his bride's face for the first time. In a gay and tender voice he said:

'You must remember, my dear love, that I have only yet seen a charming miniature of yourself. Now that we have stolen this moment alone let me kiss those lips which have smiled at me for so many days from a piece of painted ivory.'

'No—no,' the frantic protest was torn from Magda.

But Esmond laughed and picked up a fold of her lace veil in his long fine fingers.

'Your timidity charms me, but you are my wife, sweet child, and I have told you already—you have nothing to fear from me. Rumour may have reached you,' he went on in a slightly more cynical vain, 'that your husband has not always conducted himself as he should have done. At one time I gained the disapproval of her august Majesty; but all that is changed. Esmond is henceforth the faithful husband of Magda, and in the name of her whom we both so dearly loved, I vow to love *you* always, whate'er may come. So let our sweet lost Dorothea witness that promise, and fear me no longer, my child.'

Despair weighed down upon Magda and

filled her very soul with sickness. It also made of her a wild and desperate creature— a young animal at bay, just as she had been for so many years.

She gave a laugh that chilled Esmond Mornbury's heart and suddenly lifted her own veil—tore it from her head. She stood by the fireplace so that the full light from the candles on the high mantelpiece pitilessly exposed her face.

'Look then,' she said hoarsely, 'look and see what you have just vowed to love.'

There was a moment of silence. A silence that was to leave forever a sinister mark upon the souls of both these human beings who stood staring at each other.

Esmond gazed upon his bride's face at first with incredulity—then with a horror which no amount of chivalry or kindliness could quell. Indeed, he felt neither chivalrous nor kind, but only a mounting tension and indignation because he had been so hideously cheated.

This was not the sweet-faced maiden of the miniature that Adam Congrayle had sent him. Magda bore no resemblance to that painting. His horrified gaze noted the distortion of her mouth, dragged downwards by a terrible scar and the livid weals that stood out from brow to chin, down the left side. True, there were attempts to conceal the scars, but Annette's skill with paint and powder only served to make the mutilation more obvious to Esmond. It presented to him a pitiful painted mask. Blinded by indignation, the young Earl was oblivious to the misery in her eyes. Even her hair, he thought, was unattractive, lifeless, overcurled (dyed, he was sure).

He gave a low cry:

'In God's name what is this?'

Once again, Magda felt as though she was dying—one more death after the thousands which she had suffered since her stepfather forced her into this thing. She could see the sick dismay in Esmond's eyes. She had watched the tender eagerness vanish as though wiped off by an invisible hand. She knew exactly what effect her appearance had upon him. Now that it was all over a queer kind of relief, of courage began to rise in her. She felt that she had nothing more to lose. She was among the lonely and the damned for ever—doomed to walk alone on the face of the earth. She said with a bitter sarcasm:

'I fear that his lordship does not find his

bride pleasing.'

Pale to the lips, Esmond clenched his hands.

'You—*you* are not the girl in the miniature.'

'No,' she said dully, 'that was my mother.'

'*Your mother!* Great God, in Heaven, who engineered such a villainous deception?'

'You had best ask Sir Adam that,' said Magda in an utterly lifeless voice.

Esmond continued to stare at her, stupefied. He felt that he must be in some fantastic nightmare; that this thing could not be true. Gallantry could play no part now. A wicked deception had been practised upon him, and Esmond's was a nature that could not tolerate such a thing lightly. He suddenly raised his voice and shouted:

'Why was this done? With what object? How dared you? How dared Adam Congrayle ...' he stopped, choking, crimson with his rage.

In the same lifeless voice, Magda asked:

'Do you wish to send me home?'

'Send you home?' he repeated stuttering, 'I have just made you my wife. You are tied to me. You are bound to me by the laws of

God and of man. You—*you* have been made Countess of Mornbury—cheap trickster that you are!'

She shivered and put one hand to her throat. Her eyelids half-closed. The room swam around her. The handsome impassioned face of the man who was her husband was blotted out in a mist. She heard herself crying out, in anguish:

'Don't . . . oh, *don't*! . . .'

When she recovered consciousness, she was lying on the bed. Esmond stood beside her.

His first passionate anger had died down to an ice-cold rage. Mingling with it came the first faint stirring of pity. During those few seconds when she had lost consciousness, when all colour had drained from her cheeks, he had noted how hollow they were, and how thin and ill she looked. He had noted that one side of her face was curiously unimpaired and still had something of beauty. And beauty lay also in the long line of alabaster throat; the bare graceful sloping shoulders just emerging from her gown.

But except for those things, Magda seemed a pitiful caricature. Those hideous scars repelled him. All his life Esmond, who was a perfectionist, had hated any kind of deformity.

When Magda opened her eyes and looked up at him he saw nothing in them that suggested any malicious pleasure because she had carried the plan of deceit to such a triumphant end. Nothing that suggested that she would hold up the marriage ring for him to see and sneer at his frustration.

'Are you going to send me home?' she had asked him.

He spoke to her in a low, cold voice.

'I want an explanation. God knows it is not your fault that you are mutilated. But the sending of your mother's miniature was a deliberate act of treachery. The whole of our correspondence has, I presume, been deliberately planned to deceive me. Maybe you did not even write those charming letters yourself.'

She struggled into a sitting position. Her curls, her ribbons were disarrayed and made her all the more grotesque. But she answered hotly now.

'I did. I did—every one of them.'

His lips curled.

'In them all, you spoke of your high regard for me—your wish only to serve me.

175

Was it love, then, that made you pretend to be someone whom you are not?'

'I cannot answer that,' she said dully, 'it is all too hopeless. I can only say that I am indeed Dorothea's cousin.'

Esmond's face crimsoned.

'*She* abhorred lies and deceit. She was pure and truthful. It is hard for me to believe that the same blood runs in your veins.'

Magda winced and hid her face in her hands. She had expected such things to be said, yet now when she heard them, they destoyed her.

Suddenly Esmond asked on a less harsh note:

'When did you receive this hurt?'

She answered:

'When I was a child. In an accident. I was thrown by my horse.'

Esmond turned and scowling, began to pace up and down the room. He remembered that he had seen her veiled at Shaftley Castle but had imagined it was on account of her mourning. Never had he expected the 'tragic child' spoken of by her aunt, to have had this sort of tragedy in her life nor that she could be of a nature as to agree to such base deceit. His whole being was in revolt. He wanted suddenly to rush from the girl, saddle Jess and ride away from Mornbury, never to return.

He was doomed. This house was doomed. Last time death had kept him from the arms of his bride; to-night *this* thing was like a hideous farce. He had fallen into Adam Congrayle's trap. Too late now he realized that he should have made personal contact with Dorothea's cousin before the marriage day. But that miniature, her association with Dorothea and those letters, had helped to build up in him a totally erroneous picture of a girl whom he could easily love, and would be proud to own as his wife.

That poor creature sitting there on the bed, he thought, could arouse nothing but pity of a kind. Did he not know, personally, what it was to suffer after being thrown from a horse? Yes—he could pity her. And the more he thought about it, the more terrible he felt it was that one who might have grown to great beauty should be so dreadfully scarred.

That paint and powder . . . that pulled-down mouth . . . those weals . . . oh God, how could *he* ever be a lover to *that*? How could he get over his revulsion?

Send her home? Was that the answer?

Then the thought what this would mean. He would become a laughing stock in the eyes of the world. Queen Anne herself might find it humorous, and chortle. The whole Court would buzz with the amusing scandal. His enemies in particular, would look at him with eyes of derision every time he entered a Club or coffee-house in London.

The Earl of Mornbury—he who had been so proud, so sure of himself—had been nicely hoodwinked and had been fool enough not to see through it. Adam Congrayle, that cunning fox, had tricked him into marriage with an unmarriageable daughter.

All Esmond's pride rose up in arms. A thrill of fresh horror went through him at the memory of Magda's face and what people would say about it. Yet if he discarded her now, the truth would get around and he would become the fool of London. *He could not survive it.*

Suddenly he stopped his restless pacing and marched back to the bedside.

'I can see what has happened,' he said harshly. 'Your redoubtable stepfather kept the truth from me in order that he should

178

gain for a son-in-law a godson of the Queen and the Earl of Mornbury. He aimed high and resorted to the lowest of methods to gain his prize. And *you* were party to it. You, who wrote in tenderness to assure me of a devotion in which I no longer believe. If you had cared one particle for my feelings, you would not have permitted such a thing to happen.'

Magda let her hands drop from her face and stared at him with great sullen eyes.

'Bully me all you wish,' she said, 'I am used to bullying and to pain.'

For an instant her words shamed him and then he scowled, his lower lip thrust out.

'I bully only when I am aroused and affronted. Do you not consider what you have done has been sufficient provocation?'

'I admit that I am no beauty,' she said with a terrible little laugh.

'You are not responsible for your scars,' he said roughly, 'but for the abominable deceit. No doubt were I truly noble in character I would pretend I saw nothing untoward in your face and continue to smile. But I abhor betrayal, and you have betrayed every instinct of honour that should adorn the character of a decent

179

gentlewoman.'

Her finger-nails dug into the palms of her hands. She had been through so much. She began to be conscious of an appalling weariness; feeling as though at any moment her weighted eyelids would droop and she would fall asleep even while Esmond was saying these terrible things to her. She supposed she deserved them. Of course she might tell him of Sir Adam's brutality and his threats but she could do so only at the risk of her mother's life. For if Esmond Mornbury was further enraged, he might vent his anger upon Sir Adam who would then take drastic revenge upon her wretched mother.

She whispered:

'I will go back to Stroud.'

'You will do what I wish you to do,' he said violently. 'I will not be made a laughing stock. I must pay the price of my folly but you shall stay here and play *your* part as Countess of Mornbury.'

She gasped and sat up, staring at him, wide-eyed.

'You could not want me to.'

'I do not want you to,' he said brutally, 'but you shall stay. You have connived at this thing with your atrocious stepfather, and mother who cannot be worthy of that name since she, sister to Lady Shaftley, aunt to the most noble being who ever drew beath, must also have consented to this wickedness. *Her* miniature, not yours ... ye gods what an imbecile I have been! but the world shall never know it—that I swear. You shall stay and pay the penalty.'

Magda gasped again.

'What are you going to do with me?'

He looked down at her. His face was convulsed. She saw now that demon that had always been hidden in the depths of Esmond Mornbury's nature and had for so long lain dormant. The demon that Dorothea and, later, his sojourn in the monastery, had almost banished for all time. But in the heat of his anger and resentment against the trick that had been played upon him, the black devil was abroad again. Esmond felt a craving for the wine that would at this moment be served to his guests downstairs. His lips were dry; his eyes inflamed. Magda read not one spark of pity or kindness in them; yet a little while ago they had gazed at her with tolerance and even pride. All the deep emotion that the young unfortunate girl had felt towards him—all the vanquished love in her own sore heart culminated in a low anguished cry.

'Esmond, Esmond, forgive me, forgive this thing which seems so unpardonable. You do not understand ... you cannot know ...' she broke off, running her fingers wildly through her hair, tearing away the ribbons, the laces, the tragic furbelows of her wedding finery.

Just for an instant the man's gaze travelled from the scars to the undoubted magnificence of the big hazel golden eyes swimming with hot tears. He saw the pathetically immature curve of a snow-white breast; the delicacy of wrists and ankles and truly exquisite hands. Horror seized him. For he saw *her*, too, the Loved One lying on her bier; remembered the iciness of that other little hand, which he had kissed in death.

Like a drunken man, he turned and stumbled out of the room.

CHAPTER SIX

The guests were assembled in the handsome panelled dining hall. Servants were coming in with silver crested trays bearing goblets and wine. The trio of musicians played a Viennese waltz. The atmosphere was gay and there was much laughing, chattering, and speculation among the guests as to when the bride would reappear. None so far had seen her.

Then the Earl came into the room.

Archibald St. John was quick to note the change in the bridegroom's demeanour and the deathly pallor of his face. The honest young man's heart sank. He hurried forward towards him.

'How is your wife, Esmond?'

Esmond gave a low laugh—a humourless sound which further dismayed St. John. Esmond said under his breath:

'My wife? *Oh, God!*'

St. John glanced to the right and left, frowning.

'Ssh! Come with me into the library. Let us talk. Something terrible has happened. I can see it.'

'Wait,' said Esmond, and walked across the crowded room to Sir Adam Congrayle who stood talking to General Corsham. His boasting voice could be heard:

'I do assure you, General, that my daughter is one of the finest horsewomen in

Gloucestershire. Unlike many young gentlewomen of her age, she has been known to ride bareback—yes, without saddle—upon a newly broken-in colt and keep her seat.'

'Miraculous,' murmured the General, stroking his white moustaches. 'But dangerous, surely.'

'Dangerous to the extent that she might have had a fearful accident,' cut in the cold voice of Esmond Mornbury.

Sir Adam turned. His protruding eyes blinked and he coughed and tittered.

'Yes, indeed, yes, indeed, my lord.'

'You, being my father-in-law, should surely call me Esmond,' said the Earl in the same freezing voice and with a look that spoke volumes to the guilty man. Sir Adam bowed, conscious suddenly of acute indigestion.

'Indeed, Esmond, I thank you. I am most lucky to own you as such.'

'As lucky as I am,' said Esmond in a ringing voice, 'to have so fair a wife.'

'I trust the bride is now fully recovered,' put in General Corsham.

Esmond made no answer. He looked straight at Adam Congrayle and then at Archie.

'Might I ask that you two gentlemen accompany me for an instant to an adjoining room. Lady Mornbury is unwell and will not, I regret, be coming downstairs. She has a slight indisposition. Nothing serious. But I must take care of her—you will understand. Let the meal begin. I shall be with you all in a moment but first must join these gentlemen and my legal adviser who has to return on urgent business to London. There are papers to sign. The marriage settlement ... you understand ...' he bowed to one and all, with that set smile on his handsome pale face.

There were immediate little cries of sympathy and the ladies began to whisper about Lady Mornbury's health. Naturally, one and all were struck with the same thought; it was earnestly to be hoped that Magda would not follow in her cousin's ghostly footsteps and that there would not be a second tragedy in the young Earl's matrimonial career.

Now in the library, without the lawyer who was in fact told to produce his documents in the morning, Esmond faced Sir Adam and his friend alone.

Archie, completely mystified, began:

'What has happened? Magda is not really ill, is she?'

Esmond broke in.

'She's not ill at all, except with a sickness of the soul. A sickness which you'—he pointed a finger at Sir Adam—'must have nurtured and allowed to spread through your entire household. The sick miasma of deceit, lies and chicanery. I can only hazard a guess at your vile purpose. Money. The need of this settlement which I am about to make upon Magda and the financial support which you, I know, require. It was made plain to me that you have fallen upon hard times.'

St. John stayed speechless, staring from his friend to the older man whom he could see now wore a sickly grin on his sallow face.

'What have you to say to me?' Esmond asked in a terrible voice fixing Sir Adam with his gaze.

He has seen Magda, thought Sir Adam, *devil take it! And Mornbury has a quick temper and is a fine swordsman. If I am not careful I shall be a dead man before this night is out.*

He started to mumble. Archie broke in:

'I implore you, Esmond, tell us what has

occurred?'

Esmond kept his furious gaze upon Sir Adam as he answered.

'My wife is not the girl of the miniature, Archie. That was a likeness of her mother, Jane Congrayle.'

'But great heavens, why—' gasped St. John.

'For reasons I have already stated,' broke in Esmond, 'Sir Adam needed a rich son-in-law and a husband for his disfigured daughter or stepdaughter or whatever he chooses to call her.'

'*Disfigured?*' repeated St. John in a tone of horror.

'She was thrown from her horse as a child,' said Esmond stonily. 'The left side of her face is mutilated. She is as unbeautiful as the miniature was the reverse.'

'The poor, poor child!' gasped the kind-hearted St. John.

'It would be more pitiable,' said Esmond, 'if she had not been so eager and willing to play this trick upon me.'

'Yes, that is true,' said St. John nodding, and pulling out a handkerchief mopped the sweat from his forehead. This was a tragedy he had never expected. An abominable, unbelievable affair.

'Now, I know,' continued Esmond, 'why Sir Adam made it seem impossible for me to visit Wildmarsh Manor. His sons had the pox, he said. I begin to wonder if even that is true. I am not going to deny that mine is the folly for believing what I was told, but I must be excused for trusting in my own eyesight, and had Magda been like the girl in the miniature—like the person so often described to me—I would have pardoned the miserable greed of this vulgar, bragging fellow . . .' he pointed at Congrayle again. 'I would have gladly helped him. But he sends me Magda—veiled, hidden until it was too late to undo the marriage service. Poor child, indeed! And what of me? What will be said of *me* when England knows?' Esmond beat a clenched fist on his chest, his face working.

'Great God, this is indeed catastrophic,' muttered Archibald, and tugged at his neck band, overpowered by the warmth of the room, the wine he had just drunk and the awfulness of his friend's revelation.

Then Sir Adam fell upon one knee, a craven, grotesque figure, weeping, wagging his chin, moaning excuse upon excuse.

He had passed through evil times. He

had been robbed. He had, although London did not know it, often been at the point of starvation; so, too, his invalid wife, and his three little boys. The land tax was heavy. He had had trouble draining the land. Often they ate only rough oatclap-bread. He had banked with a one-man concern, a Jew, who had absconded with his money. He knew that he had done wrong. He craved the Earl's indulgence. It was an abominable trick but Magda had, herself, suggested it. She had fallen in love with Esmond when she first saw him at Shaftley Castle. She had set her heart on marrying him and begged Sir Adam to help her achieve her desire. Sir Adam coughed and spluttered, plucking at the satin brocade of Esmond's sleeve.

'One side of her face is still fair, I do assure you. If she is told to do so, she can dissemble and arrange for the world to see her only from the best angle; or keep herself always veiled; or wear a mantilla like a Spanish *grande-dame*, half concealing her features. She has a beautiful form. She has intelligence. Indeed, all her letters were of her own writing. I saw to it that she had a splendid education. She is well instructed in the classics, and in the arts, and what I said just now to the General is true. The whole of Gloucester will tell you that she is second to none on horseback. Even after her accident she rode again. She is fearless and spirited. She—'

'Hold your peace!' Esmond thundered, breaking in on this diatribe. 'I have heard enough. I want no more of your disgraceful efforts to foist your daughter upon me.'

But even in the heat of that hour it flashed through his mind that he could be thankful, at least, that Sir Adam Congrayle's loathsome blood did not run in the veins of that young girl upstairs. She was not his daughter.

Sir Adam blew his nose and wiped the crocodile tears from his sweating face.

'You cannot be so brutal as to spurn my poor child,' he said snivelling, 'it will break her heart if you send her home again. Besides,' he added with a cunning look, 'Esmond Mornbury is an honourable gentleman who will not break his word and you have taken your vows to cherish Magda whate'er betide you in this world.'

'Hold your peace, you miserable scoundrel,' said Esmond again.

But he was reminded painfully of some words he had spoken to Magda before she was unveiled. He could hear his own voice: *'I vow to love you always whate'er may come. So let our sweet lost Dorothea witness that promise. . . .'*

Suddenly he put a hand across his burning eyelids. Oh, God, what would Dorothea have said to all this. What would she tell him to do now? Was that sweet ghost here at his side to witness his betrayal and her uncle's shame? And would she, who had been a saint, beseech him to feel some degree of compassion towards that unfortunate scarred girl who had stepped into her shoes? For Dorothea had loved Magda; he knew that. She had spoken of her always as her 'poor little cousin' whom life had treated so ill. But he had hardly listened at the time; uninterested as to what kind of ill should betide Magda Congrayle.

He heard Archie's voice:

'Esmond, my dear fellow, what can I say or do to help?'

Esmond looked up. He gave a hoarse laugh.

'I am the most unfortunate of men where marriage is concerned, am I not, Archie?'

'The marriage can be annulled.'

Esmond set his teeth.

'I've already thought of that but I tell you

191

that I would become the laughing stock of England and this miserable creature,' he inclined his head towards Sir Adam, 'would strut around like a vain peacock, telling the world that he had cheated Esmond Mornbury into marrying a girl whom he could tolerate neither in his bed nor at his board.'

'But Magda is very fair of body—' Sir Adam began to whine.

Archie turned on him.

'Hold your foul licentious tongue, or I, myself will run a dagger through your base heart.'

Sir Adam turned green and laughed nervously.

'I will do whatever his lordship thinks best,' he whimpered.

Esmond stared hopelessly at his friend.

'We must return to our guests. I cannot permit them to think that anything is seriously amiss. You, Archie, go up to my ... my wife's room,' he stumbled over the word, 'and acquaint her of my decision to keep her here. But she is to say nothing to anybody and I will inform her later, to-night, what I intend to do in the future. I have married her and I will not back out of the bargain. Her Majesty the Queen shall never live to hear it said that I have been so shamefully duped.'

'Perhaps that will be for the best,' said Archie with a sigh, 'and perhaps some good surgeon, or physician, clever with herbs, might help to restore the unfortunate girl's appearance to such an extent that you might no longer find her repellent.'

Sir Adam piped up:

'Indeed, she is not repellent, sir. When she is at her best she is even now a good-looking girl.'

Esmond went close to him.

'You,' he said, 'listen to me. I could kill you but I do not wish to add another death to my record. When I caused the unfortunate end of Philip Senthill I vowed never to be the murderer of another man. Because of that vow, *you* will live. But if you do not as I command I will see that you are hounded out of every decent man's house in all England.'

Sir Adam unbuttoned his coat and puffed and blew.

'I will agree to anything—anything—that your lordship wishes.'

'You will play your part at the banquet this evening and you will say nothing, now or ever of the accident that caused your daughter's misfortune. You will leave Mornbury Hall to-morrow at daybreak, and never return. Neither will Magda be permitted ever to visit you or her mother at Stroud.'

Sir Adam choked.

'But you would not allow your wife's parents to starve . . .' he moaned. 'My poor wife has just miscarried and is near to dying. I cannot even afford to educate my sons. People, knowing we are related, you and I, will talk—'

Esmond cut in roughly.

'I will send my legal advisers to inquire fully into your affairs. If you are, indeed, without means, I will see to it that help is given to your family, otherwise you will not get one gold piece out of me.'

Sir Adam bit his thumb-nail, his mind festering with the problem of how to conduct his affairs so that he could establish proof of his poverty. He would have to empty his coffers—his store of gold— before they could be discovered. He would give most of it into the safe keeping of his favourite mistress in Cheltenham.

He dared not anger Esmond further. He realized that he had, in truth, chosen the wrong man to affront, and made a dangerous enemy. He agreed to hold himself at Esmond's disposition and behave exactly as was required of him.

After he had shambled out of the library, thankful to be alive, Esmond almost collapsed.

'Bring me a restorative, Archie,' he said, 'for this has been a terrible blow.'

Archie, himself, fetched a goblet of wine, and while his friend drank it, offered his commiserations.

'Is she—is she so awful to look at, Esmond?' he asked in a low voice.

'Now that I am calmer, I suppose not,' said Esmond. 'One side of her face is ruined, torn to shreds. Her hair is not good. It is too black. I think dyed; and she was smeared with cosmetics which I abhor in a young gentlewoman.'

'Perhaps,' said Archie, 'when you see her washed, she will look better.'

'Or worse,' said Esmond bitterly, and added: 'There was some truth in what that scoundrel said about the girl being fair of form. All the world could see that in the chapel to-day. She moves like a swan and has a lovely throat and her hands ... oh, God, Archie, her hands are like Dorothea's! So too, her voice.'

'And maybe it is true that she is intelligent and instructed. You know how her letters charmed you,' St. John tried to console him.

'But what of her character? Would any girl of decency and good upbringing have consented to play such a trick?'

'Maybe she was forced into it by that terrible stepfather of hers. Who is to know what brutal power he has wielded over her?'

'True,' admitted Esmond.

'And remember,' added the optimistic St. John, 'that one of our own monarchs was so tricked and weathered the derision.'

Esmond gave a harsh laugh.

'If you are speaking of Henry Tudor and the Flanders Mare, yes. Holbein's lying miniature did, indeed, trick him into marriage with Anne of Cleves, but I am not Harry Tudor, who so blithely got rid of his unwelcome bride. I cannot reject Magda Congrayle—nor behead her, nor kill her snake of a stepfather,' and he laughed again.

Archie tried to echo the laugh.

'Come, my dear fellow, we must join the others if you do not wish tongues to wag. Already the guests are disappointed because the bride is not to receive them.'

Wearily Esmond gained his feet.

'Above all, let us avoid a scandal. That is my first thought. Later, other thoughts and ideas may come. Meanwhile go you upstairs, Archie, and tell *her* that on no account is she to leave her room. Report later to me what you think of her.'

'I will go at once.'

Esmond returned to the dining hall where he was at once surrounded by a crowd ready to drink a toast to him. Chantal LeClaire was there. He saw her agate, alarmed eyes gleaming at him and her red lips smiling. How beautiful she was, he thought, compared to that wreck upstairs. He shuddered. He could not bring himself to look once in the direction of Sir Adam.

'Will we not see your Magda to-night at all?' asked one of the ladies who had come down from London for the marriage ceremony.

'Alas, it is her physician's wish that she stays in her room and rests,' said Esmond in a voice of forced brightness. 'You will understand I am sure. After the events of the past I am taking especial care of my . . . my wife,' again he stumbled over that word as though it burnt his lips.

General Corsham raised his goblet.

'To Lord and Lady Mornbury.'

'Bride and bridegroom,' murmured a dozen or so voices, and the toast was drunk.

Esmond drained his own glass and drank another . . . and another . . . full of feverish regrets for the sweets that had been denied him once again; full of resentment against the whole world. Let the monks say that there was another and better life for which one should prepare one's soul. There was *this* life, too, and it must be led. It was like those candles, he thought, burning down rapidly from the moment they were lit. The light must be savoured before it flickered out forever.

He moved among his friends, uttering ready lies about his wife's sudden indisposition, assuring everybody that she would soon be better, apologizing for her absence. He found himself finally sitting beside Mlle LeClaire.

Recklessly he reached under the cover of the embroidered tablecloth for her hand and pressed it.

'We will dance together when this meal is over.'

'*Enchantée*,' said the French girl in her

198

own language and gave him a long significant glance from the fine eyes which he found so disarming.

Upstairs, Archibald St. John sat at the bedside of Esmond's newly made wife, feeling himself flung suddenly into a tragedy, the magnitude of which he had not guessed before he entered her room.

Magda had fainted after Esmond had marched out of her bedchamber. Annette had come and applied burnt feathers and vinegar and then undressed her ladyship and put her to bed.

Magda lay motionless, looking, Archibald thought, piteous and tiny in the huge fourposter. It was as though all life had been drained from her, she was so pale. She had lain thus since Annette left her.

'What is to become of me?' she kept whispering, 'what is to become of me?'

If Archibald had been shocked by the news his friend had broken to him, he was even more shocked by Magda's appearance. Not only because of the scars, although he could see, of course, that her beauty was sadly impaired; but he had found no painted harpy here, anxious to fasten upon a wealthy husband. No hardened female who cared not that she had played so dishonourable a trick. Despite Annette's coaxing and bullying, Magda had scrubbed and washed her face and refused to touch it again.

'I have finished with deceit. Let *him* see me as I truly am,' she had said. So it was that Archie saw her. A young, pitiable girl who looked incongruous in the fine primrose-coloured wrapping gown which covered her loose silk bedgown. She had refused to put a cap on her head. Her dark hair tumbled about her shoulders in the ebony ringlets. Yet there was a breathtaking beauty in the big sullen eyes in that ruined face. Her voice had that velvet quality which Archie remembered Dorothea, too, had possessed.

'Why did you do this thing?' he asked her.

She had refused to answer. Then he said:

'You can confide in me. I am Esmond's oldest friend.'

'Then you cannot be mine,' she retorted bitterly. 'You must hate and despise anybody who has done what I have done to him.'

'Was it of your own free will?' he persisted.

The sullen eyes turned towards him

glowering, with a bitterness that he found terrible in one so young.

'Of my own free will I took the marriage vows before God and man, did I not?'

'But why? *Why?*' Archie asked many times, mystified, feeling that there was something hidden in all this that neither he nor Esmond knew about. But Magda was not to be drawn into explanations. He had a strong feeling that she was afraid of her stepfather and unwilling to admit it. She bit her lips in the effort to keep silent. For when she had heard that Sir Adam was to be banished to-morrow and sent back to the Manor she knew that he would revenge himself upon her mother should she expose him.

'I cannot believe that you were voluntarily so unscrupulous in your determination to marry Esmond,' said Archie at last. And although she still withheld her explanations, he was interested to note that the only time she became impassioned was when she begged him to see that Sir Adam was properly treated.

'It is imperative,' she said, obviously flustered, 'that my stepfather should have some help with money. We are . . . we are

... very poor and have much come down in the world at Wildmarsh. However ill you may think of me for being mercenary I do beg you to persuade my ... my husband ...' she covered her face with her hands, 'to pardon Sir Adam on account of his crying need and not to let him return home empty-handed.'

When Archie had begun to expostulate that the squire of Wildmarsh had scarcely earned Esmond's benefaction, she continued to implore him.

'My mother may die. Please, please, Sir Archibald, see that she is aided.'

So insistent was she that he made the promise.

It was with that plea ringing in his ears that he finally left her and went back to the party. Just before going out of the bedchamber, he looked at the young figure in the bed, so lost, so lonely, so abysmally unhappy—and said:

'You would do well to pray for Heavenly guidance in your sorry plight. I cannot vouch for what Esmond will do. He is sorely disappointed and tried by the gross deception. But will you permit me to tell him that you regret it?'

'I've already said so,' was her answer.

'He will not believe me. I have been put to bed here but I would prefer to return to Wildmarsh with my stepfather.'

Archie affirmed that it was Esmond's wish that she should remain where she was.

'It is essential there should be no breath of scandal. Esmond is too well known a figure—too close to the throne. There cannot and must not be gossip which would evoke derision. Knowing Esmond as I do, he could not tolerate that.'

Magda had turned her face away. In a voice that sounded tired to death, she said:

'I will do as I am told.'

After he had gone, she remembered Archibald St. John with some slight comfort, for he had seemed a gentle and kindly man and not too wrathful with her. But she laid her face on the pillow and wept long and bitterly. The prayers he had told her to utter would not come. She felt deserted by both God and man.

This was her wedding night.

She lay alone, rejected, weeping, accused of a villainy she had not meant to perpetrate, while her bridegroom feasted and danced without her. When she remembered the look in his eyes once she had removed her veil, her very heart seemed to wither up. She put a hand to her scarred cheek and suddenly moaned aloud:

'I want to die. I want to die. *I want to die.*'

She did not know how long it was before Esmond came to her.

Faintly she heard the sound of music from below, and once, outside her window, she saw flickering lantern lights from the terrace as a window opened and one of the couples came out and stood laughing at the wintry moon. She could hear their gay voices. She wondered what it must be like down there in the beautiful reception room with the lights and the laughter and the dancing—she who had never danced in her life and for whom there could never now be laughter.

Annette came in with food and when she refused, snapped at Magda:

'Your ladyship must have sustenance or in truth be ill. Is there not enough trouble here already without his lordship having to call a physician for you?'

Too tired to argue, Magda choked down a little of the excellent fish cooked in white wine which Mrs. Fustian had sent up to her, but refused the rest. Finally she told Annette to snuff the candles and leave her.

The evening's entertainment seemed to go on interminably, although the last phaetons and coaches rolled down the drive before midnight. At last Mornbury Hall lay wrapped in dignified silence.

Archie St. John had retired to his room.

Now Esmond, the bridegroom, stood alone in the hall watching a great log burn to ash in the grate, while the yawning footmen whom he had permitted to enter, snuffed out the hundreds of candles all through the rooms and corridors, leaving at his request, only the one candelabrum which his lordship would carry upstairs.

Esmond had removed his wig and unbuttoned his coat. He passed a hand constantly, nervously, over the cropped boyish head. He was a little drunk and feverish. Hazily he remembered the many dances he had had with Chantal LeClaire and how she had clung to him and inflamed his passionate fancy; how he had pressed her against him and murmured in her ear that they must meet again soon.

Chantal was his for the asking. Of that he could be sure. And if he had waited he might have married her; he knew that, too. She came of a fine patrician French family and had good blood to offer as well as her charms.

Then he had thought of the girl upstairs.

Archie had not spoken too ill of her; on the contrary he had suggested that she was little more than a scared child who had been driven into this for the sake of her family. Archie had also surprised him by saying that Magda's one honest cry had been not for herself but for her mother, begging that Sir Adam should receive tolerance and that whosoever Esmond sent to inquire into the state of affairs at Wildmarsh should see to it that Lady Congrayle's burden of penury be made lighter.

Esmond had made no promises save to 'think about it'. He was still in a state to send Adam Congrayle about his business without a farthing.

He poured himself out a fresh glass of wine and carried it unsteadily to his lips.

'I must be on my way to the bridal chamber,' he said aloud with a drunken laugh, 'to my beautiful wife. . . .'

Magda heard that low sinister laughter as Esmond finally climbed the handsome staircase, letting the wax spill from the candles which he carried in an unsteady hand. She heard that muttering voice, for it came ever closer and woke her up from an uneasy sleep.

She sat up, her heart pounding, her eyes straining through the darkness towards the door, waiting for him to enter.

CHAPTER SEVEN

The door of Magda's bedchamber was pushed open. She sat up in bed holding the covers tightly up to her chin, staring up at the enormous shadow of Esmond cast upon the ceiling by the light of the candles he carried. She could not see his face. He could not see hers. He was bemused with wine. He sang in a pleasant baritone voice thickened by alcohol, laughing and hiccuping.

'In delay there lies no plenty,
   Then come kiss me sweet and twenty,
      Youth's the stuff will not endure . . .'

Magda began to pant. Her heart-beats clamoured through her thin tired young body. She felt as always when she was upset, that those weals on her cheeks were rising and burning.

Now he was beside her. He set the perilously held candelabrum on a table. She could see his shorn chestnut head. He looked a total stranger to her without his formal wig. Younger and yet terrifying with so livid a countenance and those eyes that mocked and menaced her. His white brocaded coat and fine waistcoat were unbuttoned and stained with wine, his Steinkirk untied. He thrust his face so close to her that she gave a little cry and hid her face in her hands.

He half fell upon the bed and grabbed at her dark flowing curls, pulling them so that she was forced to look up. She had suffered much in her life but never so much as now, for those brilliant handsome eyes seemed to bore like gimlets into her very soul and his expression was one of loathing for her.

She moaned aloud:

'It was not my fault. I did not want to do it.'

He heard the words but only as from a distance. He continued to pull at her hair. He laughed.

'My bride. My beautiful wife. This is our marriage night. Most of our guests have gone. The others are snoring in their beds. But we are alone. Is it not romantic? Have I kept you waiting overlong, my Pretty One?'

Now her eyes blazed at him, and the spirit in Magda that was indestructible even now, flared up.

'I am not pretty and you know it. You mock me. You whom I thought the most chivalrous of gentlemen.'

'Chivalrous; I?' he laughed. 'Why should I be so to a common trickster? What right have you to expect quixotry from me—your victim?'

Her young breast heaved. She had to sit still and upright because the long cruel fingers clutched fast to her hair so that she could not bow her head nor break away. She was subjected to his merciless scrutiny, but she retorted:

'I, too, am a victim—oh, God, why do you not leave me alone.'

'What!' he exclaimed in mock dismay. 'Is my dear wife unwilling? Have I married me to a spouse who objects to the amorous advances of her bridegroom?'

'You are pleased to mock,' she said between her teeth, and her fear of him was replaced by a bitter resentment. She moved her head from side to side. 'Oh, leave me alone. To-morrow I will go back to my old home where you will never see me again.'

'To-morrow and the day after and the day after that you will do as you are told by *me*, your lord and master,' he said thickly. 'You will not leave this house. Those who know the truth shall be silenced. I have formed a plan of action. Your stepfather has said that your brothers have the pox. You, too, shall have it.' He gave an ugly laugh. 'It shall be spread abroad that you brought the pox with you. Let those who are scared of the plague drink nauseous draughts and bathe themselves in vinegar and say their prayers. Who cares? Not I! But *you* shall stay closeted here in your rooms, Madame, until the physician who is in my pay, permits you to leave them. After that your face shall be veiled and those that see you so will imagine that it is because that fair face has been pitted, and must be hid. Esmond Mornbury can tolerate sympathy when misfortune is discussed, but for him to be laughed at, *never*! You have done this thing to me and you shall pay for it by helping to prevent that laughter.'

Magda stared at him dazedly. He had loosed his hold of her hair now. She put a hand up to both her cheeks, shaking her head from side to side.

'What will this benefit you? Why go to so much trouble to keep me?'

'Not for any love, but because it shall not be said that I am Adam Congrayle's dupe. The dastardly game that you and he have played together shall continue to be played—in *my* way.'

Resistance died in her. She whispered:

'As you wish, I am so tired ... I care little now what becomes of me.'

For a moment he railed and ranted, accusing her of this, and Sir Adam of that, stalking up and down her bedchamber, slashing at the roses, pulling at the curtains, acting like a madman. Her gaze followed him, hunted, terrified. This was a terrible stranger bearing no resemblance whatsoever to the Esmond her cousin Dorothea had loved; of that she was sure. Then he came back and seizing the bedclothes, stripped them from her and looked down at the long lovely lines of the girlish body trembling in the transparent sheath of ivory silk. She turned her scarred cheek to the pillow, moaning. Like this he saw only the fair profile, pure and untouched. In the candlelight, she looked suddenly beautiful; with a defencelessness, a child-like touching slenderness that could not do otherwise than appeal to the better side of his nature. For a moment his wrath exploded into a thousand fragments leaving him almost as defenceless as herself. He stood there, staring down, wondering, bitterly unhappy. He saw two great tears hang on her lashes and pearl down her cheeks. He heard her sobbing. Then he pulled the covers over her again and said:

'God forgive me for the brutality I have shewn you this night. My dead mother, and Dorothea, would abhor me for it. Whatever you are and whatever you have done you are still a woman—barely yet grown out of childhood. But it was terrible that you should have allowed yourself to be so influenced by your unnatural parent as to join in the misrepresentation.'

She said nothing only shook her head in a hopeless fashion.

He went on:

'Yet Archie is right. You cannot be all bad and I still remind myself that Dorothea's blood and yours have relationship and it was in *her* dear name that I vowed to protect you, before I learned the worst. I will not divorce you. There has never been a divorce in the Mornbury family. You remain my wife and I will not

212

torment you further although you have robbed me of the affection and companionship which was my due. You shall show your penitence by helping to ensure that my name is neither mocked nor dishonoured. To-morrow, Dr. Ridpath who attended my birth, shall receive my confidence and be sent to examine you. If there is aught that can be done to improve these terrible evidences of your childhood's accident, no money shall be spared in order to do so. That is all I have to say to you to-night.'

He spoke coldly now, sober as a judge. Magda, alive to every word, turned and stared up at him. He saw the magnificence of her eyes, golden in the candlelight, swimming in her tears. With a little sob she said:

'I will do all you ask ... anything to prove to you that I am not as bad as you suppose.'

'It is no longer of any account what you are. I am interested only in the future and the preservation of my pride.'

'My lord ... Esmond ...' she stumbled over the word.

But he gave her no time for further words. Nervously he passed a hand over his head. He was beginning to feel sick and weary to death. Impossible, he thought, to believe that this was his marriage night and that that sobbing, terrified girl in the big bed was his wife.

'Good night,' he said abruptly and turned on his heels.

'Esmond . . .' she spoke his name again. Her whole soul desired to hear some word of pardon or kindliness from this strange violent man. But when he turned at the door and asked what she wanted in his ice-cold voice, she had no heart to plead for herself, but whispered the thing that was uppermost in her mind.

'My mother . . . my young brothers . . . for their sakes will you please not to anger Sir Adam too greatly.'

Esmond scowled. Somewhere, vaguely at the back of his mind, he seemed to remember Archie suggesting that this girl had been terrorized by Congrayle and feared reprisal against her own flesh and blood. He could not sort it out now. He had been through enough for one day. And he still felt a scorching hatred of Adam Congrayle which was not easily to be quelled. He said:

'Pray do not concern yourself with these

matters. It is for me to deal with the situation as I think best.'

Meekly she lay down again. He closed the door. She lay motionless for a moment, her limbs so cold that she could not control their trembling.

When he had first come in, she had feared he was going to do her violence, but she had been reprieved. Now, bemused, she could not see far into the future but a glimmer of hope cut through the thick blackness of her despair. At least she was to be allowed to stay here as Esmond's wife. That, in itself, was some degree of comfort, for to return to her martyrdom at Wildmarsh would have been insupportable.

She thought of the tall handsome drunken boy who had pulled at her curls in his wine-heated fury. She thought of that *other* Esmond who might, in different circumstances, have come to her this night with love in his heart. That dream of romantic love that the young Magda had never known but only gleaned from the books she had read.

The grey desolate dawn broke over Mornbury and found her still awake, still weeping.

Then it was as though her whole life

215

changed. It began with the arrival of Mrs. Fustian in a striped gown and long white apron, bearing a tray with fruit and coffee; a silver bowl of porridge with a jug of cream and plenty of crisp baked bread, yellow butter and honey. Very different from the sordid meals to which she was accustomed under her stepfather's roof. Her head ached and she felt languid with lack of sleep and her eyes were swollen with much crying, but her young body was healthily hungry. She let the woman draw the curtains, sat up and looked with some pleasure at her tray. Mrs. Fustian bobbed and said sourly:

'Is there anything else your ladyship requires?'

Magda flushed. *She* was 'her ladyship'—the ring was on her finger and the sacred words had been said. Nothing could wipe out that fact. But she did not care much for the expression on Mrs. Fustian's face. The housekeeper looked a cross-grained woman, Magda thought, and had a nasty expression in those small eyes which were almost lost in pouches of fat. She made Magda horribly conscious of her facial defects. She picked a lace handkerchief from the pocket of her bedgown and laid it against her bad cheek.

'Is his—lordship up?' she stammered the question.

'Yes, my lady. He is out riding.'

'Then what o'clock is it?' asked Magda.

Mrs. Fustian replied that it was past ten. Magda realized with a shock that she must have fallen asleep in the early hours and that exhaustion had claimed her until now.

'I would like to rise,' she began.

'Pardon me, my lady,' broke in Mrs. Fustian, 'but you must not leave your bed. His lordship has given orders for Dr. Ridpath to call. He fears that you are not yet recovered from your fainting fit and that you have ominous signs of a grave sickness.'

Now Magda remembered the plan upon which Esmond had decided. She hung her head, crimsoning.

'Very well,' she said in a strangled voice.

Mrs. Fustian tossed her head. She had been a long time in this household and in her way was not a bad creature although she had a spiteful streak and little use for females younger and more lovely than herself. She had been sent for to interview his lordship this morning and found him in a mood which she knew well. The sort of mood that poor old Wilkins used to dread

217

and which boded ill for everybody. It suggested that all the peace of mind and change of nature that had bettered his lordship when he first returned from his sojourn with the monks, had vanished overnight.

After being questioned, Mrs. Fustian had admitted that she *knew* about her ladyship. She had been genuinely indignant on his behalf. It was an abomination, she said, that such a thing should have been allowed to happen. But Esmond had cut short her commiserations, reminding her of the long years she had served his mother. He bound her over to respect his wishes now and keep his secret.

It was to be given out that her ladyship was sickening for the pox. Nobody was to enter her rooms but a nurse attendant whom Dr. Ridpath would provide and who would be in their confidence. Mrs. Fustian would be responsible for her ladyship's meals. Her ladyship would not go out for several weeks. And when he asked Mrs. Fustian if she had already mentioned what she saw to the servants she had replied with truth that she had not done so; for which he had commended her.

In Mrs. Fustian's opinion, the new Lady

Mornbury was a lying chit who should be sent home but she could see that his lordship had his pride and *that* must be upheld.

When Magda asked her now if Annette could be sent for, Mrs. Fustian had much pleasure in informing her ladyship that Annette was already on her way by post-chaise to catch the steam packet at Harwich. She had been sent back to the Continent through Rotterdam owing to the present state of the war. The Frenchwoman had wept and railed and demanded to be returned to the Cotswolds to her master but Mornbury would have none of it. He wished her out of the country. Annette knew too much. And prior to this, he had sent a note to Sir Adam's bedchamber.

'I never wish to set eyes upon you again' [he had written], 'but my Legal Advisers will contact you and see that your debts are paid and that Lady Congrayle is given the Monetary support befitting to a Gentlewoman of her standing—on one condition.'

This condition he added was that Sir Adam should agree not to breathe to a living soul the truth about Magda's injuries, and that he would himself spread abroad the rumour that the bride had been afflicted by the pox. If he so much as mentioned to a living soul that he had played a trick on Lord Mornbury, he would be severely punished.

Mrs. Fustian knew about this, too. She was in her master's confidence, and she had been delighted when he placed Magda entirely in her charge. She thought she knew how to deal with my lady.

Magda stirred her coffee, having taken a childish pleasure in putting three or four spoonsful of sugar into it. No stinting of luxuries here. No stepfather to pry and pounce. She did not particularly mind about the departure of Annette. She had never liked the foreign woman, but the fact that Annette had been sent packing was a painful reminder of the fact that Esmond was verily going to keep her, his wife, a prisoner in her new home.

Magda made no resistance this morning. Mrs. Fustian left her meekly eating her meal. Outside the door, the housekeeper hummed and ha'ad. She felt no pity for the young scarred lady, only indignation because the Earl had been so grossly misled.

Gathering the servants together, Mrs. Fustian informed them all that her ladyship was sickening for the pox. This drew screams from the maids and grunts of dismay from the men. Some were already pitted by the scourge, others had not taken it. All save Mrs. Fustian pitied the hapless bride. For the most part they remained at their posts doggedly, praying that they would be spared. Only one of the scullions and a kitchen maid were found missing at nightfall, and it was presumed that they had taken fright and run away from the 'pestilence'.

Soon the whole village of Godchester knew. The Earl of Mornbury was unlucky, the people whispered. Death might come and claim the Lady Dorothea's cousin as it had done that other unfortunate young lady.

Neighbours—Esmond's friends and acquaintances—complained bitterly that they were subjected to this risk when they went to the wedding. But such was the Earl's importance they hastened to send letters of sympathy. Esmond read them all and listened to all the stories that Mrs. Fustian had to tell him, his face grim and expressionless. Things were working out as he had planned. No one would come near Mornbury Hall now until the February snowdrops began to push their way up through the brown frozen earth. Pity he must expect to receive, but at least there would not be the derision from which his very spirit shrank.

He visited his newly made wife that morning in the company of Dr. Ridpath. White-haired, white-bearded, the old physician had been easily managed, for he had reached the age of retirement and was only practising medicine in Godchester now by courtesy of his lordship. Esmond liked him and he had an affection for the young Earl. When he heard the sorry story briefly sketched for him, he at once promised to aid and abet Esmond in every possible way. He would visit her ladyship twice daily. He would keep the truth from everybody in Godchester.

Just before going into Magda's bedchamber, Esmond had a last word with the old man.

'Know you of any skilled surgeon who might help to lessen the evil that was wrought to my wife's face through her accident?' he asked, frowning.

Dr. Ridpath blew his long thin nose, blinked his watery eyes and pulled at his narrow neckband. His head itched under his musty wig and he longed to scratch it, but dared not, in front of his lordship whom he knew to be fastidious.

'No doubt, no doubt,' he mumbled, 'I can anyhow make inquiries of my colleagues in London. I will acquaint your lordship. Meanwhile I would like to have a look at my—er—patient.'

Esmond led him upstairs. At the door he turned and added:

'I would ask that you do not allow yourself to be drawn into any conversation with Lady Mornbury, other than on the subject of her health, and to keep strictly to the routine of the sick room. I think you will find that she will be amenable. My trust is in you and you shall be well rewarded if all goes well.'

The old doctor bowed. When the young Earl's back was turned, hastily and surreptitiously, Dr. Ridpath scratched the offending pate, then shuffled into the Countess's bedchamber.

Magda sat against her pillows, listlessly. Esmond, under scowling brows, thought that she looked truly ill enough to receive medical attention, so shadowed were her huge eyes this morning. Their gaze met. He saw the shamed red blood creep under the skin and immediately repelled, turned his fastidious gaze away from those hideous scars. But he spoke in a voice of cynical, formal courtesy:

'Good morning, my dear. I bring our well-loved family doctor to examine you. Mrs. Fustian also is here to attend. The report on your condition will be made to me.'

She made no answer but kept a sullen and despairing silence. Neither did she answer save in monosyllables when the old doctor sat down beside her and began to question her, rather foolishly.

Old Ridpath knew that he was in a ticklish position. The whole thing must be treated with great delicacy. But within a few moments he had satisfied himself that Lady Mornbury was an exceedingly strong and healthy young girl suffering only from exhaustion which could soon be remedied. She just wanted feeding up and rest, he could see that. He felt some pity for her and was surprised to find that she was not the scheming young person he had expected. She was, he supposed, the victim of some dire plot out of her control. As for her face; carefully, Dr. Ridpath examined every portion of that sadly altered profile. Forced to do so Magda described her accident and exactly what had happened and how rudely her wounds had been sewn up at the time.

In his youth, Edwin Ridpath had been interested in the treatment of injuries and malformations. When the Earl first questioned him he had forgotten—but remembered now—a certain Pieter Dyck, a Dutch surgeon of considerable talent, who had once been attached to the English Court, and was reputed to have operated with such skill upon a certain beauty in Bath that few traces of her accident had been left. He could consult Mynheer Dyck. True, he was now back in Rotterdam but the Earl would no doubt be pleased to pay his expenses to come to England and visit Lady Mornbury. Not at the moment, while this scheme built around the pox was carried out, but later when she was allowed in public again. He said nothing to Magda on this subject. Neither did she ask him any questions. He felt that her silence, her moroseness, made his position even more difficult. Mrs. Fustian, with hands folded over her bosom, stood by with a smug critical expression on her face, enjoying her role as chaperone.

Dr. Ridpath finally rose and announced that he would be sending a certain Jemima Vole—a nurse whose services he sometimes used and in whom he entirely trusted—to take charge of the 'sick room'.

At this Magda's lashes fluttered. She did not relish this farce of being turned into an invalid. It irked her curiously. Down in the Cotswolds she had been used to so much fresh air. Never a day but she would run from the house, when Sir Adam was not looking, to pick fruit in the orchard or hide in the stables and give a wisp of hay to her favourite pony, or race with the children over the fields. She would not care to be kept, even in the glorious room, without fresh air, for a month perhaps, chained to her bed.

'Do I need to lie here, sir?' she asked the old doctor. His beetle-brows drew together. He wagged his beard.

'Maybe not. Maybe not. We shall see. Good day to your ladyship now. I will be back later to-night with Nurse Vole.'

Magda, after he had gone, hovered between tears and laughter. She said to Mrs. Fustian:

226

'*Vole!* What a name! Will my nurse then be a mouse? I am used to watching the mice run through the fields at home.'

'Indeed, my lady!' said Mrs. Fustian in a tone of disdain and marched out of the bedchamber.

The moment she was alone, Magda sprang from her bed, slipped into her primrose-coloured gown with its wide sleeves and fur trimming, and, like an inquisitive child, began to examine her gilded prison. She had never before seen such a room. There were many beautiful pictures on the walls. She admired them, and the fine decorated panels around the fireplace, the exquisite Dresden china ornaments on the mantelpiece. A French gilt clock inside a glass case fascinated her with its little gold pendulum swinging to and fro. It ticked so daintily.

She touched the rich satin of the curtains and felt her bare feet sink into the thickness of the carpeting. She was delighted, too, by the fine mahogany washstand on which stood a rose and gilt floral china toilet set. She sat a moment at the dressing-table with its frilled muslin hangings and fingered the beautiful bottles, she brushed her hair with the crested brushes and touched her throat

227

with perfume.

Then she got up and wandered through a communicating-door into a boudoir which truly enchanted her. It was octagonal in shape, the walls panelled in palest blue satin. Here there were some charming French water colours, and French walnut furniture, possibly sent over from Paris long before the war, to suit the late Lady Mornbury's tastes. There was a satinwood escritoire with gilt adornments. Dove-grey paper lay on the little desk ready to write upon. There were blue quills, and ink in a Dresden pot, waiting for Magda. Then, there were books. Eagerly she examined the hanging book-case filled with slender colourful leather-bound volumes. Oh, what joy! she thought. Here were authors that she had not found in the library at Wildmarsh where so many of the best books had been sold by the money-hungry Squire. Here, for her delight, were first editions of many classics that she had discussed at home with the old tutor. She took down a volume and began to glance through it. Esmond, entering her room a second time, saw her thus.

He came in an ugly mood, angry and sore because all his plans had been changed.

Had things gone as anticipated, he had meant to take his new young wife to Rome and stay at the palazzo of one of Archie's diplomatic friends, for a month or two perhaps, while the severity of the winter lasted. They should have travelled to Italy via Holland. The sunshine would have been good for Magda and Rome would have been interesting for him and kept him from any ennui which he might have to endure in his new role as devoted husband.

Now all that was impossible. He was forced into this unpleasant intriguing, and felt perpetually conscious that he had made a fool of himself.

Yet somehow, now, when he saw the slender girlish figure in the primrose gown, her dark locks tumbling to her shoulders, face bent over the book, the acid greeting he had prepared for Magda remained unspoken. Some slight interest in the workings of her stirred in him.

'What is this volume that commands your rapt attention so?' he asked.

She swung round, crimson and confused, and immediately hung her head as though she did not wish him to look at her face.

'I—your pardon Sir—I did not hear you enter. It—it is Pepys' *Diary*, my lor—, I mean, Esmond.'

'Pepys—do you read him with any pleasure then?' asked Esmond surprised.

Encouraged, she continued timidly:

'It is the description, Sir, of May-day, when he drove through the town and his *"horses' manes and tails were tied up with red ribbons and new green reins"*.'

He nodded. She read a paragraph or two aloud. He recalled the many letters sent to him by Magda, stressing her love of horses. She was certainly not given, like the majority of young girls he had met, to swooning over love sonnets and leaving the rest of literature unread. Pepys' *Diary*! A curious choice for her to have made. Then he remembered what he had come up to say and his fleeting friendliness evaporated. He said coldly:

'Pray return to your bedchamber, my dear, and await your nurse. You must remember your indisposition.'

Rebellion now stirred in her.

'Am I not to be allowed the freedom of my rooms? I am not sick and you know it.'

'You are sick of soul which is worse,' he said, scowling. 'And it is my wish that you act your part as invalid for a while, anyhow, in case some servant should get into these

230

rooms and see you walking around as though you had no pox. Then the whole thing would be known as a hoax.'

'Which it is,' she said sullenly. 'Why must I bear the brunt of it?'

'You dare to dispute with me!'

'I have been forced into disputes all my life. There have been constant attempts to brow-beat me and break my spirit. I am used to it,' she said with a violence which made him raise his brows.

This was a strange girl, of that there was no doubt. He might have expected her to weep like any weak female and fall at his feet, imploring his mercy, his forgiveness. But there was nothing like that about Magda. In ordinary circumstances he might have been amused and impressed by such display of character, but at the moment, he resented it.

He said:

'I am uninterested in what you are used or not used to. You are my wife now, greatly though it provokes me to know it. You will obey my commands without questioning.'

The wild cat in her snarled a reply. She was not at heart the gentle Lady Mornbury that she should be—receiving her orders with dignified humility. She was the Magda who had so many times crouched in a corner at Wildmarsh, spitting venom back at the man who spat at her—the stepfather who had enslaved and tormented her. She had so frequently stood in defence over her helpless hopeless mother and the half-starved retinue. Touching the laces at her throat, she said:

'You are cruel and without humanity. Much more cruel than your friend Sir Archibald St. John.'

'Oh, I am, am I?' shouted Esmond furious with her. 'How dare you utter one word of criticism against me—remembering how you have helped to deceive and ensnare me.'

'I know what I have done,' she choked, 'and I have already offered to go away.'

'We will not be drawn into that again.'

'And I will not be held by a fine gold chain in a satin-padded kennel like one of the bitches on the farm who has food thrown at her and is then left to howl alone.'

'You use words unbecoming to a gentlewoman, Madam.'

She burst into angry tears.

'I do not pretend to be what I am not.'

232

'Is that so? Your letters suggested a gentility and culture that you hardly seem to possess.'

'I am well educated, Sir, even if life has made me ungentle. I know as much and more perhaps then you'—she swept a hand indicating the books on the shelf—'but I have had a harsh upbringing about which you know nothing.'

'You waste your time trying to soften me with tales of hardship.'

'I have no wish to soften you, but only wish to say that if I am to remain here, I must be allowed some air and some exercise, or, I tell you, I shall die.'

'You little fool, do you not realize that you are supposed to have the pestilence?'

'Then I can go out by night. I have ridden by night before now. I have taken one of the ponies over the moors by the full moon many a time.'

Esmond blinked. Never in his experience had he dealt with such a female. He could not conceive of any of the finely nurtured young ladies in his circle creeping out of their houses to ride by the light of the moon. He was half impressed and wholly appalled.

He thundered at her:

233

'You are no longer Magda Congrayle residing in the wild Cotswolds. You are Lady Mornbury of Mornbury Hall. What do you suppose gossips would say if she were seen careering on horseback through the countryside at nightfall?'

Magda hid her face in her hands, sobbing angrily.

'Very well then, keep me indoors, in my bed. Maybe Dr. Ridpath will have true cause then to come and attend me and bring a priest with him to perform the last rites. Then you can lay me as my cousin was laid, in a vault, and close the door on me for ever.'

Esmond went white to the lips. He set his teeth.

'You dare to mention *that*.'

Magda made a gesture of despair, ran into the adjoining chamber and flung herself on the big bed, sobbing.

Esmond stood staring down at her. For once he was nonplussed, baffled as to what he should really say or do, but he began to see that he had not got for his wife a meek and penitent girl easy to deal with. He was not without imagination. He had a sudden and quite entertaining picture of Magda, her dark hair blowing in the wind, riding bareback on a half-broken colt as described by Adam Congrayle. It was unthinkable that any lady in her position could be allowed to do such a thing. Yet Esmond knew that he, himself, in times of stress had needed to take those long rides upon Jess. Maybe this unhappy misguided child equally longed to sweat out of her body the devil that had led her to come here, and present to him that shocking painted mask of a face.

Incidentally, he thought, that face did not seem so shocking this morning. Archie had been right. With hair unbound and cheeks washed, Magda presented a more natural, frail and even intriguing appearance. And those eyes! Heavens, how they flashed when she was enraged.

He drew a heavy sigh and said:

'Stop your wailing, for God's sake. I will consider this matter of you taking some air later on. Meanwhile pray do as I request and help to make things easier for the one you have so bitterly wronged.'

She made no answer, although her sobbing ceased. An uncomfortable silence followed. Then Esmond turned to the door.

'I am going up to London with Archibald St. John,' he said as he went. 'I shall be away for several days. It will be the worse for you if I find at the end of the week that you have done anything to upset my schemes or cast any reflection upon my name.'

He heard her hoarse little voice.

'I shall do nothing further to anger you. Good-bye.'

'Good-bye,' he said abruptly and shut the door.

After the midday meal he left for the capital with Archie in St. John's coach, and with their valets.

St. John was on leave from the Foreign Office and due to travel up to Edinburgh to further his acquaintance with his Scottish enchantress.

'You are more intelligent than I, Archie,' Esmond remarked with a short laugh as the friends travelled through the cold grey afternoon. 'You have at least seen her face before marriage.'

St. John tried to soothe him. He, himself, was carrying away an unhappy yet not unpleasant memory of the young Countess who had seemed to him so utterly lost, bewildered and forlorn.

'All may work out well for you yet, Esmond,' he had said. 'Do not let the acid

236

enter your soul. With the monks you once learned to conquer yourself. I beg of you to maintain your strength.'

'You do me good always, Archie, but the whole thing has been a fearful blow to me,' said Esmond shading his eyes with one hand.

'Your plan will work out and nobody will be the wiser,' said Archie.

'But I am left with a wife who looks as *she* looks.'

'There may even be a solution to that.'

Esmond shrugged.

'That old dotard, Ridpath, speaks of a Dutch genius who once performed a miraculous operation on a lady who was fearfully slashed in the face by a madman. We can but see.'

'I cannot help feeling some pity for your—er—wife,' said Archie clearing his throat.

Esmond folded his arms and stared at the bleak countryside while the coach rattled over the narrow roads. When he thought of the girl he had married only yesterday, he had to confess a conflict of ideas. She was, indeed, very young. Drunk though he had been last night he could still remember the pure outline of that unmarred side of her

237

face, the length of her lashes, the sloping beauty of her shoulders and the delicacy of the form he had so roughly exposed to the candlelight. He had thought of her many times since—lying there, virginal and shrinking. How he remembered her snarling at him like a young panther, earlier to-day. And that other Magda, immersed in her volume of Pepys. He knew instinctively that he could have no cause to accuse his wife of being unintelligent or lacking courage.

The devil take the whole affair. He was sick and tired of it all, and felt a much injured man.

Suddenly he said:

'I must get away, Archie. I must go for a long time—as soon as this farce of the pox is ended.'

'Do you think that you have your wife under control?'

'I think so,' said Esmond uneasily.

'Where then will you go?'

'I have made up my mind to come with you to see Lord Chesterman, and do some work for my country.'

Archie raised his brows. James Chesterman held a high position in the Foreign Office. Archie knew that he was a distant cousin of Esmond's. He raised his brows still more when he heard what Esmond had decided upon.

Through Chesterman, Esmond might procure for himself a post in Brussels. Esmond had never done a day's work in his life but he had education and brains and was quite capable, as Archie knew, of being useful to the Foreign Office.

Marlborough, after the battle of Ramillies, was now well ensconced in Flanders. Antwerp, Ostend, Dendermond had all surrendered to the Allies. But the great General's triumphs had not of late been so many or so glorious. The whole country was aware that unless Marlborough changed his tactics, one or another of the Flanders cities might eventually return to their French loyalties.

Esmond, driven by his present personal failures in love and marriage, felt a strong urge to leave England. With Chesterman's help he must, he said, try to secure a position in Marlborough's entourage.

'You know, Archie, that I have always been interested in politics and I have a command of the French language. Think you not that I might be useful?'

'I'm sure of it,' said Archie warmly, 'and

will see to it that you are given an audience by Lord Chesterman as soon as we reach the Foreign Office.' Then he added, more doubtingly: 'But will this immediate separation from a newly made wife not raise comments from your friends?'

'My behaviour has always raised comments, my dear fellow. So long as my honour and pride are not involved I do not care. I shall of course wait until Magda is "out of danger", and then use the present crisis in the Duke's campaign as an excuse for putting an end to my idleness and doing some useful work.'

With this answer St. John was totally satisfied. He now sat back, closed his eyes, and gave himself up to the happy thought of seeing his pretty lively Alison in Scotland again. Pray God he would have better luck than poor Esmond, he thought, when it came to the day of reckoning with *her*.

CHAPTER EIGHT

For three days Magda was forced to suffer the attentions of Nurse Vole, combined with the jailer-like Mrs. Fustian, which taxed her patience sorely. They seemed to take an almost malicious pleasure in assuring her that she was very sick of the pox and must lie still and be nursed accordingly. Despite all her pleas, the windows were kept tight shut and enormous fires were burned in the grate, sprinkled with aromatic herbs which filled the room with strong odours bitterly assailing the young girl's nostrils. She knew, of course, that such smells found a way into the panelled corridors and picture galleries and drifted down below, until all and sundry sniffed them and truly believed that the Earl's bride was being nursed of the pestilence.

But Magda felt stifled. These were dark days and nights of grief and endurance for her. She even began to wish that Esmond would come to relieve the monotony. When she asked to be allowed to read, her attendants said that reading would be bad for her eyes and snatched from her every volume that she procured from her boudoir. Finally, Mrs. Fustian turned the key in the door of the communicating room and took it away in her apron pocket.

Magda had never received deferential treatment in her own home but somehow this complete curtailing of her physical liberty irked her to such a degree that she began really to feel ill. She was not however allowed to forget that she had become the Countess of Mornbury, and was waited upon as such. But all the time she was conscious of the wrong she had done in consenting to come here. She kept thinking about the man who was her husband and who despised her.

Her one compensation was when the post-chaise brought a hastily scrawled letter from Stroud. Her mother had sent it to tell her that things were improving a little at Wildmarsh Manor.

'Sir Adam returned in no fine Humour but has left me severely Alone for which I praise God. Sir Adam appears to have been made some monetary offering by your Husband which has Delighted him. I fell on my knees and blessed your Name, my Child, when I heard that the Earl had no intention of sending you back to us. I can get no details from your Stepfather but so long as He remains away in London, I am left in peace and can stand even the Riotous Behaviour of the boys who join with me in sending

242

your their Brotherly Love, and our trust that we shall one day look upon your face again.'

When Magda read this she felt relief and almost a sensation of justification because she had not sacrificed herself in vain. She was also conscious of a half-shamed gratitude towards Esmond who seemed not to have visited his malice against Sir Adam and so spared her unfortunate family.

But now Magda wondered how long she could bear to continue with her imprisonment and eke out this farce.

Jemima Vole was exactly like her name, Magda thought; a tiny mouse of a woman with greying hair and sharp nose and bright little eyes. She was forever nibbling at the bits of food—cakes or jellies—sent up by Mrs. Fustian who had become her dearest friend.

The two women spent a lot of time whispering either in the corner of the bedchamber or outside her door which drove Magda nearly mad. Not that Nurse Vole was unkind. But she fussed the girl unmercifully. She must be stripped and washed. She must have her bedgown changed. She must drink copiously of cups of herb tea or drink the medicines prescribed by the doctor which brought her out into sweats and seemed to produce strange fevers. Sometimes Magda feared that they gave her opium for she went into long trance-like sleeps from which she awoke heavy-headed, furry-tongued and panting for breath. They tried to keep the heavy satin bed-curtains drawn closely around her bed but she cried out against this so loudly that they dared not insist. When she was meek they left her alone. If she complained or protested they threatened her.

'Dr. Ridpath shall be sent for immediately. Your ladyship is worse. Do not pluck at your face or you will be further marked . . .'

And so forth until Magda would scream.

'I have not the pox and you know it. Leave me alone. Get out of my room.'

When she demanded to see the Earl she was told he was not returned from London.

Only when she was alone could she behave in normal fashion. When Jemima Vole went downstairs to the housekeeper's sitting-room for a glass of ale and a private chat, Magda would rise and pace up and down her room like a caged young tigress,

244

her large eyes glowering, her lips sullen and set. She would stop and stare at herself in the mirror. The enforced rest and the good food with which they plied her, had certainly helped her to put on a little weight. She was no longer quite so painfully thin. But there was not a vestige of colour in the face and she felt giddy and always tired.

She would stand with her face pressed to the window looking longingly down at the classic beauty of the terraces, the statues and the pillars in the garden and the beautiful lake.

Motionless she would watch the swans gliding with their effortless grace across the shining water. After the wild unkempt acres around the Manor at home, Mornbury Hall seemed a dream of beauty. Magda longed to go out, to walk down those green groves of tall limes; to explore the wooded parks in which now and then she could glimpse a spotted fawn moving on its dark delicate hooves.

She longed to wander through the colonnades and step inside that little Italian garden to the right of the house with its black pointed cypress trees; she imagined how exquisite it must look in the spring when it came into flower. As for the sculptured figure of the man on the horse, that was a constant delight and fascination to her. She yearned to step out of this hot room and bathe her body in that sparkling water which gushed from the stone animal's nostrils.

As the days and nights passed she began to lose all sense of time.

Esmond had in fact meant to return to Mornbury within the week but changed his plans. After his interview with Lord Chesterman it became imperative that he should remain in London for further conferences. The news coming through Holland from Marlborough was none too good. England was in need of useful men. It looked as though Esmond might soon be offered an important post in Bruges.

Esmond half forgot his troubles at home, having satisfied himself, after sending a man to the Hall for news, that his ruse was working. Mrs. Fustian returned word that 'her ladyship was giving no trouble', and so Esmond turned his thoughts to war and politics, rather than his disastrous marriage.

It was the beginning of February before he drove back to the Hall. A crisp, cold but lovely day of sunshine melting the frosts.

Once home—almost before he had time to unbutton his long travelling coat—he was attacked by two gabbling hysterical women. Mrs. Fustian on one side and a small woman in cap and apron, whom he had never seen before, on the other. He presumed her to be Dr. Ridpath's sick attendant.

They both started to speak at once.

'Oh, milord, it is not our fault. We kept the door locked. Her ladyship must have climbed out of the window. We are not to blame. She was very refractory. We are terrified and helpless. We dared not send men to hunt for her until your lordship came because of the gossip. . . .'

These and other statements were hurled at Esmond. He muttered an oath which made both the women shrink back, and flung his tricorne hat on the floor.

'To the devil with you both,' he said, 'I told you to watch her.'

'I'm sure I did my best,' squeaked Nurse Vole, 'but it was an awkward dilemma for me. Her ladyship did not always accept her position with equanimity.'

Esmond bethought him of the little tigress who had blazed at him up in her

247

room a few weeks ago. He pursed his lips. No, there was certainly nothing very humble about Magda—one knew that when one came down to rockbottom truth, he decided grimly.

He questioned Nurse Vole and Mrs. Fustian. Snivelling, terrified of the Earl's wrath, they said that her ladyship had remarked last night that unless she got some fresh air and exercise she would go into a decline. She had become hysterical and mentioned something about being as agile as her brothers and that she would not stop at climbing down the wall.

'*Climbing down the wall!*' repeated Esmond in a voice of thunder. 'You knew this yet did not prevent her attempting it?'

Together they chorused that her ladyship had gone before ever the house was roused early this morning.

Esmond looked at the tall Dutch marquetry clock in the hall. It was midday. That meant that Magda had been gone for several hours.

His rage cooled. He said to the valet who was at this moment taking his boxes down from the coach.

'Leave those. Attend me. Get me into my boots and riding attire.'

A few moments later he was ready for the ride. He told Mrs. Fustian and Nurse Vole to go back to their quarters and say nothing. Grudgingly he commended them for their tact so far in not spreading the news of her ladyship's escape.

He stood for a moment frowning up at the windows of his dead mother's bedchamber. This was the side of the house, of course, which was festooned with thick creeper. He had meant to have it cut away. Devil take it, the mad girl must have climbed down here. No mean feat. He could not but feel a slight tinge of admiration for her.

Then he marched round to the stables. He saw, immediately, that the doors of Jess's particular stable were open, then found that his cherished grey was not there. Now the blood surged through Esmond's cheeks and he let forth a volley of oaths, both hands gripping the crop until the knuckles showed white.

'*Jess!*' he exclaimed.

Magda must have saddled and taken *Jess*. Ye gods, what colossal impudence; and what nerve. And now Esmond questioned the grooms, who glanced at each other, lied and spluttered and gabbled a dozen explanations, none of which satisfied Esmond. Jess had gone, that was all *they* knew.

Esmond began to feel apprehensive as well as enraged. Nobody save himself had ever ridden Jess, nor was anyone permitted to do so. She was not only the swiftest of mounts but a highly nervous creature with a mouth that needed extra care. Under him she was a lamb. At the hands of a stranger she might be dangerous.

That mad girl had possibly killed herself and broken Jess's legs as well.

Esmond gulped. If there was one thing he cared for deeply in this world, it was Jess.

If Magda has caused her death, I shall kill *her*, he thought.

In a fine rage he ordered one of the grooms to saddle a handsome chestnut from the adjoining stables, and touching the satin flanks with his heels, galloped down the drive. There were only one or two roads which Magda could have taken. He must find her—or her corpse—he thought, in a positive ferment of mind.

But on the road to Godchester he saw nobody, passed nothing save a couple of farm wagons trailing into market. He knew a pathway through the woods on the brow of the hills that looked down upon the village. He turned his chestnut's head. In the wood the big horse picked his way daintily over the rich oak soil, dusted with dry leaves of long past summers. But here there was only silence. No trace of Jess's hooves. Anxiously he rode on, taking yet another route towards London. He was passed only by a post-chaise and a phaeton pulled by two spirited bays. He recognized General Corsham, driving with Mlle LeClaire by his side. Esmond had almost forgotten Chantal. She waved her muff at him prettily and looked as though she might wish to stop and talk, but he had too much on his mind. He bowed low in the saddle and rode on. He had no time just now for women, he thought. The devil take all of them, and especially Magda!

After an hour's hard riding and vain searching he turned the chestnut's head for home. He was really anxious now. More, he thought cynically, about Jess than the girl. At the big wrought-iron gates of Mornbury Hall, he stopped, dismounted and stood a moment looking to the right and to the left in helpless fury.

And then suddenly he heard the faraway

251

clattery-clack of horse's hooves striking against the hard ground. Somehow it was a familiar sound and set his pulses jerking. *Then he saw her.*

She came towards him at what he thought a crazy pace, *on Jess*. He had a moment of wild relief when he sighted his handsome grey and knew that she was unimpaired. Nearer and nearer came rider and mare. Esmond drew the chestnut on to the grass verge, and watched, dumbfounded. Ye gods, how Magda rode! He had never seen anything like it!

When she came near enough his dazed sight took in her appearance. And that in itself was enough to astound him. From somewhere she had dug out a riding habit which had belonged to his mother. He recognized it at once. He remembered that he had never allowed it to be given away, because the late Countess had been painted in it, and he cherished the memory.

One of the oil paintings that hung in the gallery was of Catherine Mornbury on horseback. The habit had been put away in the cedar chest in her bedchamber. This madcap Magda must have unearthed it. It seemed to fit her. She looked dashing enough to stir any male heart in that coat and waistcoat of blue camlet trimmed with silver; a cravat of fine lace, and a little beaver hat with a sprightly feather in it. But he was shocked to see that she had pulled the long skirt up to her knees and was riding astride like a boy, showing long coarse woollen hose.

Her dark hair was tied back with a scarlet ribbon; and thank God, he reflected grimly, she had taken the precaution of tying a gauze veil over her face. Astride his Jess, she cantered towards him. He rushed into the road and shouted:

'*Jess* ... whoa ... *whoa* there, girl. ...'

The mare pricked up her ears and, recognizing the beloved voice, skidded on all four hooves to a finish. Her nostrils flared. Her eyes rolled. Her neck and flanks were white with the foam of her sweat.

Esmond took the bridle. The face that he raised to Magda was almost demoniac in its expression of anger.

'You devil! How dared you take my horse?'

She slid from the saddle. Lifting her veil he saw that she was flushed from the exercise and her eyes were brilliant with excitement. She gave a wild laugh.

'Be angry with me if you wish. Punish

me, but I have had my ride. I felt the wind against my face and got the smell of physics and burning pastilles out of my nostrils. So was I saved from going out of my mind,' she panted.

He stared down at her.

'How dared you leave your room?'

'I told you I was not a bitch to be kept on a chain.'

'You *are* a bitch and that is a certainty,' he said in a brutal voice.

'I do not care how you insult me. I got away and I have had my ride.'

Esmond ran a hand over Jess, feeling her fetlocks, and withers, slapping and soothing her.

'If you have done an injury to Jess—'

'I have done naught,' broke in Magda, 'but give her the exercise that she was needing. She is growing fat.'

Esmond gulped.

'Why, you little—'

'And she has been having vastly too many oats,' added Magda, looking up at her husband sulkily.

For an instant Esmond thought that he would burst, then suddenly he flung back his head and laughed. This was past being an annoyance. It was positively funny. Her colossal cheek appealed to his sense of humour.

Magda listened to that laughter and for an instant wondered if it boded ill for her, and she started to tremble. She had not really been fit to take so much physical exercise after the weeks in bed, but she was glad now that she had done so much walking up and down the room in order to keep her limbs supple, whenever her two jailers were out. Esmond spoke to her now in a changed voice:

'I am told you left the house before breakfast was served. Where have you been?'

'All over the place. I stopped for an hour or two's rest ten miles away,' she said shruggingly. 'I do not know the names of the villages around here but it is flat gentle country after the Cotswolds.'

'You do not seem to have been too gentle with my mare. She has been hard ridden.'

Magda shrugged again.

'I told you that she is out of condition.'

Esmond removed his tricorne hat and his lips twisted into wry smile.

'There is a grain of truth in your criticism. I am away too often and Jess does not get enough exercise.'

'Then please let me ride her,' said Magda with sudden daring, and looked at him eagerly. 'She is so glorious, so sensitive. Never have I known such perfect action from any animal.'

'You are right. Jess is a queen of beasts,' said Esmond grudgingly, 'but you had no right to take her and she does not like strangers.'

Magda turned and laid her scarred cheek against the mare's damp nose.

'She likes me. From the moment I whispered to her and gave her a handful of the sugar which I took from the tray, when they served me last night's milk, she was my slave. She let me do what I wished with her.'

'You saddled her alone?'

'Of course,' said Magda impatiently.

Esmond blinked. This was incredible. And like that, her mutilated cheek hidden against the mare's nose, Magda suddenly looked almost beautiful in his mother's colourful habit. He remembered the days when he used to see his beautiful mother ride to the hounds with his father, surrounded by a bevy of admiring gentlemen. Nobody in this district had ever seen Catherine Mornbury's equal on a horse. He recalled his own sense of regret and loss because his Dorothea had been too delicate to ride. He recalled also the bragging of Sir Adam who had spoken of Magda as second to none in Gloucestershire on horseback. Now he could believe it. Anybody who could have saddled Jess, managed her so deftly, and come with her at a canter as he had seen Magda come just now, could not fail to stir a hunting man's admiration. Suddenly he said:

'Whether I allow you to ride Jess or not is problematical, but I will see to it that you are properly mounted.'

She gave a little gasp.

'Oh . . . thank you, *thank you*, Esmond.'

As though ashamed of his weakening, he snapped:

'But you took a risk and disobeyed my orders. Cover your face and we will ride back together. You must return at once to your sick room.'

'You are not over-angry with me?'

He avoided the large eyes.

'I will help you mount, Madam,' he said coldly.

She bit her lip. Her blood was stirring and her heart still racing from the joy of exercise, and the beauty of the grey. But

257

now the fun was over. She said:

'Please, *please* do not condemn me to much more of that farce about the pox.'

'It will continue until the doctor says that it is the appropriate time for you to be seen out, Madam.'

Suddenly she felt depressed and miserable again.

'Must you call me *that*?'

'Be thankful that I do not call you worse,' he said and lifted her on the saddle none too gently.

They rode up the long lime-bordered drive in silence. Magda's head was downcast. Esmond scowled. Never before had he seen Jess mounted by anybody save himself and although he grudgingly acknowledged that the girl sat the mare as bravely and straightly as a boy, he still could not forgive the outrage.

When they reached the nobly built steps leading up to the portico of the house, he said brusquely:

'Go straight indoors and up to your bedchamber.'

'Can I not talk to you for a moment longer?' she began.

'Later I will come to you,' he cut in.

She bit her lip and obediently slid from

the saddle, patted Jess's velvet twitching nose, and whispered:

'Dear beautiful creature, farewell ... thank you for the golden hours of freedom spent with you.'

Esmond did not hear the words. He saw only the coarse inquisitive faces of one or two menservants at the windows. He rang the bell furiously. A lackey opened the doors. Then Esmond sent for Mrs. Fustian.

The house-keeper approached him, red-faced, sullen but obsequiously bobbing and mumbling her excuses. He cut her short.

'The incident is closed. You were not to blame. Her ladyship needed fresh air and exercise. Let nothing more be said about this escapade, but see to it that in future her rooms are less suffocating.'

Mrs. Fustian stared, amazed. The Earl flung his gauntlets and crop on to a chair and continued:

'Being kept all these weeks abed has been too great a strain on her ladyship who is young and strong. Bid the nurse allow the patient to dress and walk about her rooms and do as she wishes there. See to it also that the servants think that I myself took her ladyship to ride with me this morning, and if they become muddled or too

259

inquisitive, shut them up.'

'Yes, my lord . . .' Mrs. Fustian panted.

'Send for Dr. Ridpath,' added Esmond. 'I shall ascertain from him how much longer it will be before we can allow her ladyship, veiled, to come downstairs.'

'You are home for good now, my lord?'

'For one week only. I go abroad to the war.'

Mrs. Fustian gulped. The Earl going abroad? *To the war?* What news, indeed!

She hastened to impart it to her new confidante, Jemima Vole, and cautioned her not to be too hard on her ladyship in future as his lordship seemed to have undergone some change of mind concerning his disfigured bride.

She scattered those of the staff who had watched the Earl and Countess dismount and were chattering and making wild surmisals. Her ladyship had made a more speedy recovery than was anticipated and except for some facial markings, was well enough now to go out, she told them, and sent them about their business.

Up in her rooms, Magda took off the riding habit and the little beaver hat which she had discovered in the cedarwood chest and which had greatly appealed to her.

Reluctantly she replaced the garments in the chest, and put on her hated wrapgown again. That unattractive mouse, her nurse, was pattering around, scolding and bullying in her fashion, trying to get her 'patient' back to bed.

But Magda, heartened by her ride, snapped at her.

'Let me be, for God's sake. . . .'

In the midst of the dispute, Esmond knocked on the door and marched in. He was still in his olive-green riding clothes. He looked tired and worried, Magda thought, as soon as she saw him. He motioned the nurse to leave. When he was alone with Magda, he said in his iciest voice,

'Where did you find my mother's clothes?'

'In yonder chest,' said Magda, pointing to a far corner of the room.

'It was an impertinence to wear them.'

Now she stuck out her small chin.

'What else could I wear Sir? I could not ride in a bedgown. When I found the habit, I borrowed it. Was it so great a crime?'

His lips twitched. The anger in which he had come died a natural death. The way this chit who had behaved so outrageously, dared to defy and argue, amazed Esmond. He had to admit he had married no spiritless, boring creature, and that there was a strange dignity in Magda which he was just beginning to discover, setting her apart forever in his mind from Sir Adam Congrayle. He began to suspect, also, that Archie's conjectures had foundations and that this child had possibly been the innocent tool of an unscrupulous man and nothing much worse.

He said:

'I do not wish my mother's things disturbed. I loved and honoured her.'

Magda bowed her head. Against her will sudden tears stung her eyelids.

'Naturally I can expect neither loving nor honouring from you, Sir.'

'You are still, however, my wife,' he reminded her, 'and I wish you to receive the attention and respect a Countess of Mornbury expects.'

'Thank you for that much,' she whispered and surreptitiously wiped away a tear.

He saw the action and made a gesture of irritation.

'You repent your behaviour too late, my dear,' he said in a tone of sarcasm.

She lifted her head, revealing the stark misery in her great eyes. But it was the hatefully scarred cheek he saw.

'Then I shall not repent,' she said chokingly.

'Behave as you wish. I am uninterested whether you pray to God or to the devil,' he said in the same irritable tone. 'Only I will not have my name bandied about and as we have so far managed to make a success of this supposed illness of yours it would be a pity to undo it now and set tongues a-wagging.'

'I will not climb out of the window again,' she whispered forlornly.

He marched to the window and stared down.

'You could have tumbled to your death. That creeper might not have held your weight.'

'I do not weigh much,' she said.

He turned back, his gaze travelling over her. Her head was bent. Now he noticed with some surprise that since her hair had been washed, a pure white streak shewed in the dark threads running from the top of the small skull down to the pure forehead. He gazed at it, fascinated and said:

'No more dyeing or crimping of your

hair, please.'

'As you wish.'

'And you are still too thin,' he added with grudging interest in her condition, for he had noted the excessive slenderness of the young white arms where the wide sleeves of her wrapping gown fell back, and the hollows in her long fine throat. (That swan-neck reminded him so painfully of Dorothea's, it both touched and maddened him.) 'Did you hear me, Magda?' he shouted. 'I said that you might have crashed to your death when you climbed out of the window like a vulgar stableboy—then consider the scandal!'

'Would my death not have been a relief to you?' she flashed, 'and made the scandal worthwhile.'

He found himself suddenly abashed. He could not help now but see the stark unhappiness on her small ruined face. More gently he answered.

'No, Magda. Let us not speak with exaggeration. I would not wish your death.'

'Then you are different from myself for I would welcome it as a release,' she choked.

'From what?' he asked curiously.

She did not answer but hid her face in her hands. Now he came and touched her hair, lightly, with his finger-tips.

'Peace! Tears are a waste of time. What has been done cannot be undone.'

She wept uncontrollably.

'I cannot live to be so hated and despised.'

'I neither hate nor despise you.'

'You do. You do,' she said childishly.

'I repeat that I do not. I am—without feelings,' he said and began to walk up and down the big room. He felt it to be so hot and stuffy and full of the unpleasant odour of some bitter herbs Nurse Vole had sprinkled on the logs that he turned to one of the windows and flung it open.

'I have to agree with you that it is abominable in here. You need fresher air,' he muttered.

She made no answer. She sat on the edge of the great bed, quietly crying. It seemed to Esmond that she was no longer the shameful deceiver but a lonely, tragic child who could not help her injuries, either of body or soul. He made a movement towards the bed as though to put an arm about her but drew back. No, he was damned if he was going to show any weakness towards her, or any other member of her sex. He was finished with

265

females. This marriage was a sterile bitter farce into which he had been tricked. He would not soften towards Magda. She should not have come to Mornbury.

He said:

'You will see little of your husband in future, my dear, so you must learn to play your part as Countess of Mornbury and to uphold my name and my honour in my long absence.'

Her head shot up. He averted his gaze from the tear-wet, flushed young face with its frightful scarring.

'Why ... where ... are you going?' she asked desolately.

'Abroad—one week from now,' he said abruptly.

And he told her of his interview with Chesterman at the Foreign Office, and that he was being sent to join the Duke of Marlborough's entourage in Flanders.

The tears dried on Magda's lashes. She sat very still, making no sound or movement save by the nervous clasping and unclasping of her exquisite hands. He spoke of the present grave troubles surrounding England's great military leader; of the Queen's consent and approval of his, Esmond's, plans for making himself

266

useful rather than continuing to lead an idle existence in this country. He told her of the storm clouds billowing on the horizon for the Allies.

'You will understand nothing of foreign affairs,' he added, frowning, 'but they are serious. The King of Sweden has allied himself with France and he is a formidable enemy—one of the military geniuses of our time.'

Now she suddenly spoke, her sad eyes glistening.

'I know. I used to read the papers to Sir Adam at night. I have also talked over the present world crisis with my brothers' tutor. I believe that it is essential that the Duke of Marlborough should stop King Charles of Sweden from conniving with Germany.'

Esmond, amazed, turned to stare at the young girl.

'You know so much?'

'I realize the implication if the Swedish monarch's plans were to succeed, Sir.'

'It is a fact,' agreed the astonished Esmond. 'The French have gained far too many victories in Spain for our country's good. They will be altogether heartened if Sweden joins against them.'

'You say you go to Flanders. Are not Bruges and Ghent two danger points on the map?' asked Magda, forgetting her personal miseries for a few moments. For she had always had a strange love of maps and examined them with Mr. Bacon and listened to his rhetorics about history, both ancient and modern.

She used to tell her halfbrothers long stirring stories of the battles already won by the great Duke of Marlborough and weave a tapestry of her own thoughts and desires; longing to be a youth, free to ride into battle, instead of a defenceless girl.

Esmond, unused to any such discussions among the tittering, swooning flirtatious females of the day, listened to her now, thunderstruck. He let her talk and talked to her as man to man. Once, when she misstated a fact, he corrected her. But he was surprised and even pleased by the clear analysis she made of the present situation and the extent of her knowledge. He began to see that this extraordinary girl had, in the confines of her wild Cotswold home, never allowed her intelligence or aptitude for acquiring knowledge, to lie fallow.

He said:

'I join the Duke at Bruges. It is, as you

say, a possible danger-zone. Trouble may fester at Oudenarde which is where the French may decide to strike at us. But I shall not be in actual conflict for I am not a soldier.'

'But you may, like other gentlemen attached to military headquarters, be cut off in case of a sudden attack.'

Now he was amused and laughed aloud.

'Poof! You speak like a loving wife who fears for the safety of her lord and master. Let us not be hypocritical.'

Magda flushed and turned away her head. Was she being a hypocrite, she wondered. Was it not true that she had no wish to see Esmond leave Mornbury and travel to the seat of war? Whatever had transpired, she was, as he himself had just said, his wife. And he was still the noble Esmond she had idealized and dreamed of and upon whom she could have lavished all her love. Oh, why, why, she asked herself drearily, could she not have presented to him a face he might have liked to touch and to kiss. It was terrible and bitter as gall to her to know that she was repellent in his sight.

She bit on her lips until a trickle of blood came and she had to wipe it away with the back of her hand. But she would not cry in front of him any more.

She suddenly asked:

'When do—you go?'

'I have already told you—a week from now.'

'And what are your wishes concerning me?'

He stood in front of the fire, scowling into it, drumming his fingers on the mantelpiece.

'You will remain here, naturally, and behave as an ordinary wife would do in the absence of her spouse. When you are pronounced well you can take normal exercise on horseback, or be driven out in a phaeton. I will leave suitable orders with the servants to carry out your wishes.'

'Mrs. Fustian dislikes me,' Magda said in a strangled voice, 'I wish she need not serve me.'

'She was good enough for my mother. She shall remain here with you,' was Esmond's cold reply. 'The doctor—old Ridpath—has a Dutch surgeon in readiness to look at your—ahem—face ...' he coughed and frowned, half ashamed, suddenly of harping on her misfortune, 'and it is my wish that you see him and do whatsoever they think may help to reduce the effects of your accident.'

Magda whispered:

'Very well.'

'You will also remain veiled in public and let it be supposed you are pock-marked.'

'As you say.'

She winced.

'You will do your best to avoid mingling with my old friends. Those who call can be told you are delicate and not receiving.'

'Am I then to have no friends? No one to talk with?' she asked forlornly.

He bit his lips. He hardly knew what to answer. Then he hardened his heart.

'If your life must be solitary, it is a penance which you deserve, Madam. You must content yourself with your embroidery, or spinet, or these books which you ask for. Mornbury boasts a fine library.'

'I shall like reading, but I have done little needlework in my life, nor do I understand music.'

'Then you can learn both. I will arrange that you take lessons from a music master and from a sewing instructress,' he said icily. 'It is right that a Gentlewoman in your position should be proficient in such

271

things. Were you so idle then, and your upbringing so neglected, at Stroud?'

She made no answer, remembering bitterly, how she had been kept with her nose to the grindstone from dawn till dusk in hard menial labour. She could not speak of these things to this husband of hers who was husband in name only. She saw not a glimmering of real kindness or sympathy in his conversation. The fleeting pleasure of their discussion on the war had vanished. She was faced now, she thought, with a loveless, lonely monotonous future while he was abroad and for heaven knew how long. It was a cheerless—nay, an appalling vista—for a girl not yet seventeen summers.

He found suddenly that the staring of her large mournful eyes made him uneasy. He turned and walked to the door.

'I bid you good day, Madam,' he said.

'Good day,' she said under her breath.

After he had gone she slid between the silken sheets of the bed and felt suddenly a raging misery and anger against her fate. She rang the bell violently. When Jemima Vole appeared, Magda was sitting upright, two hectic spots on her cheeks and her body shivering.

'I wish a warming pan and a bowl of hot

soup to be sent up,' she said. 'And then pray draw my curtains and leave me in peace.'

'But your wash, my lady—' began Nurse Vole.

'Do as I say,' broke in Magda, more furiously than she had ever spoken to Tammy at home in her life.

The woman gulped and obeyed. She ran down to the housekeeper's room and told good Mrs. Fustian that her ladyship had gone into a tizzy and was casting her orders right and left.

'Do as she bids,' counselled Mrs. Fustian with a grunt, 'and continue to do so until his lordship leaves, or lose a good job. A plague on that ugly young woman who has inveigled herself into this household is what I say.'

But none dared flout Lady Mornbury's wishes that night or for many nights to come.

CHAPTER NINE

Esmond spent the next few days setting his affairs in order, discussing the business of the farms and estate with his bailiff and even sending for his legal adviser in order to add a codicil to his Will. It was not to be denied, he told himself, that Magda was right in assuming that it might be dangerous to follow Marlborough in any campaign, even if not as officer in Her Majesty's Army. 'Twere well to die in order, if die he must.

Once or twice during that final week left to him at Mornbury, he felt a pang at parting from his country home. The house in St. James's had no particular meaning or sentiment; but Mornbury he loved.

He had meant to have a loved wife, too, and an heir to inherit the title and estates. He thought gloomily of that strange defiant girl upstairs. How could he ever make her the mother of his children? How could he begin to feel physical love for one so afflicted?

Over-much thinking and regretting made him morose and ill-humoured. It did not do to cross him as the inmates of the Hall were quick to find. He disliked the enforced silence and sedateness of the house, but dared not invite a guest to share a glass of wine, lest he reveal what had really transpired with his newly made wife.

Once or twice he felt a latent urge to look into Chantal LeClaire's velvet brown eyes again and feast his gaze on her perfect face but he could not do so. So he chafed against the enforced solitude and boredom.

On the night prior to his departure for Bruges, he went up to Magda's rooms.

She was now formally permitted by Dr. Ridpath to dress and walk from bedchamber to boudior.

Esmond found her seated at her walnut escritoire. He stared at the slim straight back. Her hair was looped back with a blue bow. The heat of the rooms in which Nurse Vole kept such large fires, had led her to put on a thin banyan of Indian muslin billowing into frills to her slippers. She did not hear him arrive, for her quill was scratching busily over the paper before her.

Esmond stood in silence, frowning. He had just finished a rich dinner washed down by his favourite claret. He, himself, was simply attired in sober grey and wore a small peruke. His face was pale and tired. A deep depression had settled on Esmond. He had drunk the last drop of wine, brooding in solitary state at the head of his dinner table, irked by the whole turn of events. In one way he longed to be off to the

Continent to-morrow. In another, he felt a strange unaccountable sadness at the idea of leaving England. A nostalgia for the past when he had held magnificent parties here in this house and in London; filled the rooms with light and music and laughter; diced and gambled in the clubs; drunk with his friends and duelled with his enemies. Spirited, vital days, full to the brim with all that life could offer a sybarite. Days when he had paid his respects at Court and been a prime favourite of Queen Anne who, as royal godmother, had afforded him many privileges in his golden, misspent youth. Days when he had passed from vice to virtue and ridden joyfully to Shaftley Castle as the betrothed of the loveliest girl in England.

How was it possible life could change in so brief a while? He felt that he had been dogged by misfortune from the time of Dorothea's death and his accident, to the awful revelation on his marriage day.

To-night he stood, unseen, unheard by Magda, staring, ruminating, wondering bitterly what the future could hold for him. Perhaps, he reflected, he was over-fatigued and had drunk too much claret, but he felt furiously befogged in his mind, and resentful that he could not come to grips with his very Destiny and defeat it as he would do an enemy who had affronted him.

How youthful Magda's back looked! What was she writing? He had seldom known a young female spend so much of her leisure with pen and paper, or studying a book.

She had done no more climbing out of windows, but he had seen to it that she rode every morning before breakfast. He, himself, rode at her side. Never would she mount Jess again but he had found a small but strong strawberry-roan that suited her, and had been pleased to remark upon the excellent way in which she had handled it. She rode out always closely veiled, and he had little or nothing to say to her but made it obvious that he went with her only as a necessary escort. He did not see her again during the day.

This morning they had not gone out at all for a sudden fog had descended upon Godchester, and flung it into a melancholy shroud. He had strangely missed that early morning canter with Magda and was positive she, too, would have been disappointed. From to-morrow, he had told her, she would ride with two of the grooms—men he knew and trusted.

He realized that this time was the last time he would see her for months, perhaps years, perhaps *ever*. The idea did not cause him pain yet it increased the acute discomfort of spirit that had weighed him down for the last few days and nights.

He marched across the little octagonal chamber, which was charming in candlelight, with the wood-fire leaping, and smelling of a perfume which she had started lately to use.

He asked loudly:

'What is all this scrawling about?'

She jumped, swung round, and put a hand to her heart.

'Oh . . . I . . . did not hear you, Sir.'

'Let me see your papers,' he said.

She looked red and confused and shrank back, putting a hand over the desk.

'Oh, no—it is—they are—nothing. I assure you—nothing that could interest you.'

'I will see for myself, nevertheless.'

'My writing is private to me,' she said, scarlet-cheeked.

'Anything that belongs to my wife cannot be private to her,' said Esmond irate now, and curious. 'Come, Madam—hand your scribblings to me.'

Magda tried to tear the sheets of paper in half but in a trice he had prevented it, and twisted her delicate wrist so that she cried out and the papers fluttered to the floor. As he bent to pick them up, she cried out again:

'It is ungentlemanly of you ...'

'Tush,' he broke in, a smile twisting his lips, 'you and I cannot talk of gentle behaviour. There has been far too much licence on the subject.'

Helplessly and pale now, Magda watched him scan what she had written. She had been working on a diary—writing down her own personal feelings and the events of each day since she had left the Cotswolds. Some of the matter lay in a drawer. This latest entry was the very last she would have wished Esmond to read. Dismayed, covered with confusion, she watched him, knowing every line he was perusing.

Esmond read only a few paragraphs of the piteous diary. It was so frank and revealing—so much a *cri de coeur*, it both surprised and troubled him. It left no room for doubt in his mind as to the extent of her remorse and the present heavy burden of her woe; her intense loneliness.

'It is the waking hours when I lie watching the dawn creep through the chink in my bed curtains and remember where and what I am. There is so much beauty here in Mornbury and so much pain. It is a paradise and it is also the island of the damned—and I am an exile, wandering upon it, condemned to suffer without hope of relief. I did wrong when I consented to cheat Esmond. I know it full well but it is too late to repent. He was once the chevalier idolized by my sweet dead cousin. I, too, thought of him as an ideal. In those days when he lay half dead in the care of the monks, I felt drawn to him, irresistibly. Without ulterior motive, I communicated with him, and without hope of reward. I could well have loved him. But he has become cold and as cruel as the grave. That grave in which I wish to God I lay buried, out of sight of him and the rest of the world. Now he is leaving me and I shall be worse than dead, alone with servants who must secretly mock at me. I feel a bitterness that can never be wiped out of my soul. Why did I not die when I was flung from my horse as a carefree child? Why had I to live with my disfigurement and endure the look of hatred in my husband's eyes? What Life has done to me is undeserved and unforgivable. I shall not forgive Life. But what Esmond Mornbury has done to me, is worse. He has been a monster. Would God I were a man who might duel with him and slash his cheek open with my sword, then make of him what he has made of me—an object of derision. A scarred, hateful scarecrow rejected in the very name of Love.

'I am as good as dead, and left here to dance in the dust of a dead saint whom my husband should have married instead of me. O, I hate him. I hate—'

Here it broke off. The last two words were heavily underscored in the violet ink in which they had been written. A blotch shewed where the quill had trembled in her fingers when she turned and saw him.

He was considerably shocked by that candid revelation of Magda's feelings. One or two of the phrases stung him:

'*What Esmond Mornbury has done to me is worse . . .*'

How dared she? What had he done—he who had—in blissful ignorance and a folly

281

born of laziness rather than ignorance—married the girl before seeing her? His cheeks burned. He had to recall his harsh treatment of her after the wedding. He could picture her, crouching on the bed, one hand against her scarred face; his rejection of her which must have left no room for doubt in her mind that she was too unbeautiful for any man to touch her.

He was glaring at the diary with its freshly entered paragraphs, and his fine nostrils flared. His temper rose. He was on one hand, moved by the anguish in those pages; on the other, enraged because she accused him of being the cause of her misfortunes. He had been rudely disillusioned. He was not going to climb down now and apologize to the one who was in fact the cause of all *his* recent unhappiness.

Esmond Mornbury had never, indeed, been anything but an egotist. One woman in the world and one only had appealed to his better side, and she lay buried in the vaults at Shaftley Castle.

Suddenly he tore Magda's diary in half and flung the pieces at her.

'You waste the hours, writing such trash, Madam,' he said thickly, 'and if you hate me, I am indifferent, believe me.'

She was ivory white now save for those pink ugly ridges across her young tired face. She got up and ran into the adjoining room.

'I shall always hate you,' she said, speaking as harshly and violently as he had done to her. Her deep longing to rouse some tenderness or understanding in him was drowned now under a storm of resentment because of his implacable hatred towards her.

He followed her into the big room where the six wax candles in their tall candelabra burning on the mantelpiece cast gigantic shadows on the ceiling, and left the curtained bed in darkness. A darkness to which Magda fled, burying her tormented face in the pillows as though they were the last, the only refuge to her. No sound come from her. But she lay there in stark dumb misery, her muslins crumpled, the ribbon on her hair untied.

Esmond approached the bed.

'I came to see you,' he said curtly, 'and bid you farewell, for by the time you waken I shall be gone.'

She turned to him, no longer caring whether her convulsed face was hideous to him or not.

'Go, then . . . go . . . I do not mind. I shall not grieve for you.'

'Excellent,' he laughed. 'It would seem we share a hatred of each other.'

'I would almost rather return to my bullying stepfather in Stroud than remain in this house,' she choked.

'Nevertheless remain you shall,' he said coldly. 'You are Lady Mornbury and must remember the fact and act accordingly. Have you not done enough harm to me and caused me enough trouble already?'

'What of *me*? Do you ever consider my side of things?' she asked, beating one small fist against her pillow, pushing the hair back from her hot face.

'No, Madam. I consider only my own,' he said frankly. 'But we will not go into that. It is too late. I merely leave you with my final instructions. Dr. Ridpath is bringing the Dutch surgeon to see you after I have gone. I insist that you obey them and do whatsoever they might consider best.'

She broke into mirthless laughter.

'Are you so anxious to restore my beauty?'

'For my sake, personally, no. Only in order that we should not be looked at

284

askance when we take up our lives together after my return from the war. *If* I return...'

She was silenced by this thought but broke out suddenly:

'I may refuse to allow these medical gentlemen to torment me afresh. I do not believe my face can be bettered.'

'That is for them to say. If you refuse their aid, I will make you regret it,' Esmond said in a warning voice.

She gave another wild laugh, her fine eyes flashing at him.

'You can no longer make me regret anything. At one time I was penitent because I had helped to deceive you. I prayed God to forgive me for permitting you to believe I was the girl in that miniature. But now I am glad if I brought you sorrow and trouble. You are as I wrote in my diary—a monster. Crueller than death itself. I am glad that Dorothea died before she could call you "husband" ... *glad!* ...'

Magda broke off, hardly realizing what she was saying. She shrank back. She had seen suddenly, the savage look that had sprung into Esmond's eyes. She put her hands up as though expecting him to strike

285

her.

He snarled:

'I will never forgive you for those words.'

She sprang from the bed, clutching her muslins against her.

'Let me go. Let me depart from this house. I can bear no more.'

He caught her as she tried to pass him. She fought a moment like a wild cat, out of control, kicking, struggling, biting at his hands. He, too, inflamed with a night's drinking, acted without restraint. He shook the slim girl as though she were a kitten, clawing him. He was amazed by her physical strength. Her resistance bred in him a desire to defeat her—to conquer her for good and all. No woman should say such things, do such things to him and get away with them, he decided. She had gone too far.

Now Magda's mantua fell away. He saw the white beauty of her unblemished skin and her rose-tipped breasts. The white streak of her hair fell across her injured cheek, hiding it. Esmond, all male, responded suddenly to a primitive awareness of the fact that *this was his wife*. Legally his. He had the right to master her. Every instinct of chivalry, or gentleness for

286

the weaker sex, lay in this moment buried under a hot welter of fury, of passion. He pinned Magda's arms against her sides, carried her to the bed and flung her down upon it.

'You shall not defy me, neither shall you think that you can say and do as you wish. You shall learn that Esmond Mornbury is your husband and your master,' he said. 'You who vowed less than two months ago to love, honour and obey me shall do all three . . . at my command.'

She was reduced to panic-stricken silence. His livid face, his sudden sensuality, terrified her.

He snuffed the candles, plunging the room into darkness save for the red glow of the log fire. Then he came back and drew the red handsome curtains around the bed.

For a moment he made love to her madly, his kisses burning her lips. She lay unresisting. But gradually he tasted the scalding heat of tears trickling slowly down her cheeks. And suddenly the tempest of fury left Esmond. Relighting the candles he got up and dressed again, poured himself a goblet of water from a carafe on the table beside her and drained it. He could see his own reflection in a long cheval mirror; it disgusted him. He knew that he had conducted himself like a boor. Now reaction had set in and he was filled with a remorse which was to burn in him like a slow fire for many a long month ahead.

He ruffled his shorn hair and muttered an oath.

On her pillows Magda lay motionless, her face swollen, her mind exhausted. Through half-closed lids, she watched Esmond, half in fear, as though he might turn back into the devil again; half in wonderment. Whatever he had done, or said, he could never wipe out this night, she thought, and the memory of his embrace. But those violent kisses had added yet another scar to her hurt soul. They had spoiled for her the very essence of the word '*love*' as she had in her childish dreams imagined it.

She lay weeping quietly, hopelessly.

He came to her side, bent down and touched her hair. A few moments ago his blood had leaped at the touch of her. Now he turned embarrassed, from the sadness in those deep eyes. For the first time he saw this tragedy from her side, as well as from his own, and it was as though in a strange fashion the ugly side of her face became suddenly less objectionable to him. He said quietly:

'I did wrong. What you said about Dorothea drove me mad.'

'I regret it . . .' she whispered.

'What has been done is irrevocable. Let us not hurt each other further,' he went on with difficulty. 'To-morrow I shall be gone. I may never see you again. I ask only that you uphold my name and my pride in the eyes of the world that knows us.'

She turned her face to the pillow and sobbed.

'I will do so. But oh Esmond, try not to hate me so. I am so weary of hatred.'

He put the back of his hand against his eyes.

'I—will try not to hate you any more. I can pity you if it is pity you want, my poor child.'

She could scarcely believe her ears. These were the first truly kind and gentle words she had ever heard from him. She said:

'I do not ask for pity—only for your pardon.'

'Then I pardon you, Magda, as you must pardon me, also, for my appalling behaviour a while ago.'

She turned, caught one of his hands and laid her wet flushed cheek against it.

'I wronged you first—in league with my stepfather. One day maybe you will listen to what I have to tell you about it all and understand me better.'

He hardly heard those whispered words but dragged his fingers from her lips.

'You cannot kiss the hand that struck you so cruelly. You must not,' he said thickly.

She said:

'When you go to-morrow I shall be utterly alone.'

'Perform the tasks I have asked of you and wait in patience until I return, and we will try to put this ghastly muddle right,' he said softly. 'I—I will communicate with you by letter from time to time,' he added, turning away.

He did not see the tragic hope that flickered into her wounded eyes.

'Farewell, Magda,' he said.

She sat up, her heart throbbing, a heart full of a yearning that was stronger than her resentment against all that he had done; stronger than death itself.

'Esmond   ...   *Esmond*   ...'   she whimpered.

But he had gone.

She crept back into the bed, hiding her face under the blankets. The fire had died down. The room was growing cold. Her body ached and the wild ache of her heart and confusion of her thoughts kept the solace of sleep from her. When at length she shut her eyes and oblivion came, it was in the form of a dreamless stupor from which she was roused by the voice of Nurse Vole, calling her:

'My lady. My lady. Please to wake up.'

Magda sat up; her rapid pulse beats jerking her back into remembrance. A slow flush burned her face then her whole body. She averted her gaze from the inquisitive eyes of the little mouse-like woman. She saw a letter in her hand.

'What is this?'

'From his lordship, my lady.'

'Where is he?'

'He left Mornbury, my lady, two hours ago, by coach for London and the Continent. He asked me to give you this.'

'Gone—already gone—' muttered Magda desolately.

While the nurse bustled around, opening curtains and calling for a maidservant to light the fire, Magda broke the seal on the letter and scanned it. It was brief but poignant enough to set her pulses leaping to a new and even joyful tempo.

'Magda, last night shall ever be a memory to bring a blush of shame to my cheeks and in the name of your sweet cousin, herself, I crave your forgiveness once again, even as I forgive you. Let the past be past. You are my wife. Conduct yourself as I would have you do. What lies ahead of us when (and if) I return from abroad, remains on the lap of the gods.

'I wish you good fortune with your Physicians. I have given Mrs. Fustian orders that your every wish is to be humoured until my return, on pain of her instant dismissal. You are free to come and go as you wish in Godchester. While I am gone, comfort Jess for me and ride her, daily. I trust her to you. I shall rely on your Word of Honour to preserve mine in our joint Names. Meanwhile, fare you well and I sign myself what in truth I am.

'Your husband,
'Esmond Mornbury.'

Magda read this letter twice, three times, savouring every word as though unable to credit her sight. Such a *volte-face* was truly unbelievable. He did not, could not love her and her disfigured face must surely remain repulsive in his sight, but he no longer wished her ill. He trusted her and signed himself *her husband*. And greatest of all compliments—he had asked her to ride his adored mare.

With true feminine ability to forgive the man who had most hurt her, Magda suddenly put Esmond's letter to her lips and passionately kissed the signature. The insane cruelty she had suffered at his hands last night became to her a warm and thrilling memory of love; as of a marriage night.

All her immense capacity for deep feeling surged up and welled over. She jumped from the bed, rushed to the window and stared out. It was a fine frosty morning. The tops of the far-distant Surrey hills were still white with last month's snow. The stone basin of the fountain below was rimmed with ice, sparkling in the pale sunlight.

Magda strained her gaze northwards whither Esmond had gone, as though yearning to catch sight of him. She would have given half her life now to know that he would soon return and take her into his arms and comfort her.

'Esmond, oh Esmond, my husband,' she kept whispering.

Jemima Vole crept up behind her.

'My lady—you will catch cold. Come back to bed.'

'No,' said Magda, swinging round, her cheeks rosy. 'I will not take cold. I never do. I am strong. Tell the grooms to saddle Jess and fetch me my new riding habit.'

'But the physicians are coming, my lady—' began the nurse.

'They can wait,' said the Countess of Mornbury with a new hauteur and self-confidence, her cherished letter pressed to her bosom.

Nurse Vole rushed to inform Mrs. Fustian of this. That good woman was in a poor humour. She had been astonished and crushed by her master's threat to dismiss her unless she satisfied every whim from the new Countess. But she dared not disobey him. And she was annoyed, too, because her friend the nurse was leaving this morning, and a new personal maid was to be engaged for Magda.

'She says we are to tell the grooms to saddle Jess,' went on the nurse, sniffing.

'Jess!' shrieked Mrs. Fustian. 'Never such a thing. His lordship would not permit it. This is too much.'

She marched upstairs to Magda's bedchamber and as politely as possible, suggested that her ladyship should order the roan she had been recently riding. She whined:

'His lordship permits nobody to ride Jess in his absence save the head groom who exercises her, my lady.'

Magda, seated at her dressing-table, turned and said sharply:

'Do you dare to question my orders, Mrs. Fustian? I have his word here . . .' she picked up Esmond's letter, 'that I, and I alone in future shall ride Jess.'

Mrs. Fustian swallowed and retreated. What had transpired, she did not know. But she decided that Lady Mornbury must be a witch. She had obviously cast a spell upon his poor lordship.

An hour later, Magda, in the dark blue riding habit trimmed with gold lace which had been hastily ordered for her by the Earl, rode forth from Mornbury on the famous grey.

Her face was veiled but she sat proudly, her chin tilted. The two grooms who had been ordered by his lordship to accompany my lady rode a little behind her. Now and again they grinned at each other, whispered and gossiped. They admitted that the Countess managed Jess superbly and had wonderful hands with a horse. It was also considered by them (and by all the staff) that it was a miracle that my lady had made such a complete recovery from the pox; and that she was well enough to ride. But one and all wished they might look upon her face. However, nobody here had ever done so. The little maid who attended to the fires in my lady's rooms could never tell them anything either, for that much discussed face was always hidden from her while the girl was there.

On this brisk cold morning with the wind whipping through her veil and bringing the blood to her cheeks, Magda felt quite ridiculously happy. She rode with a pride, a feeling of splendour that had never before been hers. She rode, knowing that she was his wife—whether he loved her or not. But at least the bitterness of hostility between them was at an end. And when she came back from that ride to find the two

296

physicians waiting for her she behaved regally in truth, like the Countess of Mornbury.

With excitement she welcomed the gentlemen in the library and rang for some wine to be given them. The ride had done her good and she felt strong and glowing. Dr. Ridpath looked upon his erstwhile patient with some astonishment. The sullen weeping young girl he had recently attended was transformed into a lady of considerable determination and proud bearing. She greeted him in a friendly way and gave a gracious welcome to the famous Dutch surgeon.

'You have come to make me beautiful, sir?' she asked merrily.

The Dutchman, small, rotund, dressed in sombre grey with a narrow white neckband and wearing a bag-wig, bowed low. He had heard enough about this unusual patient from Dr. Ridpath to arouse his curiosity. But he was not prepared for what he saw when the young Countess, so graceful, so apparently attractive, whipped off her little beaver hat and veil. She was smiling. He noted that brave smile but her distorted mouth was pitiful and her big eyes were full of nameless fears.

297

'Nothing can be done,' she added, breathing fast, 'You will tell me it is all too late.'

A moment's silence. Dr. Ridpath put his hands at the back under his coat and coughed. Mynheer Dyck came near to her. His own face was expressionless but his little shrewd eyes under bushy brows, peered long and intently at that ruined face.

Ach, gott, he thought, what butcher's work had been done here, and what a frightful accident it must have been. Poor child! Poor child!

He examined first one side and then the other, noting the pure beauty of that good profile which had been left unmarred. Using his right thumb he touched the corner of her lip, lifting it as delicately as a butterfly's wing. With the same thumb he traced the outline of the little welts and lumps and the long ridged scars. Then her ears, small and well shaped, moving aside the dark curls. Then he nodded once or twice and stepped back.

Magda closed her eyes. She had put on a gay front but her whole being was filled with an anguish of longing to hear the surgeon utter one word of hope. She trembled, physically, her right had

298

gripping the riding crop which she still carried. She had a sick feeling in the pit of her stomach. She thought of Esmond, travelling in his coach to London. She thought of last night and that wild terrible moment of passion in his arms. She thought of all the cruelties that had ever been performed upon her in her brief tempestuous life. She thought of the hideous suffering she had endured as a child through the accident, and the derision and mocking which had been her fate since then. She thought of Esmond's face when she stood unveiled on her wedding day, and what it would mean to her if he could come back from the war and find her not as her mother's miniature, but the Magda she *should have been*. She had to conquer the mad desire to fall on her knees and pray to this great surgeon as though to God, Himself, to make her whole.

Then she heard his voice, guttural but kindly, speaking in his broken English.

'You haf an unfortunate accident had and bad vos the vork done upon you. But I haf seen vorse.'

Magda's head shot up, her heart bounded.

'You have seen worse?' she breathed.

'Mooch vorse. A Mevrouw in The Hague, a so beautiful yoong Mevrouw, smashed in a turnover coach ...' Dyck passed a hand over his plump face and nodded, 'Vorse than you, Countess, but now mooch happiness is hers vid a goot husband. I, Pieter Dyck, have cured her.'

Magda let the crop fall on to the carpet. She cupped her burning face with her hands and her big eyes looked beseechingly at the doctor.

'Oh, how, *how*? What did you do?'

He gave a chuckling laugh and glanced at the older physician.

'Vot did I do? Ach! That voud my gr-reat secrets give away, voud it not, Mynheer Ridpath?'

'Indeed, sir, indeed, yes,' nodded the other man, echoing the laughter.

In the stress of her emotion, tears gushed into Magda's eyes and began to pelt down her face. Forgetting her dignity as the Countess of Mornbury, she clutched at Dyck's arm with small frenzied hands.

'Oh, please, please tell me that you can do something for me, sir. I will gladly suffer any pain, any torture, if only you will restore my lost face to me.'

His intelligent eyes were very kindly now

and he patted her shoulder in a fatherly way.

'Poor child, poor child . . .' This time he said the words aloud. 'A long time it vill take and maybe moocli pain for you, and mooch money for your husband,' he added with a laugh, 'but the Earl, I oondustand has said no money moost be spared. Even if I notrink receive I voud wish me dis vork to do.'

She sobbed now, unashamedly.

He led her to a chair and made her drink some wine to calm her.

The methods with which he worked, he told her, were very new and very secret. Little doubt that in the far distant future many surgeons would follow in his footsteps and improve upon these operations which he now performed. He promised no miracles. He was no sorcerer, he said. But he had given his life to his work and was the only one in Europe who had ever dreamed of using knife, needle and thread for such purposes.

There must always be scars for her, but they would be faint and no longer these hideous welts. He would also lift the corner of that drooping mouth. His stitches could be so small, they would never be seen by ordinary eyes. Working with him was an Italian physician who had his own secrets; strangely effective salves which, the Dutchman said, were favoured in the days of the Borgias. (By the medicine-minded Catherine de Medici, herself.) All these secrets, and his skill would now be used upon the young Countess of Mornbury's face.

'In von year's time from now, you vill no more recognize yourself,' he ended.

Magda did not answer. The two doctors, who had much to talk about, moved quietly to the end of the room and discreetly left her alone to sob out her anguish—and her joy.

CHAPTER TEN

It was Midsummer's Day in the year 1709.

The Queen was at Windsor.

On this particular golden bright morning, the forests around the Castle wore the young unspoilt green of early summer. The day was calm and warm. But Anne had remained in bed. She had refused to see her ministers. She had had a bad night.

Her legs were more than ordinarily swollen with the dropsy that was gradually sapping her health and strength. She would see nobody, she declared, but Abigail Hill, her friend and favourite attendant.

Abigail, Mrs. Masham, sat beside the Queen's great canopy bed, reading to her a letter which had just arrived by special courier. The Queen turned her pale lachrymose flabby face towards the window. She looked with longing at the blue sky. She resented the imprisonment of her unwieldy suffering flesh. But all that could be done for her had been done and she knew it. She must remain a martyr to her gout and her dropsy until the end.

She was glad Abigail was here and that she no longer had to deal with the tempestuous passions and intrigues which her old friend Sarah, Duchess of Marlborough, used to raise like a cyclone, wherever she was. Anne much preferred the ministrations of the respectful and soothing Mrs. Masham. Her pale blue eyes showed a little interest as Mrs. Masham, struggling now with her own weak eyesight, continued to read the letter.

It was a despatch personally written to the Queen by the Duke of Marlborough

303

himself, sent from Tournai in France.

Queen Anne had little personal love for Marlborough—just as she stubbornly refused any attempts at reconciliation between herself and Sarah. But she had to acknowledge the immense debt of gratitude that England owed to the great man.

Following the battle of Oudenarde and the fall of Lille, Marlborough had conducted a brilliant if costly campaign against Tournai and it was from there that he had found time to write personal news to his Queen.

It was with some pride and pleasure, he said (as he knew it would be to Her Majesty), that he was able to tell her that her godson, the Earl of Mornbury, had conducted himself so well during the sieges in the past year. Esmond had become an indispensable member of his entourage, and although at one time he deemed the young man to be over-frivolous and over-ready to pick quarrels in the card-rooms and draw his sword, his opinion of Esmond had greatly changed.

'It will indisputably please your Majesty,' Marlborough wrote, 'to hear that he has not spared himself since he joined me in Brussels. After the slight flesh wound in the shoulder received when Minorca was captured, and whence Esmond accompanied my liaison officer to Admiral Leak, he rejected all ideas of leave. While he could bc of use, he would not leave us.

'I heartily commend him for whatever reward your Majesty might choose to give him. But now alack, I must inform you that he lies in hospital with a severe injury which threatens not his life, but his sight.'

There followed an account of the injury.

Anne raised herself from her pillow, panting. The look of pleasure on her face changed to one of concern.

'God's mercy; *his sight!*'

'Oh, the poor boy!' cried Mrs. Masham, who had always had a fondness for the handsome and rather wicked young man who had so often offended his Royal godmother but never been able to destroy her feminine appreciation of his fatal charm.

'Does the Countess know of this?' demanded the Queen.

'I do not know, Ma'am.'

'She must be told, my dear. Pray continue with the despatch.'

Marlborough had little more to say about Esmond. This wound had been received on the day that the English moved into Tournai. Esmond had been riding to headquarters with the military attaché bearing important documents. They had been ambushed but the enemy had been routed; it was Esmond alone who had received injury—a sabre-slash across the brows which had apparently blinded him.

The Queen called for her smelling salts and a large pocket handkerchief.

'Blind! That poor handsome youth. It would have broken the hearts of his parents who were my friends. We must write at once to his poor wife.'

Mrs. Masham sent one of the young ladies-in-waiting for Her Majesty's writing materials.

'It is your pleasure, Ma'am, that the Countess should come here for an audience with you?'

The Queen considered this but shook her head.

'No, better that she wait in her own residence for news of Esmond. It may be that Marlborough's fears are groundless and the boy will return to England less seriously injured than is supposed.'

Abigail was disappointed. She, like a great many others at Court, would have been vastly intrigued to see Esmond Mornbury's wife. It was well known throughout the length and breadth of the country that this young gentlewoman, Magda, a one time beauty had been badly pitted by the pox and that her beauty had been miraculously restored to her by a Dutch surgeon of international repute.

The Countess was never seen in London. She lived quietly in Godchester. The Queen who loved children and whose maternal instincts had been so tragically thwarted had once hoped to hear that the young Countess was to bear her husband a fine son. But no news of pregnancy had reached the Court, and now of course, there could be none, since the young Countess had not seen her husband for over a year. The Queen, feeling too indisposed to write in person, dictated a letter of commiseration to Magda, expressing the hope that Esmond would soon be restored to her. Anne munificently added the words:

'We will not deny that Esmond has at times been a Worry to Us but he has fully justified Our Affection and Belief in him. He has been mentioned several times in Despatches and has obviously conducted

307

himself like a hero for which Valour he shall in due course receive reward from Our hands.'

This missive, bearing the Royal crest, was despatched from Windsor Castle at mid-morning and delivered that same evening at Mornbury Hall.

Magda was holding a five o'clock tea-party in the small white and gold drawing-room of her home.

She was in fact entertaining Archibald St. John and his newly-made wife. Esmond's greatest friend had married his dearest Alison at the beginning of this year. There had been a fine wedding in Edinburgh, since when Archie had introduced his bride to Magda and the girls had become great friends.

The little tea-party had been a gay affair, on one of the warmest days of the year. They sat drinking tea beside the wide-open window watching the sunlight play upon the waters that gushed into the basin from the great stone horse and enjoying the vivid beauty of the flowers; in particular of the red roses which grew so profusely in front of the terrace.

Archie had never before seen Magda in

such high spirits. The only thing that dimmed them seemed to be the fact that she had not heard from Esmond since the end of May. But she knew, she said, that although the war in Europe was going well for the English, the French were making a determined effort to check Marlborough's advance. Esmond was bound to be much occupied, considering the importance of the post he now held as assistant liaison officer at the Duke's headquarters.

She had been speaking of him with a ringing pride in her voice that greatly warmed Archie's heart. She rarely went a fortnight without some word from Esmond, she told them. Apart from that wound in the shoulder which had now healed, he seemed in good health and stout heart.

'He has wasted his life so far, Archie,' Magda said, 'for he was assuredly never born to be a gentleman of leisure—he has made such success abroad and so enjoys his active life.'

'I always used to think that Esmond would have made a fine soldier had he chosen that career,' was Archie's reply, 'for Esmond was ever fearless and, as you know, the finest swordsman in the country

309

although he did not always use his talents to the advantage he is using them nowadays.'

The newly-made Mrs. St. John broke in.

'Oh, Archie, I would live in constant dread if you were abroad fighting the French,' she said with a fond look at her husband.

'Sometimes I regret that I am not with Esmond—save for the fact that I am at your side, my love,' he said.

Magda's big eyes glowed at the young couple. She had grown very fond of Archie—the more so because she knew that he was Esmond's dearest friend—and she was equally attached to Mrs. St. John— Alison, a year or two older than Magda, was a red-headed, green-eyed girl with charming freckles, a tip-tilted nose and a slight burr to her voice which was most attractive. Archie after six months as her husband was satisfied that he had made an excellent choice, and enjoyed his marriage hugely. But if he was pleased for himself, he was equally pleased now for Esmond. What a pleasant surprise awaited him when he returned from abroad! And what a surprise it had been to Archie, himself, when he had first gazed upon Magda after the long months she had spent in the care of

Mynheer Dyck.

She must have had exceptional courage and endurance, and never once complained. Archie thought her lovelier than he had ever imagined she could be.

He had known (because Magda had written to tell him so) that she was undergoing this special treatment. He had known also and been glad of it that Esmond had left her not as an enemy but as a friend and that they corresponded regularly. But now there was cause for rejoicing. Pieter Dyck's genius had made her a woman upon whom any man might look with pleasure. She was a good deal more attractive than the supposed Magda in that fatal miniature of her mother. The marriage which had begun so badly looked now as though it would end well. Thought St. John ... Magda's face could bear scrutiny even in the strong sunlight on this Midsummer's Day.

God alone knew what the Dutchman had done or how he had done it, but there were only the faintest lines to be seen on the delicate cheek that had once looked so repulsive. The tender mouth had now some shape. It was sweet and smiling. The skin looked pure and she had lost that look of savage misery which before had wiped the natural youth and gaiety from her face. If only Esmond could see her, Archie thought, as she was now—sitting in the high-winged chair in that gown of pale rose jaconet which looked cool and fresh looped over a fine silken bodice and petticoat. Perhaps doing honour to the Dutchman who had done so much for her, she had chosen a Dutch-style *coiffure*—her dark hair, unpowdered, with a raven's wing sheen of health, was looped back from her forehead and fell in loose ringlets down the back of her slender neck. The hair was ornamented with pearls. She looked very young and charming, he thought.

Esmond must come home quickly, St. John decided, for she was like a rose that has opened to the kiss of the sun. Happiness sat upon her like a benediction.

Happiness in these days did, indeed, seem to flood Magda's very soul. Life had so completely changed for her.

Following Esmond's departure she had suffered many days and nights of the old misery and thwarted longing but each time she received a letter from him, the pain seemed to grow a little less. It was not that he ever told her that he loved her or wanted her. The letters merely described his own surroundings and his new full life. But at least she knew that her husband had become her friend and bore her no ill-will. That was the beginning. She had been forgiven for the trick that had been played on him.

She answered all his letters immediately and sent him twice as many. Long missives full of anecdotes about his stately home, and particularly about Jess.

Jess had fallen sick of the colic last Christmas. Magda—terrified that the noble grey might die—remained all night in the mare's stall soothing and encouraging her, leaving her only when it was certain that she would recover.

Esmond had written back:

'If you have saved Jess's life I am greatly in your debt.'

To which she had answered:

'Never can you be in my debt, dear Esmond, for I am for ever in yours. . . .'

Sparing him painful details, she had told him of the long days, weeks and months

313

spent in the hands of Mynheer Dyck, but never once of her agony. How her nerves had been shattered almost to screaming point by the continual use of knife and needle, with little to dull the sensitivity. No—she had not spoken of that, or of the awful nights of fear that the result would be no good. The endless waiting for the wounds of the first operation to heal—then another. She never even suggested to Esmond that this had been a year that had seemed almost endless, for she had rarely been able to leave the house except to walk veiled through the grounds alone—or with her personal maid.

Magda had to forego the thrilling pleasure of riding Jess until Dyck gave her permission and she might be jolted without fear of the stitches breaking. So she had been bored and often lonely. True, she was now accepted by one and all as the Countess of Mornbury and treated with deference even by the resentful Mrs. Fustian. Neighbours had both written and called although she would see none of them.

Her mother's relations, the Shaftleys, were still in Italy. Lady Shaftley had been ill and her physicians suggested she remained in the villa by the sea near Genoa.

So Magda could not even receive her aunt and uncle.

However, the end had been so triumphant that it was all worth while. Now at long last she could look in her mirror without that old sensation of sick grief. Now she could wear a new dress with a jaunty air and watch the renewal of her youthful beauty gaining in measure day after day. Now, too, she could pray for Esmond's quick return, confident that when he looked upon her it would be with delight.

If only she could see him ride into Mornbury Hall this very day—hold out his arms, and gather her close—then the whole of her life's anguish would seem worth while.

'We must be going, dear Magda,' Alison said after another half-hour in the delicious warmth of the sun, although the ladies shielded their complexions by sitting well back in the cool of the flower-filled drawing-room. St. John added:

'Indeed yes, we have to call upon General Corsham.'

That name brought a slight twist to Magda's lips.

'Mlle LeClaire is still living at the Manor,

is she not, Archie?'

'So I believe.'

Magda turned to the Scottish girl who had become her confidante.

'I think Esmond found Mlle Chantal greatly alluring.'

'How do you know that?'

Magda recounted the story that when out riding one morning—she was still veiled then—she had come upon the French girl, also mounted. They had stopped to exchange courtesies. Chantal had made a point of commiserating with Magda for, of course, the neighbourhood believed the tale of 'the pox', and the treatment the poor bride was undergoing. The continual visits of Mynheer Dyck and his medical assistant to Mornbury were also common knowledge.

'I told *Mademoiselle* that I hoped that she need have no cause to be too sympathetic in the future,' Magda said to her friends, 'but she made a point of telling *me* that she hoped the efforts would be successful because she knew dear Esmond's reputation as a lover of female beauty.'

Alison clicked her tongue against her cheek.

'What insolence! She must be both

unkind and malicious.'

'All the same,' said Magda with a smile, 'she is beautiful. I know that Esmond found her so.'

Now Archie said:

'But he will find you still more so, dearest Magda.'

Her eyes sparkled, her lashes drooped modestly.

'I cannot get used to flattery.'

'Nevertheless your own sweet face evokes the words,' said Archie gallantly.

'Oh, Archie, I long for Esmond's return!' sighed Magda, clasping her hands together, 'for I know that *he* must remember me only as he saw me last, one year and three months ago—and it was not like I am now.'

'It will be the loveliest surprise for him,' said Mrs. St. John.

A footman came into the room bearing a long-shaped paper on a silver tray. Magda gave a cry of excitement.

'Oh! Maybe it is my long overdue letter from Esmond himself. You must wait to hear his news.'

'With the greatest pleasure,' nodded St. John.

Magda dismissed the servant, broke open the seal, then noting it, put a hand

317

to her lips.

'Mercy! It is the Royal insignia. This letter is not from Esmond but from the Queen herself.'

'From the Queen!' repeated Alison in a tone of awe.

St. John put an arm around his wife and gave her a fond look.

'It will not be the first time that our Gracious Lady has written to this house, my love.'

But now a startled cry from Magda drew their full attention to her and they saw that joy had fallen from Magda like a mantle. She was deathly white. She raised her eyes full of woe and breathed.

'*Blind!* Oh, God, dear God, not *that*!'

'Oh, dearest Magda, what has transpired?' exclaimed Alison.

'Who is blind?' demanded Archie, perplexed.

Magda held out the note that had been dictated by Anne and sent from Windsor early this morning.

For a moment after perusing it, St. John stood shocked and silent. So Esmond had been injured in the head and it was a possibility that he would lose his sight. What a catastrophe!

318

He heard Magda's voice, thick with grief.

'Never to look upon the world again. So young and so vital. He who loves life and beauty and action. To be blind and helpless. Dear God, say it is not true!'

Archie took her hand and pressed it.

'Dearest Magda, be calm. The Queen has sent you this news from Marlborough because Esmond lies unable to write to you in person. But it does not state that he is forever blind—it may be but a temporary affliction.'

Magda covered her face with her hands. She felt ready to sink to the floor. Her first thought was for *him*. Of what dreadful misfortune it would be to one of his mercurial temperament to find himself no longer able to see and to have to grope in perpetual twilight.

'My poor Esmond! My poor husband!' she sobbed.

Mrs. St. John, whose Scots blood made her more philosophical, tried to comfort Magda and bade her believe that Esmond's injuries were not as bad as they seemed. Looking across Magda's bowed head at her own husband, Alison murmured with sadness:

'Alas, our poor Magda has been through so much this seems too much. The crowning sorrow.'

Magda lifted her streaming eyes.

'Think,' she breathed, 'think not only of his tragedy but of mine. For now ...' she touched her cheek ... 'now he will never see this miracle and me as I am now. He will always think of me as that Magda whom he left, and who found such poor favour in his sight.'

This so affected Alison that she, too, began to weep. St. John strove to be optimistic.

'Come, come, you two, let us not put the worst construction upon things. To-morrow when I return to London, Magda, I will go at once to friends of mine who are high up in the military service. They will I am sure, obtain first-hand news of Esmond for you. Indeed, I may hear that he is even now on his way home.'

Magda wiped her eyes, but shook her head in despair.

'Nothing would please me better than to have him home and look after him. But God forbid that he should return in blindness.'

By the time the St. Johns had left

Mornbury Hall, Magda was a good deal calmer and more philosophical. Now it was a question of awaiting the news that Archie had promised to send her as speedily as possible. Once alone, she had time to recall the fact that this was the second time that Esmond's eyes had been in danger. After his accident before their marriage, his sight had been threatened. He had lain in darkness nursed by the monks, but made a complete recovery. She could only pray this would be the case a second time.

When Phoebe, her new maid who was a gentle pleasant girl, well-trained and a great improvement upon Annette, attired her for the night, she offered condolences. Even Mrs. Fustian had just been up, panting and gasping, to say:

'I'm sure we all hope and pray his lordship will be able to see you and his home when he returns, my lady.'

Phoebe echoed the words. She had just brushed the dark sheen of her ladyship's hair before the mirror and thought how beautiful she looked.

''Twould be a wicked shame if his lordship never saw you as you look to-night, my lady,' she murmured.

The colour rose to Magda's cheeks. The

joy that could have been hers found little scope in this hour of extreme anxiety. She patted the girl's shoulder and murmured:

'We must all pray. Go now and good night, child.'

Child! Yes, Phoebe was the same age as Magda. Yet Magda had so gained in stature, in dignity, so bloomed in the knowledge of her new looks and position, she felt years older than her maid.

Before seeking the curtained bed she stood at the window looking out at the flowers. The grounds of Mornbury dreamed in white romantic beauty on this midsummer's night. There was still dancing going on in the village. This morning she had driven out in her phaeton to watch the children skip around a beribboned Maypole in the Market Square. Lady Mornbury was now a well-known figure in Godchester and the villagers always gave her a loyal and affectionate greeting. The simple people who were the Earl's tenants had quite taken her ladyship to their hearts and were genuinely pleased because she had made this miracle recovery from the 'pox'.

Magda knew that she would not sleep well that night. She paced up and down her bedchamber, all her thoughts concentrated upon Esmond. How deeply she had grown to love him, she hardly dared acknowledge, but to-night, like many nights, she pulled out all his letters which had been sent from first one headquarters, then another. She read them again in the candlelight. Letters full of praise for the Duke; letters extolling the honour and the glory of England; expressing his pleasure that he had learned to cast aside idleness and serve his Royal godmother. Letters full of yearning to see Mornbury again and to ride with Magda through the green woods or over the hills. Impersonal letters yet each one signed:

'Your true and Affectionate Husband.'

What more could she ask from Esmond than affection she thought, and how pleasant to read such words from one who had previously looked upon her as the slayer of his hopes and dreams.

His last letter was the one she cherished most. She concentrated on its final paragraph.

'It has warmed my Heart to read the last missive sent to me by Archie. He

Appears to have chosen wisely in his Marriage. Hard though it may be for me to think of Him in the tow of a Female, and remembering how we both of us abhorred the mere thought of curtailing our Freedom, I gauge he is content with his Alison. He tells me that I also shall be content when I look again upon my Wife. Not only he says will your altered countenance delight me, dearest Magda, but your Disposition which I am assured moves you to behave Decorously and Sweetly. I can expect no more of the One who bears my Name. I cannot deny that I am eager for my Return. Although alas our Troubles in Europe Abound and the War with France cannnot speedily come to an end.'

Again and again Magda had read and cherished those words. What more could she wish than to know he longed to return to her at Mornbury?

Her tears began to flow and dripped on the closely written sheets of paper which she held.

'Oh, if he should be blind!' she said the words aloud, 'I could not bear it either for his sake or mine.'

CHAPTER ELEVEN

Towards the end of June, Magda was still without news of her husband although she had received a brief missive from Archie assuring her that the latest despatch received at London military headquarters stated my Lord Mornbury was recovering his health although there were no details given about his eyes. But it would comfort her, Archie wrote, to hear there was no definite proof that he had forever lost his sight.

Now the days and nights dragged slowly for Magda. She received many invitations to social gatherings in the neighbourhood but refused them all. She spent most of her time, as she had spent it for so long, within the confines of her home. It seemed she could never stop reading or studying. Remembering what Esmond had once said, she had also learned to play the spinet. She practised music regularly, yearning to become so proficient as to be able to entertain her husband when he returned. She was also engrossed in a piece of tapestry which she was stitching especially for his own writing-room and which she thought might please him, for it depicted a battle scene.

But all the real joy of life seemed to have fled from her. She could not rest or settle down to anything until she knew that Esmond was all right.

It was on the last night of June, an hour after she had retired, and while alone, reading a book, that suddenly she heard the sound of horses' hooves and the clatter of coach wheels outside. Her book dropped from her hands. She got out of bed—every drop of blood leaving her face only to rush back hotly again to cheeks and throat. *Esmond*. It might be he. Dear God, how wonderful that would be!

The night was warm. She seized a mantle of India muslin, flung it around her bedgown and rushed out of the room.

One of the footmen, not yet abed, had already opened the front doors. Half-way down the staircase, Magda stood waiting and watching, all her heart in her big bright eyes. What would she see? Esmond coming in walking confidently and alone, or with eyes bandaged, led by another man?

She had no time to think further. A tall individual wearing a dark brown travelling coat that was horribly familiar to her, entered the Hall, wherein the other servants were hastily lighting candles. Magda's bitter disappointment when she saw his face was almost too cruel to be borne.

Adam Congrayle. Her loathed stepfather. He, of all men, the most unwelcome! She had no idea why he had come—what he could be doing calling here at this hour. She had not set eyes on him since her marriage day a year and a half ago.

During the period she had, in fact, received little news from Wildmarsh Manor. One or two letters from her mother, giving some scant news. Lady Congrayle was no scribe. It seemed that she was never well but said she had not been particularly molested by her husband of late and even though life was never luxurious at the Manor, things were a trifle better than in Magda's day. Esmond's bailiffs had been down in the Cotswolds to inspect the state of affairs and although Sir Adam had received some monies from his son-in-law, he did not get as much as he had hoped for. So when he was at home, Lady Congrayle told her daughter, he behaved with his customary ill-temper.

However, Adam, the eldest boy now attended the Grammar School and Mr. Bacon the old tutor had been replaced by a younger and better one who taught the younger boys.

Old Tammy had died last winter. It had been a great grief to Lady Congrayle. Even Magda had sorrowed a little for the aged servant who had never been as actively unkind to her as the rest.

But why Sir Adam should come to Mornbury to-night, perplexed Magda.

He, unclasping his coat collar, looked up at her, and all her composure seemed to desert her. She felt the old awful sensation of fear and loathing as she saw his wolfish grin and heard his hated voice:

'I am a little late. We had trouble with a wheel, before reaching the last toll-gate, my dear. Come—have you not a warm welcome for your stepfather?'

Magda before the gaping servants strove to answer him as befitted her dignity.

'Of course. Come in . . .' she turned to the footman nearest her: 'Fetch wine and refreshments for Sir Adam and bid the housekeeper prepare one of the guest chambers.'

Sir Adam took off his cocked hat, patted

328

his wig into position, and rubbed his bony hands together.

'Thank you, thank you, my chick.'

Magda turned from him shuddering. Strange that time should roll back and she should feel herself once again the thin haunted girl whom he had tortured—even as he tortured her wretched mother. She did not want to entertain him but had no option since it would raise comment if she turned him away at this late hour.

Excusing herself, she went back to her own rooms, and exchanged her muslins for a Round Gown of thick figured silk secured at waist and bosom with gold brooches. It was a decorous dress of a deep shade of blue and made her look very tall and slender. Over her head she wrapped a length of gauze since she had not time to arrange her hair, and did not wish to call Phoebe from her bed.

She joined her stepfather in the library. He was already seated, gulping wine in a noisy fashion that reminded her hatefully of the days at Wildmarsh. Her hand against her fastbeating heart, she thought of that other Magda who would be forced to sit here and read to him, half dead with weariness, until he slept and snored.

'Why have you come, Sir?' she asked coldly.

Sir Adam shut one eye and looked at her with the other, cunningly.

'Zounds! Our little Magda has grown into a gentlewoman of fashion and if I may say so, real beauty. Your mother, of course, told me of the wonders done to your face by some Dutch genius. I congratulate him—and you, my love.'

'Flattery from you is displeasing to me, Sir,' she said briefly.

'Come, have you no affection for the one who nurtured and cherished you from childhood?'

'Cherished *me*?' she repeated, her breast rising and falling. 'Do not be a hypocrite, Sir.'

He gave a nasty laugh, drank more wine and smacked his lips.

'You may have become Countess of Mornbury and be under the protection of a husband but you are still my daughter.'

'No—thanks be to God, Sir, I have no blood of yours, but am a daughter only by virtue of the fact that my mother so mistakenly joined her life with yours.'

Sir Adam guffawed.

'Tush, tush, little Magda has indeed

grown into a haughty lady.'

'Will you kindly tell me why you have come, Sir?' she asked impatiently. 'If it is only that you wish to break a journey, then one of the guest chambers has been prepared for you and pray accept my hospitality, but there can never be any friendship between you and me.'

He poured out yet more wine. He had had a long journey and a tiring delay when the coach-wheel broke and he was in one of his worst moods. He had just received a letter from the Earl's legal advisers warning him that such income as was being paid to him by courtesy of the Earl would be cancelled if he continued to neglect his estates and his home. He knew, of course, that he had been spending far too much time lately in London in the card rooms and taverns, and that half the money he received was spent in housing his latest mistress to the detriment of his own wife.

Suddenly his smiles changed to a menacing expression. He growled at Magda:

'Look you, I am not going to be treated with discourtesy by you or by your husband's agents. This marriage has turned out well, therefore the Earl owes me some gratitude and can no longer feel that same animosity that was his when he first realized what trick had been played upon him.'

'He owes you no gratitude whatsoever, Sir,' flashed Magda, 'and were he to know the full story—which I have not yet expounded to him—of your execrable conduct towards me and my mother, he would hound you from this house and bid you never return to it.'

Sir Adam rose to his feet, spilling some of the wine down his waistcoat.

'You chit! Do not dare to speak so to me.'

She felt no fear now, only a surging anger.

'On the contrary, I bid you have a care as to how *you* speak to *me*, Sir Adam. I am no desperate and hungry child now, condemned to slavery and to be mocked as you mocked her half-dying mother.'

'Well, Lady Congrayle isn't dead yet. But she's a poor sickly fool all the same, no use to any man,' laughed Sir Adam thickly.

Magda gasped.

'Say more and I will ask my husband's permission to send for my unhappy mother and bring her here to Mornbury Hall where

332

she may find rest and peace. I shall see also that the truth about your atrocities are spread throughout the whole land.'

Sir Adam rocked from toe to heel and guffawed.

'Will you tell also the truth about the bride who had the pox? Or shall it be unfolded by me that the ugliest wench in England was cleverly foisted on to his noble lordship and that he had to keep her? If the country points the finger of scorn at me, it shall also rock from end to end with derision against Esmond Mornbury.'

Magda gasped.

'After all this time, could you still be so abominable and full of malice?'

He changed his tone.

'Come—let us not quarrel. Have you no jewels? No treasures that I could sell, for I am hard pressed for money, my dear,' he began to whine.

'My wife gives presents to no man,' interrupted a voice from the doorway, 'And especially not to an individual of such loathsome calibre as yourself.'

Magda swung round; her stepfather with her. They had been standing at the other end of the room. Unobtrusively the door had opened, and their conversation had been overheard. In the heat of the argument neither of them had heard the second coach clatter into the courtyard or the arrival of the second visitor to Mornbury this night.

Magda screamed:

'Esmond! *Esmond!*'

Scarcely able to believe her sight, she saw him, travel-stained, weary, wearing a dark grey military-looking cape and with bandaged head. He stood there in the doorway drawing off his gauntlets. For an instant she stared. He had grown thin and much older. There were deep lines carved on either side his lips. His handsome eyes were sunken. *But he could see.* She thought this story of his blindness was unfounded. There were faint cuts and swellings on his face, and both lids were swollen, but *he could see.*

Magda stumbled across the library to him.

'Oh, Esmond, my husband!' she cried again.

Sir Adam crouched in the shadows, watching a trifle fearfully. That the Earl should return home this very night was the last thing *he* had anticipated. But now Esmond with his inflamed eyes turned his scrutiny to his wife. His right arm went around her drawing her close. He whispered:

'Magda. At last! And praise God I have lived to return and to look upon such loveliness.'

Wild with joy, she clung to him pressing one of his hands to her flushed cheek.

'Oh, Esmond, Esmond!' was all she could say.

His gaze rested on that sweet altered mouth with a look that burned her. Then he whispered:

'We will discourse presently ...' With a single movement he put her behind him and began to walk slowly across the library towards the older man.

'You did not hear me enter my house, Sir Adam,' he added coolly, 'but *I* heard *you*. Heard quite a deal of the vileness that spewed from your lips and polluted my wife's ears.'

Sir Adam gave a nervous tittering laugh.

'I spoke in jest, Esmond, my dear son-in-law—' he began.

Esmond cut in.

'You spoke in earnest, you miserable scoundrel, and if I had not returned, it might have been the worse for Magda—as tragic for her to-night as it used to be in her childhood, which fact I now know, and which will testify for ever to your shame.'

Sir Adam made no answer but gulped, and his small mean eyes looked from side to side as though seeking a means of escape. Esmond, he could see, had returned from the war with injuries but he was by no means an invalid. He walked with his old agility and his right hand was on the hilt of his sword.

Esmond continued.

'I've been travelling all day, sir, hoping to reach Godchester in daylight. Methinks I followed in your tracks. I heard at the toll-gate that a coach had just passed through *en route* for Mornbury. I came as quickly as was possible, the packet having brought me to these shores from Rotterdam, and hoping for a pleasant return to my home. It is, however, singularly unpleasant finding you here.'

Magda suddenly put in:

'Esmond, my husband—your eyes. Your forehead—are they paining you?'

'My head can wait,' he said with a dry laugh, 'I need only rest and that must be postponed until I have dealt with this maggot of a man.'

336

Sir Adam spluttered.

'You do me wrong, Esmond. Dear son-in-law—'

'Do not call me so,' thundered Esmond. 'I will never while I live, acknowledge any such relationship with you. You are *not* my wife's father. While abroad I have heard of your miserable activities. I might have known that you would misspend whatever money I granted to you.'

Sir Adam spluttered again and pointed a finger at Magda.

'Are you not satisfied with her? Have I not done you a service instead of a wrong?'

Esmond turned and gave a quick look at Magda. Yes, he was flabbergasted by the change the long months and Dyck's skill had wrought in her. He could not credit his own sight. The thin scarred girl had blossomed into absolute beauty. He found her face, framed in the gauzy scarf, charming. Wonderful, the deep warmth of those big golden eyes. Ravishing the curve of her bosom and the slimness of her waist in the blue silken gown. He knew now how badly he had longed to see her again and what a real attachment had developed between them during this year and a half of correspondence, and of waiting.

337

Sir Adam, thinking Esmond's attention was distracted, suddenly seized his chance.

With a bound he reached a side door that led into the reception room. It was rarely used but he found to his relief that it was not locked. He ran through and crashed the door behind him.

Esmond sprang after him. Magda cried out:

'Oh, be careful ... for the love of God, remember your injury and do not trouble with him, Esmond.'

'I shall kill him for what he has done to you,' said Esmond.

She ran after him, panting.

'No, Esmond, no. No more deaths. You vowed it. Adam Congrayle is not worth the stain of a murder on your immortal soul.'

Esmond flung off his travelling cloak. His teeth were clenched, his eyes narrowed. He was the old Esmond, ripe for a fight, hot with pride and temper.

'I cannot let him live now that it has been made clear to me how he used you.'

'Please—' Magda said with a sob.

'Wait for me here,' he cut in, and darting out of the library closed the side door between them.

It was a night of brilliant moonlight.

Breathing fast Esmond looked around and saw the figure of Magda's stepfather flying down the terraced walk that led towards the lake. He rushed after the fugitive, snarling.

'Come back, you lily-livered cur. Come back and fight.'

But Adam Congrayle had no wish to fight the man who was reputed to be the finest duellist in England. He ran on, tried to scale a wall, failed and fell. Esmond was almost upon him when he picked himself up. But he got away and ran down the path blindly waving his arms, coat flapping like a bat's wings. He screeched:

'Help! Help! I am being assassinated—help!'

They were at the edge of the ornamental lake now. The water shone like a mirror. The swans nestled among the reeds. It was a dream of beauty to the tired feverish gaze of the man who had been so long exiled abroad. This was Mornbury. This was home. And Magda, his wife, warm, exciting and lovely and full of a strange new enchantment, waited for him. Esmond gave a sudden laugh and whipped out his sword. He cried out to Congrayle:

'Wretch that you are—come back and defend yourself.'

Sir Adam had no path of retreat now. His back was to the water. He thrust out both hands as though to ward off the point of Esmond's blade.

'I am an old man. I am stepfather to your wife. Consider your reputation if you kill me.'

'Consider my reputation as you would have ruined it in your malice, had you been permitted,' Esmond flung at him.

'I take it all back. I will say nothing. I will do anything you bid.'

'You will fight for your life here and now,' snarled Esmond.

Sir Adam felt his heart beat to suffocation-pitch. His blood curdled in his veins, his eyes bolted. He was enfeebled by months of debauchery and bemused by the wine he had gulped into an empty stomach as soon as he arrived. He saw the tall pale man with the bandaged head as through a mist, like an avenging angel. He began to believe that he stood at the very gates of death. He screeched again:

'Spare me, Esmond, dear son-in-law . . .'

The reiteration of that name infuriated Esmond. He made a lunge towards the other man. Terrified out of his wits, Sir Adam tottered back. His lost his footing

340

and fell with a splash into the lake. His long dismal howl reached the ears of Magda who was on the terrace.

Esmond dropped his sword. It was one thing to duel, to engage in a clean fight; another to watch a drunken man drown. Esmond made ready to hold out a hand and drag the wretched fellow on to firm ground again.

But Adam Congrayle's hour had come. He rose to the surface once, spluttering, shrieking, wig afloat, shaven head hideous in the moonlight, then went down like a stone. His fright, and that sudden contact with the cold water, had caused a failure of the heart. He did not rise again. Esmond saw only bubbles and circles in the limpid water where once that head had emerged.

Esmond turned to see Magda running through the gardens towards him. He went to meet her.

He was pale and subdued.

'All is ended,' he said. 'Sir Adam will trouble you no more.'

'Oh, how horrible!'

'Go back to the house, my love, and send me two of the menservants to help fish him out.'

Magda shuddered again. She was

weeping, not for the stepfather who had brutally ill-treated her and who had become the symbol in her eyes of all that was mean and cowardly, but with the sheer horror of the thing. She felt that the silvery swan-lake, which she used to love, had been spoiled—polluted by this night's episode.

She returned to the library and called the men to aid their master. The whole household was now astir. Phoebe was ready to welcome her mistress with a glass of cordial and a shawl.

'You will catch cold, my lady. Although it is summer, the vapours of the early morning are dangerous.'

'Early morning?' echoed Magda dully.

'Yes, my lady, it is nearly two o'clock.'

Magda sipped the cordial and looked gratefully at the girl.

'Thank you. But return now to your bed. You need your rest, child,' she said.

Pheobe curtseyed and then added blushing:

'Might I say how glad I am for your ladyship that his lordship has returned.'

'And with his sight, Phoebe. Oh, thank God, with *his sight*.'

'We are all so glad for you, my lady.'

Magda put a hand to her cheek. She was

so dazed she had had no time to consider the true poignancy of what was happening, so little time seemed to have elapsed between her stepfather's arrival and Esmond's return. So little time, she thought could elapse between life and *death*, itself. Now, while they dragged the corpse from the lake, and conveyed it to the chapel, she found some leisure in which to consider what had taken place.

Sir Adam was dead. There could be no futher threats from him to Esmond's peace or hers. Her poor mother would be free to enjoy what was left of her unhappy life.

Dozens of thoughts and ideas leapt feverishly through Magda's excited mind.

She would ask Esmond to let her have her mother here for a holiday. Perhaps he would also permit the three boys to come. He was noble and good and he would want those ill-treated boys to have a chance in life such as they had never had in their father's lifetime.

She heard men's voices in the hall. Esmond was back. She darted to a mirror in front of which candles were burning, and examined her face and rearranged her hair. Her eyes were huge with excitement. Her body trembled.

Then the library door opened; Esmond came in. His expression was grave. He walked slowly as though utterly fatigued. She ran to meet him.

'Are your eyes all right?'

'They ache,' he said. 'Nothing more. I was badly cut about, but in hospital I had every attention and am greatly improved. The Duke's own physician looked after me.'

'I heard from the Queen. She feared that you were blinded!'

'At one time I feared it myself,' Esmond said with a short laugh, 'but it was not for long and those who sent home the news made it sound worse than it was. The injury was in fact not as grave as that one which I suffered through my accident.'

'Oh, if you knew how anxious I was, and how *I* suffered!' she breathed.

He stood with his back to the wood-fire which had just been lighted. He felt a coldness born only of his fatigue. As his grave curious gaze travelled over her, he began to feel, also, a new invigorating warmth.

'Truly remarkable,' he murmured.

She flushed rosily.

'You are satisfied with me? Mynheer

Dyck worked very hard on my behalf.'

'And on mine,' said Esmond with another look that made her pulses thrill.

'Thank God you are not disappointed this time,' she whispered.

'You make me feel ashamed that I ever showed you such discourtesy,' he said in a low voice.

'Oh, but you were justified,' she cried. 'I know how I looked *then*. You were cheated—'

'Hush,' he broke in, 'that is over and done with.'

'Then you think this—' she touched the once mutilated cheek, 'a success?'

'A brilliant success, Magda.'

She ran to the table on which stood the wine that a footman had just brought in, poured out a goblet and handed it to Esmond.

'Please drink this. You look so tired,' she breathed.

'You are very solicitous,' he smiled and took a sip of the wine gratefully. He added: 'Yes, I am tired, but a good night's rest will put that right. Ah, Magda, it is good to be home and to see my beloved Mornbury again. It has been a hard life out there in France, and I fear the bloodshed is not yet ended.'

'I care only that you are safe and back with me,' she said.

He set down his glass.

'And I, now that I see you again, know that I can stay here always with you in peace—nay, more than that—in love,' he added.

She drew a long breath.

'I have suffered much in my life, Esmond, but it is all worth while to hear you utter those words.'

'Come here,' he said and opened his arms.

She went to him, her whole soul in her eyes as he caught her to his heart. She looked up at him and wound her arms about his neck.

'I know more about you than you think,' he went on. 'I have made it my business to discover things which you once hid from me.'

'What things?'

'My agents heard from those who lived in or around Stroud of the pitiful state in which you and your mother existed and the tortures which *you* were put to as a child.'

'It is only like a bad dream to me now,

346

Esmond.'

'Nevertheless I realize that when you agreed to the trickery which almost wrecked our marriage, I should never have blamed you, but only your stepfather.'

She clung to Esmond as though afraid that he would let her go. She whispered brokenly:

'But I should have stood firm and refused to deceive you. Only he threatened my mother. He threatened to roast us all,' she added in a strangled voice.

'Now,' said Esmond grimly, 'he, himself, is roasting in hell.'

As he felt her long slim body shiver, he tightened his hold of her and touched her forehead with his lips.

'I have learned other things,' he whispered, 'a letter from Mynheer Dyck told me of his admiration for your great courage. How you refused opium and stood pain that few other women would have endured. All this for my sake, the surgeon said. When the pain was at its sharpest it was *my* name that you spoke.'

She nodded, her face hot and pink.

'I have grown to love you most dearly. I want only your happiness,' she said.

'I want only yours. I am no angel, no

hero. Much of my youth was misspent. When Dorothea died I thought my life had ended but she has cast her mantle upon you, and her saintly spirit is, I know, with us this night.'

Magda raised streaming eyes.

'Tell me that you no longer feel that I have wrongfully usurped her place.'

'You have your own place in my heart,' he said.

'All these long months I have worked to please you,' she went on. 'You shall see my sewing and hear me play. You shall see, too, how well I have cared for Jess.'

'I shall ride her in the morning at your side, my darling,' he said.

Suddenly he forgot fatigue. Passionate happiness flooded his soul. She felt his kiss long and warm upon her lips. His fingers caressed her hair. She heard his voice in her ear.

'This is our true marriage night, Magda, my beloved. All else shall be forgot.'

She had no answer save to surrender her whole heart and body, clasped close in his arms.

The painted smiling face of Catherine Mornbury in her blue and silver riding habit, looked down at them from the great gold frame over the fireplace, as though in approval because her son had at long last found his way into the light.

The publishers hope that this Large Print Book has brought you pleasurable reading. Each title is designed to make the text as easy to see as possible. G. K. Hall Large Print Books are available from your library and your local bookstore. Or you can receive information on upcoming and current Large Print Books by mail and order directly from the publisher. Just send your name and address to:

G. K. Hall & Co.
70 Lincoln Street
Boston, Mass. 02111

or call, toll-free:

1–800–343–2806